Alex Fisher is a high-li.,.... ner and busy planning her perfect wedding to Emott. _. life suddenly becomes complicated when she's faced with a hot junior lawyer on her team and an actress threatening to jeopardise the deal by exposing her dodgy cosmetic surgery. Soon Alex is forced into a series of impossible choices that are all inextricably linked and life will never be the same again.

Rachel Altman is a corporate financier with a prestigious accounting firm who's desperately trying to keep on the straight and narrow. Hopelessly led astray by her bar diving boyfriend, she gets the chance to turn things round when her boss gives her the break she's been waiting for. But when the deal doesn't go as planned Rachel panics, sparking off a chain of betrayal and lies that threatens to ruin both her love life and her career.

Meredith Romaine is an ice cool senior banker whose competitive world revolves around men and money. This deal will cement her reputation as the office rainmaker and put her in line for a huge bonus. But only if no one finds out about her relationship with a doctor at the American buyers and the completely unethical way she set the deal up. Can she pull it off without her past coming back to haunt her?

The series can be read in any order.

MIXING BUSINESS WITH PLEASURE

Never Mind
The Botox

Stella

PENNY AVIS AND JOANNA BERRY

Matador
9 Priory Business Park,
Wistow Road, Kibworth Beauchamp,
Leicestershire. LE8 0RX
Tel: 0116 279 2299
Email: books@troubador.co.uk
Web: www.troubador.co.uk/matador
Twitter: @matadorbooks

ISBN 978 1838594 503

British Library Cataloguing in Publication Data.
A catalogue record for this book is available from the British Library.

Printed and bound by CPI Group (UK) Ltd, Croydon, CR0 4YY
Typeset in 12pt Aldine401 BT by Troubador Publishing Ltd, Leicester, UK

Matador is an imprint of Troubador Publishing Ltd

For each other, as together anything is possible.

CHAPTER 1

Stella wiped the soap suds off the dish before passing it to her mother to dry. She watched through the serving hatch as the age-old debate about the relative merits of Quality Street versus Celebrations was going on in the living room. Stella could see her dad in his recliner opening the wrapper on another chocolate and proclaiming, 'Quality by name and quality by nature. Can't beat them. They're classics.'

'No way, Dad, Celebrations are miles better. There's no duds in a box of Celebrations. They're all tried-and-tested high-street favourites. No dodgy nuts or rock-hard caramels. No contest,' replied Michelle, Stella's younger sister.

'Rubbish,' he said through a mouthful of toffee. 'Nothing special about 'em. Just miniature versions of ordinary chocolate bars. Where's the treat in that, eh?'

It wasn't exactly on a par with the Israeli/Palestinian debate but both sides were just as entrenched and Stella had heard the argument at every Christmas dinner and Sunday lunch for as long as she could remember.

She turned to her mother, knowing her father wasn't listening in on their conversation.

'So apart from the big chocolate dispute how is he, Mam, really?' she asked.

'Oh, you know, pet, putting on a brave face. Still scours the paper every morning and goes to the job club on a Wednesday but there's nothing out there for a man of his age. It's such a waste. He's always been such a good worker.' Stella's mum sighed, as she reached up to put away the stack of clean plates.

Stella's dad had been in and out of work ever since he had been made redundant from the shipyard, where he had worked when Stella was a toddler. His most recent job had been at the local betting shop but now everyone was betting online, the shop had been earmarked for closure. It was six months since he had left and the redundancy money had long gone. Stella knew her mum was worried. Times were hard in the Webb household. Stella had noticed the supermarket own-brand products and the lack of little luxuries, like magazines and chocolate biscuits, which had been the few treats the family had ever enjoyed. She had bought the boxes of chocolates at Watford Gap services as last-minute presents.

'I am trying to get more hours at the surgery but Maureen's been there longer so she gets first shout,' her mum continued. Stella thought guiltily of the new designer dress hanging up in her wardrobe at home and her red sports car parked outside her parents' neat council house while her mum chatted about her cleaning job at the local GP's practice.

'I was talking to Dr Barker the other day. Lovely lady she is. Still looks immaculate for her age. I reminded her about that day at the bingo when Shirley had her heart attack. You remember that don't you, love?' How could Stella forget? Although she had only been nine at the time, the story had been retold to her so many times she wasn't sure whether the version of the story she remembered was accurate or not.

'Mm,' she said, hoping her mother might not launch into the usual monologue. It was no good. She had put her tea towel down and perched herself on the kitchen stool.

'You must have been about ten,' she began.

'Nine actually,' Stella muttered, determined to preserve some factual accuracy.

'I can remember it like it was yesterday. Shirley had just got a line and was only two numbers away from House. It was big money Friday too. She could have won a thousand pounds. It was very tense, love, I can tell you.' She took a sip of her tea.

'How is Shirley?' Stella asked. Her mum ignored her and continued.

'I knew something was up when the colour drained from her face. Why, she normally has such a ruddy complexion. It's that rosacea, I think they call it. Anyways, she was as white as a sheet and started grabbing her chest. Then she was sick everywhere. Ooh, it was awful. I knew she had angina, you know, that's why I panicked and that's when we all started shouting and you ran to the reception where they had the tannoy. Do you remember those two girls fighting over who should make the announcement?'

'Yes, Mam. It was the most excitement they'd ever had.'

'Well, it probably was. Apart from that night when the bingo went nationwide and that woman from Byker won the national jackpot. Anyway, one of the girls got knocked over in the struggle to get the microphone and the other one asked in some posh telephone voice if there was a doctor in the house. I mean, as if? They should have been dialling 999, not making silly announcements. Anyway, who should come through the crowd, as calm as a cucumber, but Dr Barker. I couldn't believe it. The last person you'd ever expect at the bingo. She was with her gran apparently.'

Despite herself Stella was gripped by the story yet again. She stared out of the kitchen window and remembered the events of that day. She had run back to her mum's table, her blonde pigtails swinging, and had watched as Shirley had slumped to the floor. Then she had looked up as Dr Barker approached, with her glossy hair, expensive jacket and capable manner. The crowd had parted with an unspoken deference and Dr Barker had knelt down, taken Shirley's pulse, popped an aspirin in her mouth and spoken to her in a quiet, steady voice as she loosened her clothes. As she was doing all this, she had signalled to Stella's mum to call for an ambulance immediately.

'And that was the moment, pet, wasn't it? I knew it when I saw your face, and afterwards you couldn't stop talking about it could you?'

Yeah, because I was nine years old and traumatised, Stella thought.

'You got your calling that day. Nothing would ever stop my girl then, would it? You knew you were going to be a doctor just like Dr Barker.' Her mum beamed at her, the pride radiating from her face. Stella smiled back at her. It was true, that was when Stella had decided. However her decision hadn't been based on the altruistic reasons her mother believed but on the fact that Dr Barker had lovely clothes, the respect of the community and had later driven off in the first BMW that Stella had ever seen. To Stella becoming a doctor seemed like the way to a new life; a safe, middle-class existence where money wasn't a constant struggle. She had never met anyone else while growing up who had surpassed Dr Barker as her role model.

'Stella. Come and get the last strawberry cream before your sister nicks it,' her dad shouted from the living room.

'I'm all right thanks, Dad,' she shouted back. She was feeling slightly sick after the full Sunday lunch with all the trimmings. 'You have it.'

She and her mum finished the washing-up and joined the others in the sitting room. Michelle was hugging the

Celebrations between her legs and handed out chocolates begrudgingly when her mum or dad requested them. Michelle was six years younger than Stella and had never left Newcastle. She had done a course on travel and tourism and now worked in the city centre in one of the better-known travel agencies. She had never had the desire or the drive to get away like Stella.

'Fancy a quick drink at the Bluebell before you head back to London, Sis?' she asked. 'All the usual crowd will be there.'

Stella was pleased to have the opportunity to get some air before the long drive home.

'Good idea. Is that all right with you, Mum?'

'Of course, pet. You go on.'

'Fancy a pint, Dad?' she asked. 'I'm buying.' She suspected her dad didn't get too many trips to the pub these days.

'No thanks. I'm happy as Larry here with me Quality Street. You have a chat with your sister.'

Stella closed the front door behind her and watched Michelle admiring her sports car.

'It's gorgeous, Stella. Must have cost you a fortune.'

'It's not brand new. It's a couple of years old,' she replied, embarrassed at the obvious display of her own success. She loved driving it around London and although it was decidedly average in the car park at work, it looked ostentatious here.

Stella linked arms with Michelle and they took the familiar walk to the local pub. The Bluebell was a flat-roofed, seventies monstrosity with a large satellite dish and shabby lawns, adorned with a selection of rickety tables chained to slabs of concrete. Stella had no idea why anyone would want to steal them.

She was conscious of the heads turning as she walked to the bar. She was the one with the expensive clothes and the nice handbag now. The transformation was complete, she thought, she was now the Dr Barker of her day but with one difference. She had left; and the unmistakeable London aura was all around her. As she spoke to the barman, she noticed that even her accent had changed. She and Michelle settled into a corner with their drinks.

'I've been dying to get you on your own,' said Michelle, sipping her lager, 'I nearly killed you when you asked dad if he wanted to come. Though he hardly ever goes to the pub anymore.'

'Why?'

'Can't afford it I suppose,' Michelle replied.

'No, guess not. Why did you want me on my own?'

'Oh yeah, right. Well you know it's Mam and Dad's ruby wedding in a month,' said Michelle.

'Yes I know. What shall we get them? A teasmade? A porcelain thimble collection from the back of the Sunday paper? A lifetime supply of Quality Street?' Stella tapped a beer mat on the faux brass tabletop and frowned. What they needed most was money but Stella knew her father would be mortified if she gave him cash.

'I was thinking we should throw them a party. They've had a really bad time recently and they never go out and see their friends. We could round up some of Dad's old mates from the shipyard and Mum's bingo pals and some of the family and have a bit of a do.'

Stella pondered her sister's suggestion. 'Yeah. Why not? That's a good idea. It's better than a posh vase or a picture frame. They need something to look forward to. Where should we do it? They won't want it at home. There's not enough room for a start and Mum will just stress about the house.'

'Well, what about here?' said Michelle.

Stella surveyed the shabby bar with its patterned carpet hiding thirty years of stains and the velvet curtains hanging erratically from the brass poles, and her heart sank. She wanted to say, 'No, let's book a private room in a smart hotel in town,' but she knew her parents and their friends would be more comfortable at their local. Her parents were proud but unpretentious.

'Isn't there a private room?' she said, dredging up a memory of a friend's eighteenth birthday in a room with a wooden floor and upholstered chairs.

'Yes there is, out the back. I spoke to Carl the manager last week and we can have it on the date of their anniversary for a hundred quid. He asked us to pay him up front today if we want to go ahead with it. What do you think? I thought we could do a bit of a buffet. I can sort that if you like. And then maybe we could put a bit of money behind the bar so the first drinks are on us.' Michelle looked at Stella, clearly pleased with her plan.

'That's a great idea, Sis. Mum and Dad will love it. Look, I'll put a few hundred quid behind the bar and then there'll be plenty of free booze. Do we need to speak to this Carl bloke now?'

Michelle smiled, 'Great. I really think Dad'll love it. It's just what he needs. I'm glad you think it's a good idea. Come on, let's go and find Carl.' Michelle finished her drink and stood up.

Carl was a stocky thirty-something who managed to have massive toned biceps and a beer belly at the same time.

'All right, Michelle. This must be your sister.' Carl looked Stella up and down as though she was an exotic creature who'd escaped from the zoo.

'Hello,' nodded Stella.

'Do you wanna see the room then?' he nodded towards the back of the pub.

'Yes please,' said Michelle and they followed him through a bead curtain into a dark corridor behind the bar. The room was as depressing as Stella had expected it to be but she could see that with a few balloons, some table centrepieces, a bit of flair and a lot of positive thinking it could be made to look less like an NHS waiting room and more like somewhere you might feel like celebrating in. It had a perfectly good bar, which her father would appreciate, and Carl promised them their own dedicated barman and a free DJ for the night.

'Okay, Carl, we'll take it,' said Michelle.

'All right. I'll need the hundred pounds today, like I said.' Michelle looked at Stella.

'I'll get this,' she said, handing Carl her credit card. He looked down at it.

'Right you are. I'll just go and get the credit card machine.' He ducked into the corridor again and returned with a pristine card machine. The regulars at the Bluebell clearly didn't use their credit cards very often. Stella tapped in her PIN while Michelle chatted to Carl.

'I'll bring the buffet food round about five then. Is it okay if I bring my car round the back to unload?' Michelle was saying. Stella handed the card machine back to Carl and waited for the familiar whirl of the receipt. She glanced at her watch. She should be heading back to London shortly. It would take her over four hours to get home in the Sunday evening traffic.

'Sorry, pet. My machine doesn't like your fancy card. Says it's been rejected,' said Carl, his eyes screwed up as he read the message on the electronic screen. Stella immediately blushed.

'Gosh. I'm really sorry,' she giggled nervously, 'here, try this one,' she said, fishing a different card out of her purse. Stella's manicured nails tapped in the PIN again and the three of them waited in silence for the verdict from the screen.

'Bingo,' said Carl, 'you're a winner.' He pulled the card and the receipt out of the machine, 'There you are, pet. All sorted. Okay, ladies, I'll see you in a few weeks.'

'Sorry about that thing with my card back there,' said Stella, as they walked back to their parents' house.

'Don't be daft. One of those things. It's always happening to me towards the end of the month, though I thought you'd be okay these days with your top job and smart car,' said Michelle, nudging her with her elbow.

'Oh, just an admin thing. Must have forgotten to pay the bill,' said Stella. 'Okay, so I'll call you in a couple of weeks about the buffet and if you need any money for food or the cake just let me know and I'll transfer some cash,' she continued, as they approached their parents' house. Two boys on stunt bikes were doing wheelies up and down the street. Stella watched as they approached her car. It had obviously attracted their interest and one of them, a skinhead in a Newcastle shirt, was peering in the driver's window and leaning his bike handle against the door as he did.

'Oi,' shouted Stella, 'watch my car.' The boys turned to look at her. They didn't move.

'It's yours? Yeah right,' one of them shouted.

'Yeah. Absolutely right it is,' Stella shouted back, jogging towards them.

'Well nick one for me next time, love,' the Newcastle fan replied, before executing a perfect wheelie and riding off.

'Very funny,' said Stella to no one in particular.

As she drove off less than an hour later, watching her parents still waving as she turned the corner, Stella reflected on why she felt uncomfortable these days whenever she came home. She had got what she'd always wanted. The great job, the house in London, the flash car and the fellow doctor boyfriend. Why did she always feel so shallow then? Perhaps it was because the things she took for granted were a daily struggle for her parents or maybe it was because they thought she was doing something really worthwhile with her life? It didn't help that she was massively in debt and they knew nothing about it. Becoming a partner at her age at the Beau Street Group had cost her dearly.

CHAPTER 2

'Look Mother, it's my decision,' the beautiful blonde was whining.

'I know,' said the equally blonde and beautiful woman through gritted teeth, 'but if it wasn't for your father, you wouldn't be able to afford it, would you?'

'Yeah, but it's my birthday present.'

'Christ, I'll kill him. It's not enough to run off with his personal trainer. Oh no. He has to bring your tits into it doesn't he?' The older woman was screeching now.

'Ladies, would you prefer to come back another day when you have had a chance to talk this through properly,' said Stella, in her best calming voice, 'there should be no lingering doubts about this kind of decision. Natasha, you are eighteen I believe, would you like the opportunity to discuss this with me in private?' she asked the younger woman.

Natasha looked at her mother. The older woman sighed and stood up. 'All I want to say, Dr Webb, is that I am firmly against this. She is a beautiful young woman. There is nothing wrong with her.' She was jabbing her finger in Natasha's direction. 'I'm all for a few nips and tucks in due course but she does not need a breast enhancement. This is her father's idea of getting one over me. It's despicable how he's dragged her and her insecurities into our divorce.'

With that she picked up her handbag and left the room, her head held high. Stella watched Mrs Courtenay-Morris leave. Stella had been treating her with Botox, fillers and chemical peels for almost a year now and she knew all about her husband's textbook midlife crisis and did have some sympathy for her.

'Okay, Natasha. Would you like to talk me through why you feel you should have an enhancement and then I can talk you through the procedure and the risks and benefits?' Stella asked.

'Well, two of my best friends have had boob jobs for their eighteenths and they look really amazing and well, I just want one too. My boobs aren't very big,' she said, cupping her breasts as she spoke, 'and let's face it, all men like big breasts. Oh I don't know. I just didn't want to look a gift horse in the mouth. Daddy's offering to pay.'

Stella managed to avoid shouting, 'spoilt bitch' at Natasha and instead proceeded to describe the procedure as graphically as she could.

'... and then after the incision in the infra mammary fold, the surgeon creates a cavity with a metal refractor and then inserts the implant into the cavity under the muscle. That can take quite a bit of pushing and shoving. Obviously the bleeding is cauterised as we go. Occasionally there is post-operative bleeding and swelling and some patients might get an infection. But really, Natasha, you are very young. Most clients end up having further surgery at some point either to reduce or increase the size of the implant and they are only guaranteed for ten years. You could be setting yourself up for several further procedures over the course of your life. Think very carefully about it, would be my advice.'

'Thanks, I have. I just can't decide how big to go. Do you have any before-and-after pictures?' Natasha asked. Stella passed her a folder.

'I can show you a selection of implants. Perhaps you'd like to hold them.' Stella passed a teardrop-shaped implant to the girl.

'Wow, it's heavy! Is this like a double F or something?'

'No that's an average-sized one.' After lots of squeezing and poking of the chicken fillet-like samples and analysis of the before-and-after folder, Natasha chose a 300cc teardrop implant. In Stella's experience many people said they wanted a natural look but when it came to the crunch they wanted something significantly bigger than where they had started from. She had learnt not to counsel them down a size. If they wanted a boob job they wanted to see a difference. She had lost count of the number of clients who claimed they wanted a subtle look and then chose an enormous spherical implant.

'If I say yes, how soon could you do it?'

Stella pulled her computer screen round, 'Mm, I could fit you in three weeks today. To confirm the date I would need full payment today.' Stella had also learnt by experience to get full payment up front so clients couldn't refuse to pay when the implant they had chosen was suddenly too big or too small.

'That's great. Here's Daddy's card,' Natasha said, handing over a platinum Amex.

'My personal assistant deals with the formalities, Natasha. Are you absolutely sure about this? What about a cooling off period and another chat with your mother?'

'Look I'm fine; it's no big deal really. I don't know why Mum is making such a fuss. She's had loads of stuff done.'

'Your mum isn't eighteen,' Stella muttered.

'Do you want my business or not?' The young woman tossed her hair as she stood up, making her designer sunglasses fly across the room. Stella watched her crawling on the floor trying to retrieve them from under the examination bed and sighed. Of course she wanted her business.

'I'll see you in three weeks, Miss Courtenay-Morris. If you could speak to Karen on your way out she will make all the necessary arrangements.'

Stella watched her leave and sighed again. More than fifteen years studying and working as a doctor for this; doing boob jobs on spoilt princesses so Daddy can get one over on Mummy. There was a knock at the door.

'Have you got a moment?' It was Karen, her personal assistant, a voluptuous woman with a laugh you could hear from across the street.

'Sure. Come in.' Stella waved her in.

'Hey, what was that last one like? A right madam. She had the nerve to ask me whether my implants were 800cc!' Karen exclaimed. Stella laughed. Everyone knew that Karen's impressive boobs were very much as God had intended.

'Did you book her in?'

'Yup. Might as well give her a loyalty card. She'll be back every time Daddy gets a bonus.'

'Yeah or has a score to settle with her mum. Bloody dysfunctional that family.'

'I've had Charles on for you. He's trying to organise an urgent meeting of the management partners. Lloyd, Christopher and Tom can all do four o'clock today. Your last patient is at three fifteen but that's just a non-surgical.' Stella had recently been elected to the clinic's management committee, which comprised four of the firm's ten partners and Tom Duffy, the clinic's finance director.

'Yes that's fine. I've got nothing on after that. Any idea what it's about?' Stella asked.

'Nope. All very mysterious. I've checked with all the other PAs and they've got no idea either. Oh, and Stella, is it still okay if I leave early tomorrow? Benji's match starts at five.' Benji was Karen's seven-year-old son. He was an amazing footballer and she tried to get to all of his matches.

'Of course. That's fine. How's he doing?' Stella knew that Karen lived for her son.

'He's wonderful. He's so bright you know. I'm thinking of applying for a bursary to send him to the private school near us. What do you think?' Karen enquired.

'I'm not sure I'm the best person to ask really. I mean, I went to the local comprehensive. I met a lot of private school kids at university though and they all seemed incredibly confident. What's the state school like where you are?'

'A bloody nightmare. Literally. Two stabbings in the last month.'

'Ah. In that case the bursary sounds like a great idea. I'd go for it.' Stella was full of admiration for Karen and her hopes for her son. She didn't blame her one bit for her ambition on his behalf. If she was honest she had always envied the private school kids at university. They had a belief in themselves which always bemused her. She would convince herself she had failed every exam she ever sat and whenever the results came through and she had beaten all the kids from Eton and Harrow, she had always been genuinely amazed. They, on the other hand, breezed through everything with an unshakeable belief they would become the doctor/journalist/merchant banker. A bit of confidence like that wouldn't do Benji any harm at all.

It was five minutes to four when Stella knocked gently on the boardroom door. Charles Sutton, their Chief

Executive, was a stickler for timekeeping and manners. She opened the door into the large old-fashioned room, which housed a huge mahogany table that could seat twenty at a push. Predictably Charles was already there chatting to Tom Duffy, the finance man.

'Good afternoon, gentlemen,' she called. They were sitting at the end of the table furthest from the door.

'Ah Stella. Glad you could join us.' Ever the gentleman, Charles stood up to greet her, 'Just Lloyd and Christopher we're waiting for now,' he said, looking at his watch. Charles was in his sixties, 'old school' and occasionally still wore a bow tie. He had worked in the NHS for years as a specialist plastic surgeon before taking more and more private work and eventually becoming a founding partner at the Beau Street Group.

'Hi Stella,' said Tom Duffy, 'your figures are looking good this month.'

'Yeah thanks. Had the usual spring rush on augmentations and other "beach ready" procedures.' Stella was the youngest and hungriest of the partners and she and Tom got on. She always hit her budgets and understood that the practice was a business, as well as a healthcare provider. Tom always said she spoke his language.

Christopher Bennett and Lloyd Cassidy arrived together. Christopher was in his late fifties and as a result of his work at Beau Street and his wife's inheritance, was already prodigiously rich. They all knew he was coasting to retirement. He practically worked part time anyway.

'Good afternoon, everyone,' said Lloyd Cassidy, nodding to them all, 'to what do we owe this pleasure, Charles?' he purred. Lloyd was shiny-suited and extremely smooth. He had his patients eating out of his manicured hands as well as one or two members of staff. He had tried his charms on Stella in the past and she was wary of him. But he was a talented practitioner and his sales figures were also excellent. Stella was acutely aware that she and Lloyd were the star performers financially.

'Right, let's not beat about the bush,' said Charles, as the latecomers settled themselves., 'I have some very interesting news which I need to share with you all. Gentlemen, and lady of course,' he nodded patronisingly to Stella, 'we have been approached by Equinox.'

'The US outfit?' asked Christopher.

'That's correct. The Equinox Practice has expressed an interest in buying us. We would become their UK operation. Apparently it is much quicker and easier for them to buy us, than for them to start from scratch and set up their own British operation. They have asked if they can undertake due diligence on our business, which means we need to provide them with details of what we do, how much money we make and so on.'

There was a brief shocked silence, then Lloyd spoke.

'And what have you said, Charles?'

'Well, obviously I said I would have to discuss it with all the partners first. I thought I would start with the management committee. I am seeing the others later. Clearly it is not a foregone conclusion that they will buy us. They will have to get accountants to crawl all over our books and lawyers to check we're not up to anything untoward. Clearly they don't want to be sold a pup. But we all know this business is sound. The decision is ours. Do we want to sell?'

'I am not sure I like the idea. What about our positions? Will we be kept on if we are no longer partners?' asked Lloyd.

'They want to keep anyone who wants to stay. Our people are one of our greatest assets. Obviously they would buy us out of our partnerships. We could all stand to make a lot of money from this,' Charles continued.

'Well, I think it is a great opportunity for the business but I have to put my cards on the table and say that if the deal goes ahead, I will take the chance to retire,' said Christopher. This was no surprise to Stella; with the money he'd make from the sale Christopher could have a very nice time for the next thirty years.

'That's fair enough, Christopher. Thank you for your honesty. I have to say I suspect I may be reaching a similar conclusion myself. What about the rest of you? Tom?'

'Well as you know I've had a couple of hours more than my colleagues to think about this. Just to be up front with everyone, Charles and I had a brief chat about Equinox's approach earlier and I would say that my initial reaction is that this is a very exciting proposal and one we should follow up. Where's the harm in allowing them access to the business? Once they have made an indicative offer, we can then consider if the price is one we want to accept. Yes, in principle I am supportive.' Stella had been waiting for Tom's reaction and was pleased that it echoed her gut feel.

'I agree with Tom. I think we should let them explore the opportunity further, give them limited access to the business and see what they come up with,' she said.

'And you, Lloyd?' asked Charles.

Lloyd tapped his forefingers together and frowned.

'I am not so sure. I like the sound of making some money, of course,' he smiled but then immediately changed his expression and said, almost to himself, 'however, I don't like the idea of lawyers and accountants crawling all over our business and our patients. But it seems I am outnumbered here.'

As the meeting broke up, Stella cornered Tom.

'So, Tom, do you have any idea of how much we might get personally?' she asked. Tom laughed, 'I wondered who'd ask me that first. Don't worry, it crossed my mind too. I've run a few numbers, just indicative, mind you, and if we get something close to what Charles and I think the business is worth, you'd get several hundred thousand before deductions.'

'Pounds?'

Tom laughed again, 'Yes, Stella, good old British pounds. Though obviously in your case your partnership loan would have to be paid off out of your proceeds and then you'd get the balance.'

'Wow,' said Stella, stunned.

'I know. It makes you think doesn't it? I can't work out why Lloyd isn't more up for it. I thought he was obsessed with cash,' Tom added.

Stella was in a daze as she drove home. Several hundred thousand pounds! She did the maths in her head. Her partnership loan was a hundred and eighty thousand, which was costing her as much as her mortgage each month and killing her. She was worse off since she'd become a partner than when she'd been an ordinary doctor, but hell, it was definitely worth it now. Her credit card debts must be about twenty grand now. Then there was the house deposit she and Ian were saving for so they could move somewhere big enough to start a family. Ian had already saved ten grand and she had told him she had too, although she hadn't saved a penny of it. She hit the steering wheel with both hands and whooped. This was unbelievable. What did Tom mean by 'several' hundred? Several was more than a couple so it must be at least three hundred, maybe four? Yeah, at least four hundred thousand she reckoned. So, no debt and maybe two hundred thousand pounds in the bank; maybe more! She might be able to buy her parents' council house for them and maybe even give them a lump sum. The man in the next car was staring at her. She smiled back, not caring. She felt a freedom she had never experienced before. Financial security was a totally alien concept for any member of the Webb family.

Stella turned up the volume on the radio and danced about her kitchen excitedly. She couldn't wait to tell

Ian, who should be home any time soon. She skipped to the fridge and surveyed the uninspiring contents. An onion, a pot of fromage frais, some Brie and a mouldy bag of lettuce. She wasn't sure even the most talented TV chef would be able to rustle up a meal with that lot. She danced over to the overflowing kitchen drawer full of pens that didn't work, random keys, old receipts and most importantly, life-saving takeaway menus. As she poured herself a glass of wine and pondered the selection of menus she found herself dreaming of a life with no debt, beautiful houses, beautiful children and no more boob jobs. She could pick and choose her work; maybe work part time in the practice and do a business qualification. Perhaps she could set her dad up in a small business? As she sipped her wine she was suddenly determined that this deal had to happen. She would offer her help to Tom in the morning.

Two hours later and Stella stared at the half-eaten curry and looked at her watch again. Where the hell was he? He wasn't on call tonight and why wasn't he answering his phone? She flipped open the lid on her laptop and started idling through her favourites and on autopilot found herself on her favourite clothes site.

Mm, if she was going to be mingling with accountants and corporate types she needed to look the part. Just a smart dress and maybe a jacket? She scrolled down the pages of 'daywear' looking for the right outfit. Too floaty, too unstructured, too red, too tarty. She frowned as she analysed each item. Then she saw it. Perfect. A classic wrap dress with a hint of sexy in the perfect corporate grey. She knew it would look fabulous on her tall, slightly boyish frame. It would give her curves in all the right places but with the right shoes and smart briefcase would look professional and businesslike. She clicked on 'Buy' and tapped in her credit card details from memory. She got a momentary high as the confirmation page popped up, before the buyer's remorse kicked in. Then she remembered the deal and reminded herself that things were going to be very different soon. This was probably the most important investment buy ever.

Any vestiges of excitement over the deal or her purchase were long gone by the time Ian finally came in the door at two in the morning. Stella had fallen asleep on the sofa, still surrounded by takeaway cartons and she opened a bleary eye as Ian burst into the room.

'Hi,' she murmured, 'you're late.' He threw himself into the armchair. He looked dreadful. His tie was loosened, his normally immaculate dark hair all over the place, and his face sallow with exhaustion.

'I've been waiting up all night. I got a takeaway for us. Why didn't you answer my calls?' she said petulantly as she sat up.

'I've had the most God-awful night.'

'Well mine hasn't been a barrel of laughs,' said Stella.

'For Chrissakes, Stella, I would have killed for a night in with a takeaway in front of the telly.' He leant forward and put his head in his hands.

'All right, don't bite my head off. Do you want a cup of tea? Then I'll tell you my news.'

He looked up at her, confused.

'What news?'

'Something very exciting is happening at work,' she replied, as she moved towards the kitchen. He didn't follow her. She banged around noisily in the kitchen, angry that he was so disinterested, and made the tea.

'Here you go,' she said, handing him the mug of tea.

'Thanks.'

'So aren't you going to ask me what it's about?' She sat on the edge of the sofa watching him sip his tea and relax back into the chair.

'Stella. I'm totally knackered. Can't your latest celebrity news wait till the morning?'

She was angry now. 'It's not celebrity news. It's much more important than that. Could you just show a little interest? I've been dying to talk to you all night.'

He looked at her, surprised by her anger but too drained to fight.

In a quiet voice he replied, 'I've been in A&E for the past seven hours. There's been a nine-vehicle pile-up on the M25. I've seen two children at death's door, one amputation and enough assorted head injuries to write a textbook on the subject. Please forgive me if I'm not hanging on your every word.'

She immediately felt dreadful. He did this every time. He always held the trump card. His work, his life was always going to be more worthy than hers. She couldn't compete with saving lives. She knew he would want to talk it through with her, download his stress and share the trauma but she couldn't cope with it tonight. It was enough that she had to bury her news until tomorrow. As she stood up she felt nauseous and realised that she was also exhausted.

As Ian finally came up to bed, he found her knelt by the toilet throwing up.

'Are you okay, darling?' he asked her.

'Dodgy bloody curry. Not ordering from them again,' she replied, wiping the vomit from her long blonde hair.

CHAPTER 3

Stella strode towards the entrance to the clinic in her sharpest suit and carrying a briefcase she had dusted off that morning. She had decided to start as she meant to go on. She would be sporting the corporate look for the foreseeable future.

'Good morning, Dr Webb. It's a beautiful day. Well – broken skies and sunny spells all day apparently,' said the security guard, opening the side door reserved for staff.

'Morning, Fred. Yes it's a lovely day. How are you?' she replied.

'Very well thank you, Doctor. You're looking very smart.'

'Thanks,' she shouted over her shoulder, as she marched through the carpeted reception area and made her way to her consulting room. She had an eight-thirty appointment, after which she planned to speak to Tom.

'Mr Evans is already here,' said Karen, laying out Stella's post on her desk as she took off her jacket and sat down, 'he looks really nervous,' she added.

'Thanks Karen. Could you show him in and could you get me a glass of water please?' She was still feeling a bit queasy after the curry episode.

A few minutes later, Stella found herself nodding sympathetically at the gorgeous man in front of her. He was tall, sandy-haired, with piercing blue eyes and despite his looks seemed to be a really nice guy without a hint of arrogance. He was wittering on vaguely about his 'problem'. It was time to cut to the chase.

'Mr Evans, do you think you could bring yourself to show me what the problem is?' She had established it was something to do with his manhood but he was struggling to get to the point.

He stood up, blushing now, and slowly undid his trousers. As his trousers fell to his knees and he slowly pulled down his boxers, Stella found herself peering at the smallest penis she had ever seen.

'Ah right, Mr Evans, I can see what your problem is,' she said. *Although only just*, she thought. *The poor sod*.

'It's all right, you can put your trousers back on now. There is surgery that can help your situation. Standard penis enlargement treatment can visually enlarge the penis by about an inch. There is also the possibility of a dermal implant which can increase girth and length but that does involve fat transfer from other parts of the body and can have mixed results. Personally I would recommend standard enlargement surgery.'

'Well, I think I'll go with your recommendation. I have read up about it online and that's what I thought

I should have. Thank you so much. It's been so hard deciding to do this but I really can't go on any longer.' He looked so grateful and relieved, Stella wanted to hug him. She talked him through the risks and downsides but she could tell this was one patient she would definitely see again.

'Here's some literature. Why don't you take that away and consider your options. If you decide you would like to go ahead, I will see you again and we can book you in.'

'Thank you so much, Dr Webb. I really appreciate it. I will be in touch.' As he was shaking her hand the phone rang. It was her direct line.

'Please excuse me, Mr Evans,' she said, and reached for the phone. She sat down as she answered it.

'Dr Webb's office.'

'Stella. It's me.' It was Fenella, her best friend from university.

'Good morning,' said Stella, as Mr Evans left the room.

'Ooh. Good morning to you too. Got a patient with you have you. Let me guess? Vaginal tightening? Nipple tweaking? Arse licking?'

'Fenella stop it!' giggled Stella, 'it was penis enlargement actually.'

'Lucky you. God, I'd love your job. I'm on a burglary.'

'Not literally I hope.'

'No, some scrote who is innocent of course, who didn't break into six houses on the same estate on consecutive nights because he was visiting his gran in hospital.' Fenella was a criminal barrister who always seemed to be defending the indefensible. 'Anyway, how's things?'

'Interesting actually. A lot going down at work. I probably can't really talk about it.' It dawned on Stella that the deal was probably highly confidential. She would have to be careful who she told. 'But it looks like I might be in the money.'

'Gosh, lucky you. That's great. So, you won't have to tell Ian about the invisible house deposit.'

'Hopefully not.'

'Look, I'm missing you. Can we get together for a drink soon? I'm surrounded by posh private school types here and I feel like the poor relation. I need to compare my growing-out, working-class roots with yours.'

'Thanks. Feel like roughing it again do you? Got bored of your rich mates then,' Stella joked.

'You know how it is. You need a reality check sometimes and I'm still Jenny from the block you know.'

'Ha ha. What about Saturday?'

'It's a date. See you then. You get back to your penis.'

'Yeah, and you get back to your scrote.'

Stella took the stairs up to Tom's office two at a time. A good thigh workout, she thought, as her long legs effortlessly bounded up the two floors to the management corridor.

'Morning, Tom.' She poked her head round his door searching for her colleague. He was kneeling down pulling files out from a grey filing cabinet.

'Ah, Stella. How are you?' he said, a pen between his teeth.

'I'm good. Look, Tom, about this Equinox thing.'

Tom dumped two thick files on his desk and took the pen from between his teeth. 'They've already got me running round after them,' he said pointing at the files.

'Well that's what I wanted to talk to you about. Look, I'm really keen for this deal to happen and I just wanted to offer my help. I am sure I can help show Equinox how much potential our business has, you know, really help sell the place? My diary is manageable at the moment and I can wind it down a bit for the next few weeks if you need a hand. I can farm out all my non-surgical work to the senior nurses. I just want to show willing.'

Tom stood up and dumped the files on his desk. 'Stella, I appreciate that and to be honest I was going to call you anyway. Christopher's as much use as a chocolate fireguard, Charles is tied up on all the high level stuff, and Lloyd is, well, Lloyd, so really there's only you and me to deal with everything. I've just been told I need to hire lawyers and accountants for the due diligence and hopefully the deal in the next week or so and then they are going to be going over the business with a fine-tooth comb. We will need to pull together all the facts and figures they are going to need and prepare a really top notch plan for the business going forward. As you say, make sure we show them how much we are really worth.'

'Well, I am happy to help. You just let me know what you need me to do.'

'Will do. Thanks. Though don't let your figures slide. We still need to be bringing in the money too.'

'No pressure then!'

'It could be worth it in the end,' Tom said.

'So how do you go about hiring the lawyers and accountants?' she asked.

'I've got a firm of accountants in mind. Payne Stanley? You heard of them? An old mate of mine is a partner there. He's a good chap.' *Ah, the Old Boy Network,* thought Stella, *so that's how it works.* She wasn't sure her mates in Newcastle would come in quite so useful in her career.

'I haven't got a clue about the lawyers though. I suppose I need to ask around a bit and find out which law firms know the first thing about cosmetic surgery.'

'I've got a client who's a partner at one of the big firms,' said Stella, keen to do all she could to push things forward, 'she's had the full works, although she's paranoid about confidentiality. She told me that everyone she works with thinks she's forty-nine. I know for a fact she's pushing sixty. Looks good on it though after my handiwork.'

Tom laughed.

'By all means give her a ring. I'll work my contacts too. And Stella, thanks.'

In between Botox, buttocks and boobs, Stella called a few contacts from her university days, including Fenella again and her lady lawyer patient. Fenella couldn't really recommend a commercial law firm as she only dealt in crime and the lawyer client was horrified that she had called her. Although she said she would desperately love her firm to win the work, she was so petrified someone might uncover that she had been a patient at Beau Street, she refused to give Stella the name of the right contact. So far Stella had drawn a blank. By early evening she had decided to call it a day. She wanted to see Ian and clear the atmosphere after last night.

Stella pulled up outside the main entrance to the hospital. Ian was already there, his headphones dangling from his ears. He waved as he saw her and jogged over to the car. He folded his tall frame into the bucket seat next to her and leant over and kissed her.

'Hi, darling. Thanks so much for the lift. Couldn't face the bus.'

'That's okay and I'm sorry about last night,' she replied.

'I'm sorry too. It's was a hellish night and I was in a foul mood. Let me buy you dinner. Why don't we go to the Mexican?' Stella smiled back at him. She couldn't hold a grudge against him. He was such a positive person most of the time. It was one of the things she both loved and admired about him.

'Great idea.'

'You feeling better now?' he asked.

'Yeah. A bit dodgy still this morning but I'm starving now. Come on, let's go straight there.'

They shared a small candlelit table in a corner of the trendy restaurant and sipped at their Mexican beers while perusing the enormous menus.

'I'm going for the chicken chimichangas,' said Ian, putting his menu down, 'so what were you trying to tell me last night when I was being Mr Grumpy Pants?'

Stella excitedly told him about the deal.

'And the best bit is I could make hundreds of thousands of pounds if it happens and keep my job.'

Ian was stunned.

'Okay, let's get this straight. Your business is sold but you get to keep your job and instead of an enormous partnership debt, you end up with a couple of hundred grand in the bank. How does that work?'

'It just does. At the moment, I am a part owner of the business. In the future, I'll work for Equinox. Simples.'

Ian shook his head. 'It just doesn't seem right somehow.'

Stella frowned. They'd had a fair offer for a decent business. It was hardly drug money.

'But just think what a difference it could make for us. We'd be able to get the new house so much sooner, buy you a new car, and have a great holiday, whatever we want.'

'Yeah, I suppose so. You're right. It is really good news. I think I just need to get used to the idea.' He half smiled back at her, 'I always said that you had a business brain. I certainly don't.' Ian looked a bit deflated.

'Hey, you do something much more worthwhile than me. You're the proper doctor,' said Stella, keen to reassure him.

'So are you, just in a different line of work. And a much more profitable one, it seems. But I guess you shouldn't feel guilty about that. Without proper practices like Beau Street, the NHS would be dealing with even more botched cosmetic surgery than it already does. God, we got an awful one the other day. Did I tell you? Straight off the plane from Poland she was. It must have been the surgeon's first ever procedure. I've never seen anything so amateurish.' He slugged his beer and shuddered.

Stella was thinking of Mr Evans from earlier in the day. 'I don't feel guilty about what I do. I do a good job and I do make a difference to people's lives. I just went into medicine for different reasons than you. I always wanted to do it for the money. I couldn't afford the luxury of doing it for the vocation. I just want to do a good job and get paid well. It makes me feel secure.'

'So why do you spend so much then? I just don't get it.'

He had a point and Stella knew it. She wanted to say, 'Because you are normal and I am a screwed-up kid with a chip on her shoulder.'

'I don't know. Some sort of self-destruct thing. Anyway, I've never had enough money to go really crazy.'

'Yeah, well don't go on some shopping spree from hell when you've got your paws on all the cash from the deal. I know what you're like.'

'Presuming it happens,' she said.

'I'm sure that you'll make it happen. You may be good at spending money but you're pretty good at making it too.'

'Let's hope you're right. And it will be great for us if it does, I promise,' said Stella, raising her drink. They clinked their bottles together as the waiter came to take their orders, although Stella could see that Ian wasn't really convinced.

In the early days, his faith in her had been so reassuring. He had always had the knack of making her feel capable. It had been his belief in her at university and through her years as a house doctor that had kept her going. Ian was very much from the right side of the tracks. His parents had understood what he was doing and had supported him all the way. Ian had chosen his career very carefully with the help and encouragement of his educated family. Stella had fumbled around in the dark, clutching at the role model of Dr Barker when planning her future.

'So, how's things going at work for you?' she asked him, as they tucked into their starters.

'Not bad really. I've heard there's a senior registrar post going in Reading.'

Stella stared at him.

'Reading? Why would you want a job in Reading?'

'If I could get that, then with a bit of luck I could be a consultant in two years. Then I might be able to compete in the earnings stakes with you.'

'Ian, it's not a competition!' she said, although she suspected that he thought differently.

How could he possibly think about moving out of London? What about her career? Stella suddenly began to feel rather dizzy.

'Do you think these nachos taste okay?' she asked.

'Yeah. They're fine,' he replied, wiping his mouth on his napkin.

'Mine taste a bit weird,' she replied, pushing her plate away.

'Are you okay? he aked, ' You look a bit pale.'

'I feel a bit odd again. I wonder if I've got a bug. Maybe it wasn't food poisoning.' She took a sip of her beer and took a deep breath.

'I think I need some air.' Stella got up from the table and rushed outside. Ian followed her straight away. They stood outside the restaurant door as she took in deep breaths of fresh air, Ian's arm around her waist. Suddenly their waiter appeared.

'Hey, are you okay?' he asked, 'my boss thinks you are doing a runner.'

Ian smiled politely back at him. 'You can tell him we're not doing a runner. My girlfriend isn't feeling too well. Perhaps I could get our food to take away and the bill please.'

He turned to Stella. 'Come on, let's get you home. I think you've got that forty-eight-hour virus that's doing the rounds.'

CHAPTER 4

Stella hit the snooze button on her phone alarm and instinctively reached across the bed for Ian. He wasn't there. She sat up, confused. The covers on his side of the bed were pulled down and she could see that the bathroom light was on. She grabbed his pillow and put it on top of hers and flung herself back down onto the bed.

'Cup of tea,' he said, as he strode into the room and carefully put the mug on the bedside table. He bent down to kiss her. 'How are you feeling?' He sat down next to her and reached for her hand, demonstrating textbook bedside manner.

'I'm feeling much better, doctor,' she said, exaggeratedly fluttering her lashes, 'but I feel I may need a few days' bed rest and a prescription for Pinot Grigio.'

'Mm, if you don't get out of bed soon you won't be getting any rest,' he said, as he leant forward to kiss her again. She sat up, shook her shock of blonde hair from her eyes and giggled, as she reached for her tea and cupped her hands round it.

'How's your day today?' she asked as she sipped from the mug.

'Shift starts at ten. Shouldn't be too bad. Wednesdays aren't the worst day. I might hear something about the Reading job today.'

'What about it?' she asked, vaguely remembering the conversation of the previous evening.

'Well, just whether it's for real or not. I really want to go for it, Stella,' he said, 'I need to progress, as quickly as I can.'

'What's the rush, Ian? And why Reading? Why can't you wait for something in London?'

He stood up and sighed, his body language immediately changing.

'We've been through this before. I want to make consultant before we settle down and start a family and neither of us is getting any younger. I feel like I'm holding you back already. Reading isn't a million miles away.'

'Okay, okay.' She put her hand up as though to shield herself from any further verbal onslaught. She had heard it all before. Ian had some chivalrous/dated view that he had to be the provider and that somehow all their major life events had to wait until he could call himself a consultant. She didn't get it at all but she knew it mattered to him. She got out of bed, taking her tea with her.

'As long as my ovaries don't shrivel in the meantime,' she laughed.

'Thanks for your support,' he muttered and marched out of the room.

Stella hung onto the ceiling strap as the tube train bounced along the overland section of the journey; her legs balanced either side of her latest designer bag which she'd plonked on the carriage floor. Although Stella loved her shiny new things, she treated them in the same way she had treated the cheap cast-offs she had grown up in. She was oblivious to the East London landscape that blurred past the windows as she considered what Ian had said earlier. He was clearly determined to pursue the job in Reading. What did that mean for her? She couldn't leave Beau Street. Not now there was the prospect of making a life-changing amount of money and finally paying off her debts. It didn't make sense. He wanted them to move so he could progress up the career ladder a bit faster so they could buy a house and play happy families but if she stayed at Beau Street a bit longer they could do that even quicker.

She was greeted by Karen, as she strode towards her office.

'Morning Stella, Tom's already called for you. He wants a quick meeting with you before your first appointment. Something about "Project Pout"? What's that then? A new lip plumping procedure?' she chuckled to herself.

'Can you come into my office for a moment?' Stella asked. Karen raised her eyebrows but followed obediently. Stella sat down and explained to her about the possibility of Equinox buying the business. She trusted Karen and needed her to know what was going on. Stella imagined she would be pulled in several directions once the lawyers and accountants started swarming round the business and she would need Karen on side to cover for her in case she was late for appointments or had to ask more junior staff to cover for routine non-surgical procedures.

Karen was concerned.

'Does this mean I'll lose my job?'

'Of course not. The Americans will buy the business as a going concern. As long as I am here, I will need you, so no, there is no way you'll lose your job.'

Karen was relieved. 'Okay, Stella, thanks, but please let me know if anything changes. You know my family needs this job.'

'I know, Karen. I promise.'

'Okay. Now come on, you'd better get to Tom's office. You've got Mrs Barton at nine for her regular pillow plumping.'

Stella smiled. Mrs Barton was one of those ladies of a certain age who positively wanted her friends to know she had had work. She was a big fan of the pillow face, the cat face and the trout pout and the concept of 'less is more' was lost on her.

Tom was on the phone when Stella arrived. She sat down quietly and overheard the end of his conversation. It sounded like he was arranging for some lawyers to come and present to him.

He smiled at her as he put the handset down.

'That's another item on my to-do list sorted. I've found a firm of lawyers who are coming in to tell me about their experience on Tuesday. I've had a look at a couple of other firms too but this lot come highly recommended by Rob Sweeney.'

'The guy at Vine Medical?'

'Yup. He's a good guy. I think we tried to hire him a while back. Anyway, the accountants are already on board. So it's just the lawyers we need to appoint now. That's why I wanted a word, Stella. The accountants are a firm called Payne Stanley. Seem a good bunch, Carl Stephens is the partner and the woman who is probably going to be our main point of contact is Rachel Altman. They've already given me a list of their requirements. Here's a copy for you.' He passed her a thick document.

'Wow. This is pretty thorough,' she said, flicking through the long list of questions and requests for information.

'Tell me about it, but it's standard stuff apparently. Obviously, I'll deal with the bulk of the financial requests but there are a number of areas where I'd really appreciate your help. I've highlighted them. Do you think you and Karen could start pulling some stuff together?'

'Of course,' she said, without hesitation, 'I've told you, Tom, I want to help in any way I can.'

Stella sat down at the meeting table in the corner of the office, whilst he talked her through the sections of the information request that he had highlighted. From what Stella could glean from his quick overview, the accountants needed to get to the bottom of where the business was, or more importantly was not, making its money. That meant breaking down the work that the doctors and practice nurses did by procedure and working out which of Botox, breast augmentation, toe reshaping, etc. was the most profitable. They also had to factor in issues such as theatre time, anaesthesia, nursing staff and all the other overheads which added to the costs. Stella already knew enough about the business to suspect that it was the non-surgical procedures, such as the fillers and Botox, which were the most profitable, although of course you needed to be very efficient and cram in lots of clients in a day. One boob job could probably bring in the same as ten Botox clients but was a more costly procedure because you needed more staff and more drugs to knock out the patient. Stella agreed to spend some time with all of her colleagues going through their records and getting the facts and figures the accountants were requesting.

'Thanks, Stella. I appreciate that. Oh, and one other thing. Once we've lined up the right law firm,' Tom continued, 'we will be having an "all-party" meeting. That just means that the lawyers, accountants, investment bank and of course some of us, will all get together to discuss timetable and deal progress. Charles and I have already discussed this and we want you there and we would also like you to join the two of us on an executive team to run the transaction. Would you be up for that?'

'Yes, absolutely. Of course!' Stella was thrilled to be asked and couldn't hide the fact.

'Great,' Tom grinned, 'I thought you'd say that so I've already given your contact details to Ryan Miller who is our contact at Equinox. He's based in Chicago but will be coming over at some point, if the deal doesn't crater in the first few weeks.'

'Crater?' Stella frowned.

'Oh it's corporate jargon for collapsing. Come on, Stella, get with the programme,' Tom smiled.

'Yes sir,' she mock saluted, 'I'd better get onto this then,' she said, picking up the thick document. Tom was already moving back to his desk. She left as his phone started ringing.

Christ! This was exciting and scary. She tried to remember everything he'd told her. The accountants were Payne Stanley, some girl called Rachel was her contact and the guy at Equinox was Ryan someone and was based in California, or was it Chicago? She couldn't help a slight wave of self-importance rushing over her. She was one of the gang of three who would run the deal, she had an important document tucked under her arm and she would be dealing with Ryan Reynolds or whatever he was called. This definitely called for a new briefcase and perhaps a new businesslike haircut. She pulled some strands of bleached blonde hair away from her eyes.

On the way back to her consulting room, she stopped to ask Karen to set up meetings for her with all the other doctors to go through the information she would need from them. As Karen started on the calls she made them both a coffee from the machine in the patients' waiting room and then made her way to her office. As she sipped the strong coffee she was conscious of a slight metallic taste in her mouth. A sign? Perhaps should get a pregnancy test, she thought. This was a fairly regular occurrence for Stella who often thought she should buy shares in the company that made the outrageously expensive tests. Or maybe she should be a bit more disciplined about taking her pill.

'Physician, heal thyself,' she muttered to herself. She closed her door behind her, fished her mobile phone out of her pocket and dialled the third number on her speed dial. In the meantime, she had far more important things to do than worry about another false alarm. She was making the appointment with her hairdresser and still walking to her desk, as she heard the loud knock on her door followed by the immediate entrance of Lloyd Cassidy.

'Yes, that's fine thank you. Next Tuesday at six-thirty. I'll see you then.' Before she had finished speaking, Dr Cassidy had weaved round her, settled himself into her chair and placed his expensive-looking patent shoes on her desk. He surveyed her, his hands cradling the back of his head, with a slightly quizzical expression.

'So Stella,' he purred, 'why is it I am being asked to attend a meeting with you on this deal that Charles only told us about a few days ago?' He emphasised the 'you'.

He clearly wasn't happy that she was calling the shots. He regularly reminded her that he was many years more qualified than her.

Karen had obviously called him already. He didn't mess about. She stared back at him and forced a smile.

'Tom's just asked me to help him out with collating information on all our figures. He's going to be snowed under with the accountants and lawyers, so he needs an extra pair of hands, that's all.'

'So precisely what sort of information do you need from us?'

'To be honest I'm not entirely sure, I've only just left Tom's office. He's given me this bundle of questions that need answering and the idea is that I get the facts and figures I need from you and the other doctors. From what I can gather, it's stuff like the number and nature of the different procedures we each do, the costs associated with them and the split between surgical and non-surgical. The accountants need to work out where the business makes its money.'

'I see,' Cassidy replied, getting up from her seat. 'I'll tell Audrey to set something up. Maybe you could be so kind as to email the type of questions you need answering, so we can start getting the paperwork together. I always like to be prepared.'

'Of course. Good idea,' Stella replied as Lloyd left the room, half bowing at her as he went.

Stella spent the next hour, prior to her morning clinic, reading and distilling the list of enquiries from the accountants into a couple of dozen key questions. She then emailed them to the other senior doctors at Beau Street, whilst Karen set up meetings for her with each of them over the next few days.

***

Stella knew something was troubling Ian as soon as she walked into the kitchen. She slumped into the kitchen chair and plonked her bag onto the table along with the accountants' information request which Tom had given her. She hadn't known what to do with it. She knew it was highly confidential so she'd walked round with it clamped in her hand all day. Ian gave her a glass of wine and asked how she was, without making eye contact.

'I'm fine. So, how was your day?' she asked.

'Interesting,' he said and turned to look at her. 'Look, I should have told you before but I applied for the job in Reading a few weeks ago. It's the perfect position for me and I think I'm in with a good chance. I know two of the consultants there and apparently they're putting in a word for me.'

Stella couldn't believe he'd gone ahead before they'd discussed it properly. 'When did you apply for it?' she asked.

'It should only be for a couple of years,' he said, ignoring her question, 'and then I'll look for consultant positions back in London. I've looked into the trains and it's not that bad. There's a non-stop service to Paddington that only takes about half an hour,' he continued.

'What! You expect me to move to Reading and commute?' she asked.

'Well, I thought that was the obvious solution. Look, Stella, we always knew there was a chance one of us would have to move with work.'

'Yeah, but I thought we'd discuss it properly first. God, Ian, I can't believe you expect us to leave London. I've got this deal happening. I love London. What about the house?'

'Well, if I get the job I'm moving and that's that,' he said.

'Well I'm not.'

'Stella, it's not all about you. This is my career. I want to make consultant as soon as I can for us, not just for me.'

'And it's not all about you either. This is all about your ego. You can't cope with me earning more money than you and you can't wait to catch up, whether or not that suits me.'

'That's a low blow, Stella.'

'Yeah, but it's the truth, admit it.'

'Look, I'm taking the job in Reading whether you're coming with me or not.'

'Fine.' She got up and slammed the kitchen door behind her as she left.

CHAPTER 5

Stella perched on the purple cube and sipped her ginger margarita. Fenella was twenty minutes late and Stella had already fielded several questions about whether the purple cube on the other side of the tiny table was available. She draped her scarf over it to try and reserve it. She watched the reflections of the people clustered at the bar in the grey smoked glass opposite her. There was an eclectic mix of impossibly beautiful, angular teenagers and wealthy middle-aged men, and the occasional couple comprising one of each.

She saw Fenella first. She looked great. Sleek bobbed hair, bright red lipstick, subtle but expensive clothes and a statement bag. Underneath the cosmopolitan exterior, Stella knew Fenella was just like her. Insecure, bright, but playing a part. Stella waved at her and she smiled back and strode over and hugged her.

'Sorry I'm late, hon. Horrific traffic,' Fenella gave her a proper kiss on the cheek.

'No problem,' said Stella, feeling a rush of affection for her friend, 'it's great to see you. Have a ginger margarita.' She poured a glass from the pitcher in front of her and handed it to her friend.

'Ooh, who's been naughty?' Fenella gestured at the selection of bags next to Stella's cube. Stella had squeezed in a tactical hour of shopping before meeting Fenella.

'Just a few bits. A lovely skirt from Joseph. Some make-up.' Stella pulled the skirt out of the logoed bag and held it up for Fenella to admire, whilst pushing the bag of make-up behind her handbag. There was also a pregnancy test in the bag, which she didn't want Fenella to see. The last thing she needed was a lecture on contraception.

'Nice,' said Fenella, feeling the fabric and nodding approvingly, 'so what's going down with Ian?' she asked, after taking a slug of the cocktail. 'Come on. I know something's up. He spoke to Marcus yesterday and said you two were going to live apart if he got his promotion.'

'Did he really say that?' Stella asked, stuffing the skirt back into the bag.

'Yup. Apparently he's a shoo-in for a job in Reading or Redbridge or somewhere and you won't go with him.'

'That's his version of events is it?' she asked.

'Come on then. Give me your side.'

Stella filled her in on their row.

'Mm, tricky one. Two stubborn people. Two jobs. Two egos. But come on, Stella, Ian loves you. He's such

51

a good guy. Can't you get him to wait a bit and stay in London till something comes up here?'

'You'd think so, wouldn't you? But he's really digging his heels in this time. He applied for the job before he even told me about it. His career matters so much to him. Being a consultant is his dream. He wants to be the big provider and drag me back to his cave and have babies. He thinks he's holding us back from having kids and settling down. Honestly, I'm not in any rush but I'm not moving to Reading. I've told him.'

Fenella raised her eyebrows and took another sip of margarita.

'How is Marcus anyway?' Stella asked, suddenly desperate to change the conversation.

Marcus had been at university with Stella, Ian and Fenella and had been Fenella's on/off boyfriend for a while.

'He's great. Loving his job.'

'Really? Looking in people's mouths all day. I can't imagine anything worse.'

'You know him. Really positive about everything. Like a kid. He thinks it's a miracle he can turn thirteen-year-olds into toothpaste commercial material in twelve months. He's the most evangelistic orthodontist out there.'

'And you and him?'

'Nada. Definitely all off. And yes, I'm totally fine with that. We really are just friends.'

'Really?'

'Really. We've tried too many times now. We both agree. Honestly, we are totally fine with it. It's a relief really.'

'So you're back on the scene then?' Stella asked.

'God that sounds awful but yeah, I'm out there. Looking for lurrve.'

Stella laughed. 'What does your mum think about it? She must be devastated. Hadn't she bought a hat?'

'Not quite but yes she is a bit down about it. Keeps telling me that friendship is the best start for love. Marcus and I are a great couple. It doesn't need to be fireworks all the time, etc. etc. I told her I didn't want it to be a damp squib either.'

'Good point well made,' Stella laughed.

'So, how's work? What was all the cloak and dagger stuff on the phone the other day? Which celeb is getting the Stella makeover at the moment?'

'It's not a celebrity. It's to do with the business. I'm just getting more involved in the management of it. It means extra responsibility and maybe more money,' she bluffed. She couldn't lecture the other doctors on confidentiality and then blab about the deal to her best friend.

'That sounds good. Extra money is always good news. How's things at home by the way? Has your dad found a job yet?'

'Things are okay. Dad's still looking. There's nothing out there for him. At least he still tries though. So many of his mates have given up. It's so sad. There's a whole community of men sat at home watching daytime TV while the wives are out there cleaning, working on the tills at the supermarket, whatever they can do. Come on, let's get another drink and see if we can get a table for dinner. I want to hear all about your latest case. Any juicy trials coming up?' Talking about home depressed Stella. She knew there was no quick fix and felt powerless.

Stella took the tube home. She hadn't heard from Ian all night, which wasn't like him. His shift had finished at eight. Usually he'd text or call her and tonight there had been radio silence. He was probably still sulking about Reading, she decided. She turned the key in the front door and called his name as she turned on the light. He wasn't there. She dumped the shopping bags on the kitchen table, hung her coat on the back of the kitchen door and put the kettle on. She remembered the pregnancy test she'd bought at the pharmacy earlier, rifled through the eyeshadows and nail varnishes in the carrier bag and picked out the cellophane packet. She popped a teabag in a mug before taking the test to the bathroom with her and went through the ritual without bothering to read the instructions.

Stella absent-mindedly waved the white plastic stick in her left hand as she poured the water into her mug and then stirred it and fished out the teabag with her right hand. It was an all-too-familiar rigmarole.

She glanced at the test window, her heart pumping. The reality of what she was doing suddenly hit. It was like this every time. So nonchalant until the mundane piece of plastic was in front of her about to announce its verdict. What if it was positive? What about Ian? Would he still want them to move? Her cheeks were burning. She started to feel light-headed and sat down. She'd only missed one pill. *Christ, I'm a doctor. How stupid can I be?* She berated herself out loud. Mountains of practical problems and overwhelming emotional turmoil were crowding her mind. She was supposed to be the great planner. Her escape from her childhood had been so strategically and meticulously engineered. Babies weren't on the schedule until she was married and in her late thirties. And yet a tiny inner part of her wanted to see the two blue lines. It wouldn't really be the end of the world, would it? She and Ian had always wanted children eventually. It wouldn't be great timing, admittedly. Ian would definitely have to stay now and she'd have to hope that the deal at work would be over in a few months and she'd have time to impress the American buyers before she had to go off on maternity leave. But, yes they could cope with this. Couldn't they? She looked at the stick and checked her watch again. It had been three minutes and there was still only one line. She shook the stick and waited another minute. She wasn't pregnant. Again. She then started the usual worrying about whether that meant she was infertile.

As she sat at the table reading the test instructions for the fourth time, she heard Ian's key in the front door and his cursing as he dropped his keys and fumbled around hanging his coat up. He'd been drinking.

'Hello. Stella, are you here?' he shouted.

'Shhh. I'm only in here,' she poked her head round the kitchen door, 'you okay?'

'Yeah. I'm fine. I've got some news,' he said, belligerently. He seemed to have built himself and his Dutch courage up to deliver some important message.

'Me too,' said Stella. Ian didn't seem to hear her. He continued, 'It's big news. I've got the job in Reading. I got a call today. It's in the bag.' He looked at her.

'Great, but…'

'Stella, no buts, I'm taking it, I've told you.' He held his hand up as if to stop the traffic. 'And look, I've been thinking about this really hard and I seriously think we should take a break.'

'A break?' She didn't understand.

'Not a holiday. A break. From us. I know you don't want to move to Reading and I want this job. It's not fair of me to ask you to move if you don't want to. I am taking the job. But I'm holding you back. I know I am. I think it's best if we take a break and then if you don't want to wait for me to make consultant then you don't have to. Maybe you'll find someone else?' He looked down as he said the last few words.

'No,' Stella screamed, panicking, 'that's not what I want.'

'So you'll come with me?' He looked hopeful.

'No. That's not what I meant,' she said.

'Well then, what's the point?'

'Look, I can live here and you can live in Reading. We don't have to split up. It might only be a couple of years. We can commute at weekends,' she said.

'Stella, it could be longer than a couple of years. It might be five years. You'll be pushing forty. I'm just holding you back.'

'Will you stop saying that?'

'Well it's true.'

'It isn't. Do you really think we should take a break?'

'Yes I do. I've been thinking about it. I can't see another way. The Reading job is the quickest way to progress but if you don't want to come to Reading, then we're in limbo for as long as I'm there. That's no way to live. Commuting at weekends won't work. I'll be working a lot of weekends. You're so busy too.'

'Is that what you really want?' she asked, quietly.

'Yes. I think it is,' he nodded.

His words hit her body in the second wave of shock that evening. She had to know this was what he really wanted. Ten minutes ago she had thought they were going to be parents.

'Really?' she asked again.

'Yes.'

'God, Ian. I can't believe it.'

'I'm sorry,' he said, 'I think it's for the best.'

She was too shocked to cry. She picked up her tea and went to their bedroom. She lay on their bed feeling numb. Christ, what an evening. The events went flailing around in her head. He had been drinking and yet, *in vino veritas* and all that. He had clearly made up his mind that he wanted them to split. A wave of despair and fatigue hit her.

★★★

She was on her second cup of coffee and was trying to read the Sunday papers, when Ian finally emerged from the tiny guest bedroom.

'Morning,' he mumbled.

'Hi,' she said, 'how's your head?'

It was so surreal. How could it be awkward to have a conversation with a man she'd lived with for the past four years? Everything had changed.

'Not great. Look, about last night. I know I'd had a few drinks but I remember everything and I meant it. I think it's for the best if we take a break.'

Her last hope was demolished with those words.

'It's not what I want, Ian, but if that's how you feel,' she managed to say.

'It's not what I want really either, but I can't see another way.'

She could see so many other ways that they could work things out, but the fact that he couldn't said it all to her.

'I did a pregnancy test last night,' she looked down at her coffee as she spoke. Ian seemed to freeze. He had his back to her and turned very slowly to face her.

'Christ.' She'd never seen him look so sad.

'It's okay, Ian. I was a few days late and I'd been throwing up for a few days but it was negative. Must just be that bug…'

Ian sat down.

'Are you absolutely sure?'

'Yes. I've reread the instructions on the test. I did everything right. Ian, I know what I'm doing with those tests. I've done enough of them over the years.'

'Well, that's a relief I suppose,' Ian said, 'are you sure you want to stay in London?'

'Yes, Ian. You still want that job. I still want to stay in London. You said yourself about two minutes ago that you can't see another way.'

'Christ, it's not as simple as that. We could have been having a baby together.'

'Well, we're not, and it's a good job, otherwise things would be even more complicated than they already are.'

They went round in circles for much of the day. Stella was adamant that if Ian had wanted to break up before he knew about the pregnancy test then nothing should change. A baby wouldn't have saved their relationship. It would only have put them under more pressure.

As Ian went off to start his afternoon shift, they hugged each other in the hall. After he left Stella cried for the first time. She was desolate. She'd assumed she and Ian would be together forever. It had never crossed her mind before that they wouldn't. But if he wanted to break up, then she wasn't going to stop him.

The phone started ringing and she picked it up automatically. It was Michelle.

'Hi, Sis. I need to talk about Mum and Dad's party, good time?' she asked.

'Hi, Shell. Not great to be honest.' Stella told Michelle all about what had happened with Ian. She didn't mention the pregnancy test scare.

Michelle was horrified enough about Ian.

'I just don't get it, Stella. What's the big deal about moving to Reading?' she was asking.

'Don't you start! Look, it's not Reading *per se*. It's the way he went about it. Assuming I'd move. Applying for the job without telling me. I've got a life and a job here.'

'You're mad. You've got it made with Ian.'

'He's not a meal ticket, you know.'

'He is where I come from,' Michelle replied, 'get real, Stella, you could have given up work, had babies, the works with him and still had money for highlights and holidays.'

'Christ, Shell. Have you heard of equal opportunities, women's liberation, the end of dowries? Do you think I spent all those years at medical school as some kind of finishing school? I spent years training to do my job. What am I supposed to do, chuck it all away when I bag a doctor?'

'Well, isn't that why you went into it in the first place?'

'Noooo. It isn't. I went into it so I wouldn't have to rely on anyone else and so I'd have some independence and security. And it's a good job I did because I'm going to need it now.'

Stella knocked on Dr Cassidy's door. She had already spent two hours holed up with Christopher Bennett, one of the other doctors, and had left the session with a pile of files, several pages of notes and a sheaf of patient schedules. Now it was Cassidy's turn.

'Come in,' he called.

Stella entered the office and took the seat he held out for her. There was a neat row of files, piled two high, lined up across his desk. He had obviously done his homework.

'Good morning, Stella. Audrey has put together everything you asked for, I think.' He waved his arm towards the files, like a game show host revealing this week's star prize. 'We have looked at all the questions on your list and these files contain all the information you need.' He was rather pleased with himself.

'That's very helpful, Lloyd. Thank you. Would you mind if I just cross-checked what you've prepared?' she asked.

'Be my guest.' He sat down behind his desk and examined his immaculate nails.

'Okay.' Stella put on her glasses and balanced the accountants' document on her lap whilst she turned the pages and ticked off each item. 'A breakdown of procedures over the past two years?' she asked.

'I think you'll find that in this file here,' he drummed his fingers on one of the files. 'There are schedules of procedures in alphabetical order and a summary of the total number of each procedure performed. I've even done a little report for you showing what the trends are for the future.'

'That's great, thanks. And your patient records for the past three years? We need details of procedures, payments, dates and any follow-up work or complaints.'

'And that is all in this file, I believe.' He pointed at another file of papers. And so it continued, as she worked through the list of requests. He really had prepared for the meeting, or more likely he had made his assistant Audrey prepare. Stella was grateful. She had a lot more doctors to see. After twenty minutes, she was done.

'Thanks, Lloyd, I think that's everything. I really appreciate your help.' She smiled at him as she closed the file on her lap.

'Not a problem, Stella. I'm always glad to help. And I should thank you too for helping me with Ms Meddoes the other week.' Lloyd was stacking the files into two piles as he spoke. Olivia Meddoes was a film actress who had phoned him in a panic a few weeks earlier demanding some emergency non-surgical tweaks. Stella had literally filled in for him, as he had been presenting at a conference on the latest facelift techniques.

'Not at all, Lloyd. I know how it is with these celebrities. They want everything done ASAP and with top security, although having your fillers done at nine o'clock at night and coming in the back entrance is taking it to extremes,' she replied.

'Well, the lovely Ms Meddoes has a new film out and I'm sure she wanted to look her best. Anyway, thank you again. She is quite a demanding lady and it was lucky you were able to help. You and me are alike, Stella. Good at our work but we understand the money side of the business too.' He looked at her pointedly, rubbing his forefingers against his thumb like a mafia boss indicating a wad of cash.

'Well, Lloyd, if you mean we both want to make a good living and do a good job for our patients then, yes, I think you're right.' She felt uncomfortable under his gaze, as she often did. His solicitousness always verged on the creepy. She started picking up the files from his desk.

The two doctors carried the piles of papers to Cassidy's assistant's desk. Audrey was all smiles to Lloyd as she arranged for the post room boy to take them to the room that had been assigned to the lawyers and accountants who would be crawling all over them for the next few weeks.

Back in her office, Stella sat down in her visitor's chair and put her feet up on the low table next to it. She was exhausted. She and Ian hadn't spoken again since the previous day. She was maintaining her veneer of professionalism, despite a profound empty feeling in the pit of her stomach. Her phone rang, making her jump. It was Tom. Ryan Miller from Equinox was in his office and he wanted to introduce her to him.

She straightened her skirt and applied some more lipstick before striding down the carpeted corridor to Tom's office.

'Good morning,' said the sharp-suited American as he held out his hand.

'Good morning,' she smiled back at him.

'Ryan is on a flying visit from the US so he called in to meet us. We were just chatting about the business,' Tom said, 'I was explaining how much we've grown over the past five years and I was just telling him that you are one of our star performers.'

'You don't look old enough to be a cosmetic surgeon, Stella,' Ryan said.

Stella felt herself blush. She was acutely aware he was checking her out.

'Stella made consultant, last year, wasn't it?' Tom replied.

'Yes that's right. My practice has been up and running for a year now but I already have a number of regulars for my non-surgical work and I'm building up my surgical work via word of mouth and recommendations.'

'That's good to hear, Stella. Obviously recommendations are a great way to generate business, although in the US we rely heavily on advertising and promotion. That's something we will be keen to do more of, Tom,' Ryan said, turning his eyes to Tom briefly.

'Ryan and I are going to grab a spot of lunch. Would you like to join us, Stella?' Tom asked.

Stella had three patients to operate on in the afternoon but thought this was one lunch she shouldn't turn down.

'Of course, although I will need to be back by one-thirty. I'm operating at two,' she replied.

'Great, let's go,' said Tom, grabbing his jacket from the coat stand next to his door.

The restaurant was in a nearby hotel. Stella was conscious of her heels clicking across the marble entrance hall. No matter how hard she pretended to be one of the boys, her clothes would always give her away, she thought. Not to mention the fact that instead of viewing her as a future colleague, Ryan was clearly assessing her in quite a different way.

They were shown to their table by a waiter in a brocaded Nehru-collared jacket. Ryan pulled her chair out for her and she sat down between the two men, underneath the leaves of a giant ornamental palm plant. Tom was explaining to Ryan that he and Stella were in charge of the day-to-day conduct of the deal and would be his main points of contact for queries.

'And your lawyers and accountants are working on their reports, I understand?' Ryan said, as the waiter brought their drinks.

'That's right. We'll give you their initial views at the all-party meeting on Monday,' said Tom.

'So Stella, what do you see as the big growth areas for the business going forward?' Ryan asked.

'Well, I think there will be a growth in the traditional procedures, you know breast augmentations, eye- and facelifts, tummy tucks. I think the British public is catching up with the Americans in terms of their attitudes towards cosmetic surgery, so that I think that the under-forties are much more receptive to surgery and less judgmental than the previous generation. I think that demand for those procedures will buck the economic trend and provide steady growth for us. However, there is no doubt that some of the traditionally less orthodox procedures like toe reshaping, vaginal and penile procedures, and Botox and fillers in hands and feet are taking off for us and the non-surgical work generally is almost entering the mainstream. As long as we can maintain our reputation for excellence, we will pick up work on the back of the extensive advertising and marketing by some of the more mass-market clinics out there.'

'I'm sure you're right. That is our thinking at Equinox, which is why we are so keen to move into the UK market. Don't you approve of advertising then, Stella?' He smiled at her.

'No, it's not that I don't approve. It's just that some of the most commercial of the clinics that do that in the UK are not necessarily the best in terms of patient care,' she replied.

'Well, we are looking for both. We want commercial success and excellent patient satisfaction.'

'Then we are all on the same page,' said Tom.

As lunch arrived – they had all opted for main courses only – Stella suddenly realised she couldn't face eating, especially as the smell of Tom's lemon sole wafted under her nose. She had an overwhelming feeling that she was going to be sick. This damn bug wouldn't go away.

'Please excuse me for a moment,' she muttered as she stood up, her face surrounded by the leaves of the palm plant. She brushed the leaves aside and strode to the ladies toilets as quickly as she could in her heels and without making it too obvious she was about to throw up spectacularly. She could feel Ryan's eyes burning into her back as she walked and tried not to wiggle her bottom too much.

She banged the cubicle door behind her and fell to the tiled floor and moaned. The waves of nausea were rising in a crescendo of inevitability and she was soon hugging the toilet in a way she hadn't since the last time she'd been clubbing with Fenella and ended up regretting the kebab on the way home. She cried as she retched again and again. Crying was a childhood reflex she told herself and nothing to do with the fact she was single in her mid-thirties and most definitely not pregnant.

She splashed water on her face and fixed her lipstick again. *Mind over matter*, she told herself. She could force down a few mouthfuls of her steak and then leave. She had a full theatre list for the afternoon. That would have to be her excuse.

She returned to the table where Ryan and Tom were talking about the advisers.

'Yeah, Meredith will manage the process,' Ryan was saying.

'She seems very formidable,' Tom replied.

'And some,' Ryan laughed. He looked at Stella as she sat down, and smiled, 'Meredith is the banker at Clinton Wahlberg who identified Beau Street as a target for us.'

'I see,' said Stella, not really understanding where bankers came in to the sale of a cosmetic surgery business.

An hour later, as she scrubbed up for the forthcoming breast augmentation procedure, she wondered how she could brush up on her business skills. Much of what Tom and Ryan had been talking about had gone miles over her head.

'Stella, are you ready to mark up?' Amy the scrub nurse asked.

'Yup. Do you have the marker pen?'

Amy handed the pen to Stella. She examined it carefully to check it was a permanent marker. She had never forgotten the time she'd used a felt tip pen and it had been wiped off as the patient's body had been cleaned with sterile cloths before the incision and after she had been anaesthetised. She'd had to bring the patient round, wait until she could stand and then start all over again. Marking up had to be done whilst the patient was standing. It was remarkable how different everything looked when a patient was flat on their back.

'Hello again, Mrs Shaw. Now if you could just stand here for me, I'm just going to make a few marks on your skin so we know where we are working.'

Mrs Shaw stood nervously in front of Stella with her hospital gown rolled down to her waist. She was clearly embarrassed.

'Now, there's nothing at all to be nervous about, Mrs Shaw. This is a perfectly normal procedure. We'll soon be ready to operate.' What a difference consciousness made, she thought. She would be spending the next hour or so manhandling her patient's breasts but this bit was always the part that made them the most uncomfortable.

Once Mrs Shaw was in the capable hands of her trusted anaesthetist, Ahmed, Stella did one last check that all the right kit was ready, including the all-important implants which Mrs Shaw had so carefully chosen after several consultations.

Today she enjoyed operating. There was something almost relaxing about being away from her phone, her laptop, the deal, Ian and everything else. She was in the zone and the time flew by. Just over an hour after she had begun, it was time to stitch up and she asked Amy to put some music on. The rest of the team started chatting, as classical music played on the radio.

'So Stella, are you doing any more surgery for Dr Cassidy?' Amy asked.

'Er, no. What do you mean?' Stella replied.

'Oh, he just said that you'd helped him on one of his late night jobs recently and that we might be seeing some more of you. I do a late shift for him every other week.'

'Really? I had no idea it was a regular thing. I just did some non-surgical work for an actress who needed it doing in a hurry when Lloyd was at a conference.' Stella was surprised to hear Lloyd had a late clinic.

'Oh, well I'm not sure it's a regular thing but he tries to accommodate his clients with busy diaries, like the actresses, models, famous people, you know.'

This was news to Stella. The clinic had a policy of keeping the doctors informed about any famous people, so they could handle any press interest. They needed to be prepared for tabloid interest and have their statements of denial and 'no comment' ready. She didn't think Lloyd had mentioned any big names for some time. She made a mental note to check the patient records he had given her earlier in the day.

Two eye lifts and a very quick ward round later and Stella was on her way home. No texts from Ian, she noticed, as she went through the messages on her phone. She realised she didn't want to go home. If he was there it would be awful and if he wasn't it wouldn't be much better. She called Fenella before she headed down the steps of the tube station and arranged to meet for a drink.

It was a new bar that had only just opened and Fenella had been keen to try it out. Stella pushed the glass door open and peered through the gloom of the mood lighting to try and find her friend. Fenella was perched at the bar on a precarious-looking steel structure, which looked extremely uncomfortable, and was waving a cocktail menu in the air. Stella waved back and weaved her way through the high-gloss perspex tables towards her.

'Hi, hon,' Fenella said, struggling to shuffle off the stool to greet her friend. It proved too difficult, so she planted a kiss on her cheek whilst grabbing both Stella's shoulders for support. 'Don't move suddenly,' she said, 'or I'm going to hit the deck. Not a good look.'

Stella laughed and climbed up onto the stool next to her.

'How cruel are these contraptions,' she said, as she balanced herself.

'Really crap business idea. They won't sell too many cocktails to anyone before they lose their balance and fall off.'

'Maybe that's the plan. Some kind of extreme challenge. A prize for the person who can drink the most and stay on the longest. I'm not going to suggest it though,' she said, as the barman approached.

'Two glasses of white wine please,' said Fenella.

They downloaded each other's days, before Stella decided to unburden herself.

'You know that argument with Ian about moving to Reading?'

'Yeah, have you kissed and made up yet? Marcus said Ian was gutted about it.'

'Not exactly. We've split. For good.' Fenella's shocked face said it all. Stella knew that she and Ian had always been considered the rock solid couple.

'No way. I don't believe it.' Fenella shook her head.

'It's true. He was adamant about the Reading thing and it was his suggestion in the end. He kept banging on about how he was holding me back but, I don't know, I think he must have been having doubts about us for a while. All this stuff about Reading seemed to crystallise them.'

'Stella, I just don't get it. Ian's mad about you. Always has been. There's no way he's had doubts. Or if he has, he's kept them totally hidden from everyone.'

'Well, it was his suggestion.'

'Yeah, you said that, but do you think he was trying to give you an opt out? You know, make it easy for you because he thought you wanted out?' Fenella asked.

'No. How could you say that? You know I thought Ian and me were forever. How could he think I wanted out?' Stella shouted.

'Steady on, I'm just trying to get my head round it. I just can't believe Ian would call time out on your relationship, that's all.'

Stella was crying now.

'Hey. Come on, Stella. Have a drink, babes,' Fenella tried to hug her friend and almost fell off the stool in the process, 'Christ these fucking stools are a health and safety disaster.'

Stella managed a half smile. 'Go on then,' she said and took a slug of wine.

'That's more like it,' said Fenella, holding onto the edge of the bar to regain her balance.

'Do you want me to have a word with Ian?' Fenella asked.

'It won't do any good. He's made it clear he wants to go. I don't want him thinking I'm in pieces and that my friends have to fight my battles for me,' Stella said.

'He won't think that. Come on, Stella, it's worth fighting for.'

'That's what I thought but Fenella, I'm not sure he wants it anymore. He gets the job in Reading without even asking me and then suggests we take a break. It looks pretty clear to me. We even had another pregnancy scare and it didn't seem to change anything.'

Fenella lifted her glass to her mouth and promptly fell off her stool. Stella got down from hers and helped her up.

'God, I wouldn't do very well in the extreme drinking/stool competition. I've only had two sips of wine,' said Fenella, 'run that past me again. The pregnancy thing. You're not, are you?'

'No. False alarm, but I told him about it and he just seemed relieved and a bit sad.'

'And you're definitely splitting up?'

'Yes.'

'Stella, this makes absolutely no sense at all. If you and Ian can't make it there's no hope for any of us.'

CHAPTER 7

Stella was finishing her ward round when Tom paged her. He wanted to introduce her to the lawyers and accountants who were now on site at the clinic working through the files she had gathered together for them. She finished checking the bruising and swelling of a rhinoplasty patient and then hurried back to her room. She had a patient for a consultation at eight thirty. She would have to be quick.

She ran down the carpeted stairs to the basement room which had been allocated to the legal team. Tom was already there chatting to a dark-haired woman.

'Ah, Stella, good morning. Let me introduce you to Alex Fisher from MacArthur Warren and her team,' Tom said, 'Alex, this is Stella Webb, one of our consultants. Stella has been helping me put some of the materials together for you.'

'Nice to meet you,' said the lawyer, standing up and offering her hand, 'and this is Dan Furtado who is working alongside me,' she said, gesturing towards a preppy-looking colleague who had walked straight off the pages of an Abercrombie and Fitch catalogue, 'and this is Ross Livingstone, a trainee solicitor who is assisting us,' she finished. Stella shook hands with them in turn.

'I hope you have everything you need,' she asked, not quite knowing what she was expected to say.

'I think so, your colleague Albert Cheung has been most helpful. He has gathered all these files together for us and we are working our way through them.'

Like hell he has, Stella thought. Albert was one of the clinic's patient care coordinators. His job was to meet and greet potential patients and explain the kinds of treatments and surgery they could have. Stella had very little time for him and found him far too pushy. She often had to counsel patients to have less work than he'd tried to recommend.

'Has he. That's good to hear. Well, if there's anything else you need please let me know. I can get any more files or information from the doctors if you need it.'

Stella and Tom walked back up the stairs together.

'They seem a decent bunch,' he said, 'what was all that about Albert?'

'No idea. I gathered all the files together. He might have helped some of the doctors' secretaries. Trying to get the credit as usual I bet.'

'What do you mean?' Tom asked.

'Oh, I don't want to go into it now but he's obsessed with getting the plaudits for every procedure I do, trying to make out it was all his idea. More often than not he raises patients' expectations or oversells them work they don't really need doing.'

'Is that right?'

'Yup. Makes us look like those ultra-commercial outfits I was mentioning to Ryan yesterday.'

'That's not necessarily the end of the world, as long as the doctors are sensible.'

'Tell that to Lloyd,' she couldn't help muttering. She much preferred consulting with her patients who came to her direct, but anyone who came in off the street tended to fall into the clutches of Albert Cheung.

'Right, let's meet the bean counters now,' said Tom, as they approached another office.

Tom introduced Stella to Rachel Altman, the accountant from Payne Stanley, and her team.

'Hi Stella, nice to meet you. Are you ready for the all-party meeting? I see you've got a slot for a short presentation. How's that coming on?' Rachel asked.

Stella had no idea what she was talking about.

'Great, thanks. Look forward to seeing you again then,' she bluffed.

'What was that about a presentation?' she asked Tom, as she closed the door behind them.

'Ah yes, I was going to tell you about that. You know I mentioned the meeting coming up with the accountants, bankers, and lawyers? Well, they asked if one of us could do a short presentation about growth areas for the business, that kind of thing, and yesterday Ryan suggested you do it. That's okay isn't it?'

'Yeah, of course,' she said. It was a great opportunity to show Tom, Charles and Ryan her commercial and business skills, but she was apprehensive too. She had never presented on anything outside the field of medicine and didn't want to look a fool. She would need to do her homework.

Karen was waiting for her when she got back to her rooms.

'You're a bit late for your eight thirty. He's already complained,' she whispered.

'Okay. Show him in then.'

Stella was just sitting down behind her desk when a tall, very well-groomed man strode into her office.

'Hi,' he said, thrusting his hand towards her.

'Hello, you must be Mr Wallace,' she said glancing down at her patient list. 'Please do take a seat. So how can I help you?'

'Well, I would have thought it was obvious,' he replied.

She looked at his face. It all looked pretty un-remarkable to her. Rather attractive, well-proportioned, and on closer inspection showing some subtle signs of previous 'work', she thought. 'I'm sorry, Mr Wallace, you are going to have to help me out.'

'It's my nose. It's hideous.'

The alarm bells were already ringing in Stella's head when he added, 'If I had the perfect nose like Leonardo DiCaprio then I know I'd feel so much better about myself.'

She decided to humour him for a bit longer but she could sense trouble ahead. 'And could you tell me what it is you don't like about your nose at the moment?'

'Well, its size to start with. It's way too big. And then the bump in it, oh and I think my nostrils are too flared.'

'Do you mind if I take a closer look?' Stella asked, getting up from behind her desk.

'Be my guest,' he replied. Stella looked closely at his nose from the front and in profile. It was a perfectly normal size, not small but not as enormous as he clearly felt it was. It had the tiniest of bumps in it and his nostrils did flare very slightly but were hardly horse-like.

'Mr Wallace, I understand that you feel you need some work on your nose but I think the difference I could achieve for you would really be minimal. If I were to show you some of my before and after pictures you would see that my patients usually have much more significant concerns than you are presenting with.'

'Are you saying you won't operate? I had this last time with my liposuction,' he replied.

'I'm sorry, have I treated you before?' She looked down at the thin file in front of her; he wasn't registering as a previous patient of the clinic.

'No, not you. I went to the Duke Street clinic and the first doctor I saw wouldn't do my lipo. He said I didn't need it but one of the other doctors there took me on.'

Oh great, a SIMON, she thought. SIMON was an acronym for a Single Insecure Male Over-optimistic Narcissist. They were most cosmetic surgeons' nightmare. Usually, like Mr Wallace, there was very little wrong with them but they were convinced that just one more procedure would make them perfect and change their life forever. They would shop around trying to find a doctor who would operate on them and then become the bane of their life until the surgeon finally refused to carry out any more work on them. Then they would move on to the next doctor to harass. Some of them even became stalker-like. Some doctors might be tempted to take them on because of the amount of repeat work they'd get but that definitely wasn't Stella's style. She didn't need the hassle. What she would really like to do was refer Mr Wallace to a clinical psychologist.

'Let me be straight with you, Mr Wallace. There is very little I can do for you. I'm not saying that there aren't the tiniest changes we could make which would make your nose more like Leonardo DiCaprio's nose but they really would be minimal. My concern is your expectations of surgery. This won't be life-changing stuff at all. Just the tiniest of changes, which most people won't even notice. I do wonder if you have realistic expectations of the results?'

'What are you saying then?'

'Mr Wallace, please could you tell me what other cosmetic surgical and non-surgical procedures you have had?'

'I've had the lipo, some pec implants, cheek and chin implants, Botox and fillers in my face, erm, I think that's about it.' He looked up quizzically, recalling his various trips to plastic surgeons.

'And how old are you?'

'I'm twenty-nine.'

'Okay, Mr Wallace, what I would like to do is refer you to a doctor I know who is a clinical psychologist. After a course of treatment with him, I would be happy to see you again and discuss your nose further.'

'Are you saying I'm a nutcase?' he asked.

'Not at all. This is quite a common avenue to explore. I just want to get to the bottom of why you keep having surgery. Mr Wallace, you are young and have no obvious reasons for corrective surgery. I just want to be sure we can get the best possible outcomes for you and part of that involves managing your expectations. I can't change your life for you but I could very marginally improve your nose.'

Stella scribbled down the name of a clinical psychologist she knew and passed it to him.

'So you're saying you won't do it then? The nose job?'

'I'm saying that if you have a couple of sessions with Dr Scott first and then see me again we can discuss it further.'

She was confident she wouldn't see him again. He would shop around until he found someone else who didn't have the same scruples and then in about eighteen months or so he would fixate on another part of his anatomy.

As she left the clinic that evening on her way to the hairdresser's, she received a text from Ian. He was at the house, packing, and wanted to have a chat before he left. It really was happening. She sighed as she pushed the door to the brightly lit salon. Getting a smart businesslike hairdo had seemed such a great idea last week but now she couldn't care less. She muttered something to the style director about a shorter, choppier more sassy style and then left her to it.

An hour later and Stella swished her hair from side to side. She had to hand it to the style director. She had definitely given her a style. The long slightly layered bob really suited her and looked much more professional than her previous blonde mane. Stella smiled to the receptionist as she handed over her credit card and left a generous tip.

'You look great,' said the girl.

'Thanks,' Stella replied. She'd take the compliments where they came, even if it was from a girl with bright pink hair, Scouse brows and a nose ring.

As she left the salon her phone vibrated. It was Michelle again. It was only a couple of weeks to the ruby wedding party and Michelle wanted to finalise the food. Stella calmed her down and told her to get whatever she needed. She would be footing the bill and for the prices Michelle was quoting she would be happy to fork out for a few thousand vol-au-vents, crabsticks and sausage rolls.

'Will Ian be coming then?' her sister asked.

'What do you think? Of course he won't,' Stella replied.

'Only he knows about it cos I texted him when I sent out all the texts last week.'

'I know he knows about it but he's hardly going to come, is he? But Shell, don't tell Mum. I don't want it to spoil the party.'

'You'll have to tell her eventually.'

'I know but let's leave it till after the do.'

'Okay. You're probably right. She's got enough to worry about at the moment,' said Michelle.

'What do you mean?'

'Nothing really. Just, you know with Dad and everything. Money's tight as usual,' Michelle replied.

Stella felt the usual pang of guilt. She'd just spent the equivalent of her dad's Jobseeker's Allowance on a haircut. *Still, a damn good haircut*, she thought as she admired herself in a shop window. She was determined to get this deal done and sort her parents' money problems out.

She arrived home to find two large rucksacks in the hall and Ian sitting at the kitchen table.

'Hi,' she said.

Ian stared at her and she remembered her hair. She smoothed it down self-consciously. She reddened as she hoped he hadn't thought she'd already moved on and washed her man out of her hair, or something.

'Great haircut,' he said.

'Oh thanks. Thought I should make a bit of an effort for work,' she mumbled.

'No really, it's great. Really suits you.'

It was excruciating. She didn't know where to look. He stood up and walked towards her.

'I've left all the paperwork on the table. Look I'll carry on paying my share of the mortgage until we decide what we're doing about the house. I'm renting a cheap place in Reading with another doctor. If you don't mind I'll keep my key but I promise I'll let you know before I pop back to get anything and I won't just drop in or anything. Is that okay?'

'Of course it is, Ian. This is your place as much as mine.'

'If you don't mind I think I'll give your parents' ruby wedding do a miss.'

'Probably a good idea. I haven't told them though so please don't mention anything about us, you know, splitting up.'

'Er, okay,' he replied.

'Obviously I will tell them but not just yet. I don't want to rain on their parade.'

'Totally understand. Okay, I'd better be off. Bye Stella.'

'Bye Ian. Good luck in the new job.'

He picked up the two bags and left. Before she could even think about how she felt her phone started vibrating again. This time it was her mum.

'Stella. That you?'

The concept of mobile phones was a troubling one for Stella's mum. She couldn't get her head round the fact that the phone belonged to Stella and wasn't likely to be answered by anyone else, that there was really no need to shout and that talking as though she was some kind of oral telegram wouldn't actually save her or Stella vast amounts on their phone bills.

'Need to talk. Urgent.'

'Okay, Mum. What's the matter?' Stella took her coat off, poured a glass of wine and settled into an armchair.

'Embarrassing to ask. Mortified.'

'Mum, what on earth is it?'

'Money. In trouble. Loan sharks.'

'God, Mum, can you speak properly. It's like having a conversation with a robot. What loan sharks? What kind of trouble?'

'I've borrowed some money, pet, and I can't pay it back. I got it from Roy's son. He's a loan shark now and I've been paying him regular but I missed last week and now he says I owe him double what I started with. I can't tell your father. You know what he's like about debt.'

'How much did you borrow, Mum?'

'Two hundred pounds but Roy's son says it's four hundred now.'

'Is Roy's son Neil that used to play on the Sunderland youth team?'

'That's him. The football didn't work out for him and he went into money-lending.'

'I was at school with him. Can you get me his number? I'll sort him out. Did you get any paperwork with your loan? What's the APR?'

'AP what? No, no paperwork. He just put it all down in a black book.'

'Is he licensed?'

'I've no idea. I just thought as he was Roy's lad and as Roy used to be pals with your dad that he'd be all right.'

'Is he threatening you?'

'No not really, pet. He was always such a sweet lad. Lovely blond hair. He's as bald as a badger now.'

'Coot, Mum. Bald as a coot.' Stella sighed. It was amazing how much trouble money could cause when you didn't have any, 'Mum, give me his number and I'll sort this, I promise.'

She jotted down the number and tried to calm her mother down. She poured a second glass of wine before picking up her phone again.

'Hi, is that Neil?'

'Yeah. Who's this?'

'Stella Webb. We were at school together.' There was a brief silence at the other end.

'Well bloody hell, this is about as likely as Lionel Messi coming to play for Sunderland.'

'Yes it has been a few years. Neil, I'm sure you know why I'm calling?'

'Is it for me hand in marriage?'

'Not this time, Neil. It's about my mum.'

'Well your mam's a lovely lady all right but I'm really not that interested. Besides, isn't she married?'

'Ha ha. Quite the comedian, aren't we? No Neil, this is about the money you lent my mum.'

'Ah right you are. Yes, I am in the credit business these days.'

'So I hear. The local mafia boss I understand. Licensed are you?'

'Ay of course I am.' He sounded offended.

Stella was relieved. That was something, she supposed.

'Okay, so what's all this about my mum's debt doubling overnight?'

'Ah well, I'll have to talk to me boss. See it's not me own business like. I work for a company and to be honest I'm not that good with the paperwork. Can I call you back?'

'Not till you back off my mum, Neil. She doesn't need this worry. She'll pay you back the debt plus reasonable interest but don't go all hard man on her. Can you call me back with details of the loan, the APR, and how much I need to pay to cover everything she owes? Leave her alone and deal with me.'

'I'd be delighted to, Stella. You up here much these days?'

'I'm up next week and I want this sorting by then.'

'Listen, pet, I'm on to it. To be honest my maths aren't that special and maybe I got your mum's numbers a bit wrong. I'm sure we can sort this out. Maybes I could buy you a Bacardi when you're up next week?'

'Neil, just get me the numbers and we'll see.'

'I'll call you back. I might even stretch to an Asti Spumante.'

Stella couldn't help smiling.

CHAPTER 8

Stella spent most of her spare time over the next few days preparing for her presentation. Tom had said she had to focus on growth areas so that's what she did. She used her own sales figures for the previous two years as a guide and extrapolated them out across the practice as a whole. She got Karen to help her with the graphics and produced what she thought were impressive pie charts, graphs and statistics. She had called Karen into her office for a run-through.

'Keep your head up and speak clearly,' Karen was saying from the visitor's armchair where she was reclining and unwrapping a toffee.

'Okay. Here I go.' Stella cleared her throat and stood in front of her desk where her laptop was placed with the first slide up on the screen.

'Good morning, everyone. I'm going to give you a brief presentation about the growth areas we anticipate for the business over the next twelve to eighteen months.'

'Tell them who you are,' Karen muttered through her toffee chewing.

'Okay.' She started again. 'Good morning, everyone. I'm Stella Webb, consultant surgeon and partner at Beau Street.' Stella spoke to each slide emphasising the number of breast implants, facelifts and tummy tucks she forecasted they would do and finished the presentation with a section on the growth of the more obscure procedures. She got through it without any major stumbles.

'Sounds great!' said Karen, 'I'd buy the business if I could afford it on the back of that sales pitch. All the slides and graphics worked brilliantly, though I say so myself, and you really looked the part, especially with your new hairdo. You need to wear a sharp suit though and go for your red lippy, not your pink. More corporate, less girly. Well done.'

'Thanks, Karen. You sure? Not too over the top?' Stella perched on the edge of her desk.

'Definitely not. You are trying to sell the clinic aren't you?'

'I guess so.' *I think I might just run it past Tom though*, Stella said to herself.

'Are you done with me now? I'd like to get back to pick up Benji from training,' said Karen.

'Yeah of course. Have you made a decision about the bursary yet?'

'Yes. He's going for it. I've filled in all the forms about our income and he needs to sit the entrance exam and then we'll see how he gets on. I just hope he passes. I keep wondering about getting him extra coaching but it's so expensive.'

'Could be worth every penny though?'

'Mm, that's what I said but Lenny's not sure. He thinks he's either got what it takes or he hasn't.'

Stella got the impression that Karen's husband was less keen on Karen's private school ambitions for their son.

★★★

Stella spent the weekend rehearsing her presentation. By the time Monday morning came she was tired of hearing it and so was Fenella. She had met Stella for a pub lunch on Sunday and been dragged back to the house for another run-through.

'Christ almighty, if I have to hear about the changing demographic and changes in attitudes to cosmetic surgery one more time I'm going to spontaneously combust. You make the whole thing sound so run-of-the-mill and the norm that I'm beginning to feel left out. From what you're saying, by the time I'm forty, I'll be the only woman in the Western world with her own boobs, own nose and with a jawline which frankly isn't as tight as it once was. Is this really all true? Are we really all going to be doing this stuff?' Fenella asked after the fourth time she'd heard the presentation.

'Seriously, Fenella, it's amazing how much growth there's been in our sector over the past few years. I read somewhere that if the number of people who've expressed an interest in cosmetic surgery actually have it done, there will be more surgically enhanced people in the UK than people who have satellite TV.'

'So who are these people? I don't know anyone who's had work done, unless you are keeping something from me?'

Stella laughed.

'Well, obviously, I used to be a man with a crooked nose but apart from that no, I haven't had anything done.'

'Well, obviously, you can tell that by your Adam's apple and enormous hands,' Fenella replied.

'Ha ha! Very funny. Well, I don't know any friends who've had anything major, although one or two have had a bit of non-surgical stuff.'

'Ooh who? Come on spill.'

'Can't tell you, I'd have to kill you. Patient confidentiality and all that.' Stella tapped the side of her nose.

'Go on. I bet Miranda has. Her forehead's always shiny.'

'That's cause she's got greasy skin.'

'Ooh bitchy! What about Ian, did you ever feel the need to "tweak" him?' Fenella asked.

'Steady! No. Not at all. Why would I?'

'Yeah, he was pretty perfect. Why did you split up again?'

'Fenella, please.'

'Sorry. Sorry,' Fenella put her hand up as if to fend off criticism, 'I just don't understand what happened there at all. It's hard for your mates too you know. None of us saw it coming. We're all in shock.'

'Yeah, yeah, my heart bleeds for you.'

'Seriously, I mean it. You two were the beacon of hope for all of us. Marcus is pretty cut up about it, I can tell you. It makes us all insecure when the only rock solid couple we know break up.'

'Well, I'm really sorry but to be honest we weren't really thinking about what our friends wanted when we made the decision.' Stella picked up a coffee mug and made to leave the room.

'I know that. Look, I didn't want to upset you, really. It's just still a bit of a shocker. For everyone.' Fenella got up and hugged Stella, 'Are you really okay?'

'Fen, I'm fine. I've got loads on my mind with this deal at work and Mum and Dad's party coming up and I'm not really thinking about it that much. Look, I've just got to move on. And I will.'

Stella was up at six the next morning. She had a ward round to do first thing, checking on patients who'd been in the clinic over the weekend. Then she wanted to grab some time with Tom before the all-party meeting. She'd emailed him the presentation and wanted to be sure he was happy with it.

She got dressed quickly but carefully. The new wrap dress she'd ordered had come and she'd ironed the packing creases out the previous evening and hung it on her bedroom door. She shimmied into it and admired herself in the mirror. It was perfect business attire, she thought, without being either dull or overtly sexy.

Her ward round had taken longer than she had hoped and by the time she knocked on Tom's door there were only twenty minutes to go until the all-party meeting. As she entered his office it was apparent he was not alone. Charles Sutton's plummy tones boomed out.

'Right you are, Tom. As long as you've briefed everyone we should be fine. Ah, Stella, good morning.'

'Good morning, Charles. How are you?' she replied.

'Marvellous, Stella. Looking forward to this morning's little gathering I hope? I hear you're flying the flag for Beau Street today.'

'That's right, Charles. I've prepared a little presentation. That's why I'm here actually. Tom, I wondered if we could have a quick chat first. Did you get my email?' she turned towards Tom, who was leafing through some papers on his desk.

'Sorry, Stella, which email?' he asked.

'The email I sent at the weekend. It had my presentation attached,' Stella replied, panicking slightly. She would be presenting to a room full of people in less than an hour and she needed to know that her presentation was along the right lines.

'Ah yes,' he said, absent-mindedly, 'I did have a brief look at that. It looked fine. Just a brief sales pitch will be fine. Something along the same lines as our conversation with Ryan over lunch the other day should do it. Did I tell you Ryan won't be there? He's dialling into the meeting from Chicago.' Stella was glad. As far as she was concerned the fewer people to witness the humiliation the better.

Stella was more nervous than she could remember being for a long time. The room was full of sharp-suited professionals who seemed totally unfazed by the number of people present. She scanned the boardroom as she sipped her water. Apart from Tom and Charles there were the accountants; she recognised the woman, Rachel, but there was an older important-looking man next to her. An elegant super-efficient-looking woman seemed to be running the show. She guessed she would be the Meredith character Ryan had been talking about the other day. Meredith had a male assistant with her who also exuded confidence in a low-key manner. She watched as the lawyer Alex and her good-looking American assistant arrived. It was a full house now. Meredith was patching in Ryan on the speakerphone and the lawyers were being asked to give them all an update on their work.

Stella watched. She felt like an observer at some sort of gentlemen's club or a social member at a cult meeting. They were all the paid-up members and she was the girl from the council estate who had somehow sneaked in. She watched the women in their fitted suits and the men with their double cuffs and silk ties and wondered at this corporate world where they all knew the language, the ritual dance and the agenda. She shook her new hair back from her face and held her head up. She deserved her place at the table, she told herself, and without her and the other surgeons there would be no business to sell.

The lawyers had finished their part in the performance and were nodding and shaking hands as they left. The accountants took over now. Meredith was barking questions at the advisers and Ryan's more silky tones echoed around the room with follow-up queries. There was no doubt that Equinox seemed serious about the deal. Stella felt a flutter of excitement amongst the nerves.

The accountants were finished now and Charles and Ryan were chatting about the timetable. Meredith was looking at Stella and pointing at her agenda. She was clearly up next.

'Thank you, Charles,' Meredith said, 'It seems from all the advisers' comments that we are still on track for our preferred timetable. Now I believe it is Dr Webb's turn to give us a short presentation on the management's view on the growth prospects for the business. Over to you, Dr Webb.'

Stella cleared her throat and stood up. She set up her laptop in front of her and gave a thumbs up to Meredith's assistant who had set up the screen behind him, which everyone else in the room was now facing. She clicked to the first slide.

'Good morning, everyone. As you know I am Stella Webb, consultant cosmetic surgeon and partner in the clinic.' As she said this, her confidence increased. She was a professional too; just in a different field. She might not understand a balance sheet or a sale and purchase document but she was sure none of them were too hot at performing a tummy tuck.

'This first slide shows Beau Street's sales figures for the past five years. As you can see…'

'Stella, I can't see anything,' it was Ryan, 'I'm sure your slideshow will be magnificent. But not for me. Can you talk me through the numbers?' Damn. She hadn't factored in the speakerphone when she'd drafted the presentation. All her beautiful slides and graphs wouldn't be seen by the one man she'd been hoping to impress. She saw Meredith smirking to her assistant.

'Ryan, I'm so sorry. Of course, I'll give you the headline figures and talk round the slides so it all makes sense for you. I'll email them to you later.'

She continued. It was much harder work and more long-winded now she had to talk through all the statistics rather than let the visuals make the impact. As a result, she talked up the numbers a bit more so the extent of the growth in the traditional procedures was more obvious and was more ambitious about the take-up of the toe reshaping, hand rejuvenation and other more obscure lines of work. She grew in confidence as she continued and despite the early setback seemed to have everyone's full attention by the end. Meredith was leaning forward taking notes and Rachel the accountant looked suitably impressed as she and her colleague exchanged nods of approval.

As she returned to her consulting room she could see Karen, her hand over her telephone receiver, waving to her and mouthing, 'It's the American. For you.'

Stella sprinted into her office and picked up the phone.

'Hey, Stella, that was fantastic,' Ryan purred, 'I had to call you straight away to let you know. The guys here were really impressed.'

'The guys?'

'Yeah, I had a few colleagues listening in. Frankly they were thrilled by your forecasts and projections.'

'Great,' she replied.

'I can see big things for you, Stella. We need a man, or in your case, a woman on the ground once Equinox is in charge. Your name keeps coming up.'

'Really?' Stella had no idea what he meant.

'Yeah, with Charles Sutton stepping down, there's a vacancy to fill.'

Stella was stunned. Her? Run the business? She'd only been a consultant for a year. She had no business background.

'Ryan, I'm not sure…'

'Honey. Trust me. You can do it. Maybe we could fund a part-time MBA for you or something. You're a natural. It's either you or someone from the States. Don't tell Tom but no one else at Beau Street has what we're looking for.'

Stella sat down. She had thought the presentation had gone reasonably well but hadn't been expecting this.

'Ryan, I'm really flattered but…'

'Stella, we don't need to discuss this now. The deal isn't even done yet. But keep it in mind. We need someone to run the show and at the moment yours is the only name on my list. By the way, you will be able to warrant those facts and figures in your presentation won't you?'

She had absolutely no idea what he was talking about.

'Of course,' she bluffed. She'd ask Tom what 'warrant' meant later.

'Great. I'm looking forward to getting to know you better, Stella. I'm going to be over in the UK in the next couple of weeks. I'd like to buy you dinner.' It was a statement not a question.

'That would be lovely,' she said, and meant it.

***

It was Friday night and Stella had allowed plenty of time at Heathrow before her flight to Newcastle took off. She had left her travel arrangements to the last minute and had decided that as it would only cost her a little bit more to fly up, she'd take the chance to travel in style. It also meant she wouldn't be driving back to London on Sunday with a raging hangover. Well, those were some of the reasons she used to justify her shopping spree at Terminal 5. The main reason she'd arrived early was to make the most of the designer brands all under one roof. She'd already picked up a pair of black patent heels and was now perusing the handbag section in a boutique so minimalist that she felt like she was cluttering the place. She suspected the supercilious shop assistant felt the same way. She wondered if that was part of their sales strategy: to make you feel so small and unstylish that it made you want to prove a point to them by buying the most ridiculously overpriced bag in the store. *Well, it wouldn't work today*, she thought, as she attempted her best flounce out of the store, knocking over the discreet umbrella stand by the door with her wheelie bag as she went.

Next was the perfumery. Stella loved this bit of every trip. She had deliberately not worn perfume that morning, so she could go mad with the testers. And she did. Her nose was soon so overwhelmed by the changing cocktail of scents that she didn't even bother testing the perfumes before spraying them liberally behind her ears, in her hair, on her wrist, down her cleavage and all over her linen jacket and cotton scarf. She grabbed a bottle of her mum's favourite Chanel, a celebrity scent for Michelle and chose an aftershave for her dad with very traditional masculine packaging. He wouldn't go near anything that looked too metrosexual.

Stella swung her shopping bags in one hand and pulled her wheelie bag in the other, as she headed for the gate. She was still early. She was approaching a small bar with several free bar stools. A gin and tonic would be nice before the flight.

Two large G and Ts and a lovely chat with the Filipino barman later, she heard her name being called and set off running to the gate, her perfume bottles banging against her leg. She veered round several plus-sized ladies with similar-sized luggage, her wheelie bag cornering on one wheel, and skidded up to the desk, whilst the irate steward continued to berate her over the tannoy. He got his own back as he explained how she would have to face the walk of shame as she boarded the plane, which was ready to depart, ten minutes after everyone else.

CHAPTER 9

The party was three hours away and it was panic stations in the Webb house. Stella's mum was redoing her hair after a disaster at the hairdresser's. They'd straightened her hair, which she had politely said she loved, and then she'd come home and put her Carmen rollers in. Michelle was slapping on her third layer of fake tan and Stella's dad was dressed and ready to go and was pacing the small downstairs rooms looking at his watch.

'When did you say the food needed dropping off, Michelle?' he shouted from the bottom of the stairs.

'Not till five, Dad, and you don't need to do it. I'll take it,' she shouted back from the bathroom.

'Shall I start loading it into your car?'

'Dad, just leave it. I'll be down in a bit when this tan has dried.'

The front door slammed as Stella returned from a last minute dash for candles.

'Where've you been?' her dad asked, 'you've not even started getting ready.'

'Secret mission, Dad. Can't tell you.' She gave him a hug and hung her bag on the bannister, 'Don't stress, we've got ages yet. Is my sister out of the bathroom yet?' Stella charged up the stairs two at a time.

'Shell, are you done in there?' She banged on the bathroom door, which swung open. Her sister was standing in the bath in a pair of paper knickers trying to rub fake tan onto the middle of her back and failing miserably.

'Christ, Michelle, you look like you've got a target on your back or a stencil of the Japanese flag or something. Here, let me help.' Stella grabbed the bottle of fake tan and started rubbing it onto the white patch in the middle of her sister's back. 'Why didn't you get a spray job done?'

'Wasn't organised like you,' Michelle replied, 'while you're there would you dry me?'

'What? How?'

'Get your hairdryer and plug it in on the landing and just dry that tan on my back for me. Dad's stressing about the food and I need to get dressed before he starts stuffing it in my car and dropping it everywhere.'

Stella did as her sister asked. As she stood there blow-drying her orange sister, her mother emerged from her bedroom in a bright pink shower cap which encased her heated rollers.

'How's the hair, Mum?' she asked.

'Nearly done, soon be as good as new. Don't know what that girl was thinking of. Straighteners on me! I'm sixty-two years old, for heaven's sake!'

'That's not old. Lots of my patients are older than you and they straighten their hair.' She had many clients her mum's age and older who with her help looked about fifty and wore the clothes, make-up and hair of women decades younger, some more successfully than others.

'That may be so in that London but you're in Newcastle now, pet. None of my friends do it. Anyway, can you come and look at my dress? I want to decide which earrings to wear with it.'

Once Michelle had finally got into her short, strapless blue dress and started loading up the buffet and her mother had finally settled on which earrings and necklace to wear, Stella had a moment to herself. She cleared some space on the dressing table in the bedroom that she and Michelle had always shared and which Michelle had subsequently appropriated. She applied her make-up expertly and more subtly than her sister and then unzipped her frock from the travel bag she had hung up on the back of the bedroom door the night before. She had chosen a red linen dress that was fitted around her waist and bust. She was having second thoughts about it now she'd seen what Michelle was wearing and hoped she wouldn't look underdressed. Still, it was a bit late to change her mind. She slipped the dress on and ran a brush through her hair.

'Stella, are you nearly ready? The car's all packed now,' called Michelle.

'On my way,' she called back before applying her lip gloss.

'So Ian's not coming then?' Michelle asked, as Stella climbed into the passenger seat next to her.

'No, he isn't. But don't tell Mum and Dad why.' Stella straightened her skirt; it was already starting to crease. She always regretted wearing linen.

Michelle was leaning forward over the steering wheel, crunching through the gears now.

'Okay, understood. Is anything coming your way?' Michelle was craning her neck to see the traffic coming in both directions as they tried to pull out onto the main road.

'You're okay,' Stella replied. Michelle swung out into the road and within two minutes they were pulling up outside the back of the pub. Someone had erected a hand-painted banner on an old sheet above the front door of the pub which said 'Happy Rooby Wedding June and Bob!'

Michelle jumped out and knocked loudly on the back door. Eventually it was opened by Carl.

'All right, pet, you're early aren't you?' he said, looking at his oversized diver's watch, which Stella guessed had never been anywhere near a coral reef.

'It's five o'clock like we agreed. Here, give us a hand.' Michelle was already pulling trays of cling-film-wrapped sandwiches out of the boot and thrusting them at him.

Stella and Michelle went back and forwards for the next fifteen minutes bringing out sausage rolls, sausages on sticks, cheese and bacon flans – their mum wouldn't let them call it quiche, in case the men refused to eat it

– crab sticks, pork pies and an array of artery-hardening desserts. Once they had them inside on the trestle tables that Carl had hastily erected, they arranged them into savoury and sweet items at either end of the table.

'What about knives and forks?' Stella asked.

'It's a finger buffet, isn't it?' Carl chipped in.

'What about the quiches, I mean flans, and the trifle? We're going to need a few forks and spoons at the least. Shall I go back?' Stella turned to Michelle.

'We've got a few spoons in the back. Let me go and have a look.' Carl walked towards the bead curtain that separated the function room from the main pub, waddling from side to side, his overdeveloped upper body threatening to topple him over at any point.

Stella and Michelle fiddled around with the buffet for a bit longer. Stella made little signs on cocktail sticks indicating what each item was; her mum had insisted on that, although Stella thought it was all pretty obvious. *Most people know their crab sticks from their vol-au-vents*, she thought. Michelle emptied out the tins of Celebrations and Quality Streets into several bowls and fanned out the napkins like she'd seen in an item on *Entertaining Like a Lord* on breakfast TV. Carl returned with a basket of spoons and forks and plonked them on top of Michelle's napkins.

Next the two sisters set about transforming the room. They had banners and balloons and a montage of old photos which they had put together the previous evening after their parents had gone to bed early in preparation for the big day.

'Mum's been dead excited about tonight. It was deffo the right thing to do,' said Michelle, in between blowing up balloons.

'Yeah, you were right about the party. They both seem really pleased about it. I never had them down as liking being the centre of attention but I think they're quite enjoying it.'

'Well it's taken Mum's mind off the money worries that's for sure. You know she's had some loan shark hassling her?' Michelle said, as she pinned up the balloons in the traditional obscene arrangement of two round balloons and one long thin one.

'Yeah I did,' Stella muttered between the drawing pins in her teeth. Neil had texted her once since their conversation but seemed more bothered about letting her know that he was coming to the party with his mum and dad.

'It's not good. She's been really stressed about it. The worst thing is that she can't talk to Dad about it. She hates having secrets from him. It's eating her up,' said Michelle as she climbed on a table to pin up a banner.

'Shell, don't worry, I'll sort it,' Stella said, wondering how she could sort it if it was more than a couple of hundred pounds. She had maxed out all her credit cards and had no money in the bank until she got paid at the end of the month. All her cash was going to Carl to pay the bar bill tonight. She rolled her eyes as she remembered her airport shopping.

When they had finished decorating the room and had lit some scented candles to dilute the smell of stale beer, they went through to the main bar and ordered a drink. All they had to do now was wait for the DJ to set up and for Michelle's best friend, Stacey, to bring the cake she'd made.

By seven-thirty everyone had arrived. The DJ was playing background music, the cling film was off the buffet and the cake was on a stand in a corner. Stella's parents had turned up early, as expected, and had greeted everyone as they arrived. They were in their element. Stella's mum kept saying it was the wedding reception she'd never had and was already on her third Bacardi and Coke. Stella's aunts and uncles were already gathered close to the buffet. Stella's contemporaries from school were crowded round her admiring her dress and firing questions at her.

'Could you sort my tits out then?' said Jill who'd recently given birth to her fourth baby, 'talk about headed south, my pair's practically in Antarctica now.'

Stella talked her through a breast lift operation and told her the ballpark cost, which seemed to put her off.

'What about my frown lines?' asked another friend Sasha, as she frowned to illustrate the vertical lines at the middle of her brow, 'should I do that Botox? I look like I'm permanently pissed off. The girl who does my nails can do it apparently.'

'I'd go to a doctor if I were you, Sash. You need someone who understands the facial structure and muscle interaction. I'm not sure how much training your nail woman would have had.'

And so it continued. They asked about tummy tucks, liposuction, and fillers. It was amazing how much they knew about her industry and how comfortable they were talking about, in some cases, quite major surgery.

'Testing, testing,' called the DJ tapping his mike and clearing his throat, 'can I have some quiet please? June and Bob would like to extend a big welcome to you all and declare that the buffet is now officially open.'

'Christ, he's not launching a ship,' Stella said to the girls.

'He did used to work on the shipyard,' said Jill.

'Look at the stampede,' said Michelle, 'you'd think they hadn't eaten for a week.'

The girls watched their parents' friends and family jostling to get to the front of the buffet. It was dog eat dog out there. The women were the worst. Stella's Aunt Brenda already had two plates, one piled high with sandwiches and sausage rolls and the other with trifle, profiteroles and gateaux.

'The irony is they'll all be back here on Monday evening. They hold the weekly slimming club weigh-ins in this room,' Stacey commented.

The girls joined the queue when it became obvious that this wasn't a buffet they would be able to go back to throughout the evening. The tables were being stripped bare, as though a plague of locusts had descended.

Stella felt a tap on her shoulder. She turned round to face a tall, slim bald man wearing a purple shirt with the familiar dancing polo pony embroidered on it. Initially she didn't recognise him but when she heard him speak the penny dropped.

'Hi Stella,' he said, 'good to see you. You look great.'

'Thanks Neil. How's business?' Her mum was right. He looked totally different from the Neil she'd known at school without his surfer dude hair.

'Ah,' he coloured slightly, 'wahay, business is all right I suppose. Look, about your mum…'

'Not here, Neil, not now. I'll meet you in the car park in ten minutes.'

'Er, okay then. Can I get you a drink?'

'Yes please, a white wine. I'll meet you out there,' she replied.

Stella gradually made her way to the front of the queue and grabbed a piece of 'flan' and some salad, which seemed to be the only thing which hadn't been decimated. She sneaked out of the fire exit, as the DJ started to crank up the music.

Neil was already waiting for her, pint in one hand and wine in the other. He looked nervous. Stella took the wine from his outstretched hand and took a sip.

'Thanks for the wine,' she said, 'look, about my mum. What do I have to pay to make you go away?'

'Charming. Last drink I buy for you,' he smiled nervously.

'You know what I mean, Neil.'

'She borrowed two hundred to start and she paid back twenty-two pounds three weeks in a row. So that takes it down to… er, twenty-two times three…' he was counting on his fingers, 'two hundred less sixty-six, erm, a hundred and thirty-four?'

'Sounds about right, so why did my mum say it doubled overnight?'

'Well, she then missed a payment, which incurs a penalty charge, and none of those figures include the interest. When she pays back the twenty-two, only some of that is repaying the loan.'

'How much?' Stella asked. Trust her mother to get embroiled with a loan shark with no grasp of figures.

'What do you mean?'

'How much is the interest? What's the total repayment amount? What's the APR?'

'I think the APR is about fifty per cent I heard the boss say the other day.'

'It's daylight robbery, Neil. This is such a scam. How can you do your job if you don't know how much people owe?' she asked, taking a large slug of wine, 'All I want to know is how much I have to pay to finish this? That isn't so hard is it?'

'I just collect the money, Stella. All I really know is the weekly amount I'm supposed to come back with. Honest, Stella, it's not a dodgy outfit. We're better than all the rest. Some of their APRs are in the hundreds. We never get violent or nasty. Honest.'

'Well, that's something I suppose,' she replied. She did some quick sums in her head. Sixty pounds for the DJ, a couple of hundred behind the bar, she probably had another hundred in cash on her. She'd emptied her bank account before her flight so she could pay for the party. 'If I give you a hundred now, can you promise to email me a full schedule of the debt, the repayments, the interest, everything? I'll settle what else is left then and that should be the end of it. Oh and Neil, do me a favour.'

'Anything, Stella,' he looked more relieved than she did.

'Never lend any money to Mum again. Call me instead. Here's my business card with all my details,' she passed him her plate of food to hold, whilst she rummaged in her bag and fished out a card and handed it to him.

'I'd be glad to. Are we done?'

'I think so if you give me back my food,' she nodded to the plate he was still holding.

'Sorry. Here you go. Can I ask you something, Stella?'

'Er yes, I suppose.'

'Do you do much surgery on men?'

That was one question she hadn't been expecting.

'Yes, quite a lot really. I'd say at least thirty per cent of my patients are men. Why?'

'I'm a bit embarrassed really but it's about my ears. I would have thought it was pretty obvious. You must remember all the piss-taking at school,' he smiled.

'Yeah, I remember you being in all the team photos in the middle as the FA Cup.'

'I'm still known as "Wing Nut" to the lads. Look, I don't mind the teasing, I've heard them all before, but

I'm getting married soon and I'd like to look all right on the pictures. Also me and me fiancée want to have kids soon and I don't want them to inherit the ears, like,' he smiled as he spoke.

Stella laughed nervously; she couldn't work out if he was serious or not. 'Well you've got my card now. Why don't you give me a call? Pinnaplasty is a straightforward procedure and I am sure I could help you. I'd better get inside now. Here's the money, Neil,' she handed him her plate again and took the roll of money from her bag, 'please can I have a receipt for it?'

Back inside the party was kicking off. Her mum and dad were jiving and the buffet tables were empty apart from a couple of 'flans' and some pavlova. Lots of family members were gathered around the photo montage laughing and reminiscing, Michelle was on a chair downing a shot of something with Stacey shouting her on and Aunt Brenda was being tossed around the dance floor by Uncle Brian as though she was several stone lighter than she was. As the track came to an end her dad spotted her and waved her over.

'Thanks for all this, Stella. Your mam and I are having the time of our life. It's a lovely present.' Her dad gave her a big hug as her mum disappeared to chat to some of her friends from the surgery, 'Come on, pet, let's have a dance.'

They jived to the next track, her dad far more skilled than her, and chatted about the other guests as they went.

'Have you seen the size of Bill?' her dad said. Bill was his best mate from the shipyard.

'I didn't recognise him at first,' said Stella, 'he used to be so slim.'

'He sits on his backside all day eating rubbish now. He's got a pie addiction,' he said, deadpan, 'I can't get him to come out of the house. He's depressed I reckon.' He swung expertly into a turn and caught her. 'Your sister's enjoying herself,' he continued, 'I wish she'd get herself a nice lad like your Ian. It was nice of him to phone us yesterday.'

Stella jerked her head towards her dad's, 'Yesterday?'

'Yes, he phoned to apologise about not making the party because of his shift change. I thought he'd have told you? Anyway we had a lovely chat. What a gentleman. He thinks the world of you, Stella. You've done well there, pet. You two should be getting wed soon and then we'll finally see some grandkids. Now that would really cheer your mother up. Right, talking of your mother, where is she? It must be time to cut that cake.'

CHAPTER 10

As Stella stared out of the plane window she reflected on a successful weekend. Her parents had had a lovely time and were still on a high the next morning. She had left them already scrolling through the pictures on Michelle's camera and offering tea and coffee to friends and relatives who had all congregated for some post-party analysis. The consensus was that they had laid on a great spread, the DJ had played the perfect mix of oldies and new stuff and that Uncle Brian and Aunt Brenda should go on *Strictly Come Dancing*. Everyone had behaved themselves, with the exception of Jill, who on her first night out since her latest baby had got so drunk on Pernod and black that her legs had given way as she vomited onto the one remaining 'flan'.

Her thoughts turned back to work and the conversation she'd had with Ryan after her presentation. He was supposed to be back in the UK later that week and had promised to take her out for dinner. She knew it would be more than a work meeting. He'd made that clear. She felt a flutter in her tummy she hadn't felt for a long time.

As the plane taxied to the stand she turned her phone back on surreptitiously. Her voicemail immediately started calling her. As all heads turned to stare at her and an old lady tutted her disapproval she quickly turned her phone to silent and pretended to get something from her bag whilst listening to the message. There was more than one of them; in fact, there were four messages, one from her mum and dad wishing her a safe flight and three from an Anthony Wallace about 'his surgery'. She had no idea who he was or how he'd got her mobile number. By the third message when he'd moaned on about his desperate need for a nose job she remembered who he was. It was the SIMON who had hassled her for a nose job and who she'd referred to a clinical psychologist. She sighed. Just as she'd suspected. He was a stalker patient. As her phone started ringing again she threw it into the bottom of her bag and ignored it.

Stella took the tube home. She couldn't afford a taxi and realised that she had thirty pounds to live on until the end of the week when she should get paid.

After her ward round the next morning she decided to catch up with Tom. They hadn't spoken properly since the previous week's presentation. He welcomed her into his office and called Charles in to join them.

'I was going to schedule a catch-up meeting of our little deal committee anyway so we might as well do it now,' he said as Charles came through the door. 'Ah, Charles, good morning. Now can I get you two a coffee?'

After the usual formalities and chat the three of them settled down at a round table adorned with leaflets advertising the clinic's procedures. Charles promptly brushed them all to one side and put his palms down on the table.

'Right, you two. What's the latest at your end? I've spoken to their top man, Lawson Green his name is, and so far all the information from the lawyers and accountants is in order. He seems to think the deal is "on track".' He made pretend speech marks as he spoke.

'Well, both sets of advisers got a few more files to review last week. Albert Cheung came across some more information which should have gone to them earlier in the process but they don't seem to have come up with anything of a contentious nature,' said Stella.

'As you say, Charles, it would seem we are "on track". Ryan is pleased with progress so far. He especially liked your presentation, Stella. He described it as "bullish", which I have to say it was. I hope you haven't oversold us, Stella.' Tom looked at her a little sternly, she thought. She wasn't exactly sure what 'bullish' meant. Better than 'bullshit', she presumed. 'Anyway it seems the next stage will be beginning the negotiations of the legal documentation.'

'Have Ryan or Lawson talked to either of you about the management of the business after the sale goes through, assuming it does of course?' Stella fished.

'Erm no, not really. But I'm sure you know, Stella, that I have decided to bow out if it happens. I assume they will put in a man from Equinox to run it,' Charles said.

'Well, I'm staying and I've made that clear,' added Tom, 'the lawyers seem to think we might benefit from a bit of legal expertise so we may need to appoint a lawyer at some point. Good point though, Stella, I'll talk to Ryan about that.'

So Ryan hadn't shared his ambitions for Stella with anyone else, she pondered, as she made her way back to her office. Was he really serious about her running the business or was it just flattery? She would ask him outright when they met up.

'Ah, Dr Webb, the very lady I wanted to speak to.' Stella was jolted from her thoughts by Lloyd Cassidy who had just emerged from a side room, followed by his assistant Audrey who was already clicking down the corridor in front of them in her high heels.

'Do you have time for a quick coffee?' he asked, putting his hand to her elbow as if to steer her to the canteen.

'Do I have much choice, Lloyd?' she asked looking pointedly at his hand.

He just laughed.

After they had got their coffees they sat down at one of the plastic tables.

'What can I do for you, Lloyd? I don't have very long I'm afraid,' she looked at her watch. She had a consultation in ten minutes.

'Well, Stella. You remember Olivia Meddoes, the actress,' he almost whispered, looking around him to check no one was eavesdropping.

'Of course. The late night appointment for the fillers.'

'She was delighted with your work, Stella, and although I would always be her first choice of doctor…'

'Of course you would,' Stella couldn't help butting in.

Her sarcasm was lost on him as he continued, 'she is here again next week and I think she will need a Botox top-up. She also wants to talk about what we can do for her hands. They are starting to betray her age. She values her privacy highly and she wants it doing out of surgery hours again on Tuesday. Stella, can you help me out? I am busy that night and really can't do it. She was so pleased with you last time and I know I can trust you to keep this confidential. I will make sure your figures are credited with the procedure of course. And of course I still owe you for the last appointment you did.'

It hadn't even crossed Stella's mind to ask Lloyd for payment the last time but yes she supposed he did owe her.

'Okay, Lloyd, but one thing: why didn't the rest of the management board know about Olivia? You know our policy on celebrities. We all need to know who's treating who so we can deal with any publicity or enquiries from journalists.'

'Ah well, Stella. You have met Ms Meddoes. She is paranoid, no, obsessive about confidentiality and she made me promise not to tell the other doctors. It was only because she had a perfume launch coming up that she was happy for you to do her fillers. Now she has met you of course she is okay about you.'

'That's not good enough, Lloyd, and you know it. If you can't trust your fellow doctors to keep patient confidentiality then who can you trust?' she countered.

'It isn't me who doesn't trust them, it's Ms Meddoes. Look, Stella, you are right, of course. She twisted my arm. The other thing, and this is a secret too, is that she doesn't register under her stage name but under her real name, Jane Meadow, so her name isn't on any of my records anyway, so you could argue I'm not treating Olivia Meddoes at all.'

'Lloyd, that's rubbish and you know it!'

'All right, all right, I'll say something at the next management meeting. Is that enough?'

'And you won't do it again?' she almost smiled. It was as if she was talking to a six-year-old.

'Stella, I swear. Now, will you do the Botox for me?'

She couldn't see any reason why not.

'Fine. Get Audrey to let me know the time of the appointment and I'll come to your rooms. Will Audrey be working late that night?'

'Yes, she'll be there. Thank you very much, Stella. I knew I could count on you.' He kissed her hand, got up and left.

Stella immediately wiped the back of her hand on her skirt.

Karen had left two telephone messages from Mr Wallace on her desk when she got back. She sighed when she saw them. She was certain he wouldn't have been to the clinical psychologist she had recommended. She dialled the number on the yellow sticker.

'Mr Wallace, Dr Webb from the Beau Street Clinic returning your calls.'

'Ah, Dr Webb. Thank God you called. Look, I'm really desperate about this nose job. Please can you book me in?' he pleaded.

'Mr Wallace, did you see Dr Scott as I suggested?'

'Yes, yes I did.'

'Really? Shall I check?'

'Well, not exactly but I have made an appointment. It's next week but I just wanted to get something in the diary with you so I had something to look forward to.'

'Mr Wallace, I've already explained. See Dr Scott and then make an appointment. You've had your nose for over twenty years I'm sure you can wait a few more weeks.'

'But you'll do it then?'

'Let's see how it goes with Dr Scott first shall we?'

'Okay. I'll book another appointment for a consultation after I've seen Dr Scott.'

'Fine.' She put the phone down and banged her head onto the desk.

By Thursday evening Stella was down to her last fiver. She had travelled by tube all week, brought in sandwiches for lunch and generally had a miserable existence. She hadn't been out once or bought a single takeaway coffee or newspaper. Tonight she was meeting

Ryan for dinner. She would have to take the tube again and would bring her emergency credit card. She wasn't going to let Ryan pay no matter how bad her financial position was.

She was wearing the red linen dress again. She had nothing new, which depressed her. She liked to wear at least one new thing whenever she went out, which was probably why she didn't have a house deposit, more than five pounds in her purse and a pile of credit card bills. Neil, the world's worst loan shark, had been in touch and her mum still owed more than a hundred pounds because of the penalty fee. The first thing she would do next week would be to pay him off and get him out of her life.

On the way to the station a group of bare-chested men drinking outside a pub wolf-whistled at her, which immediately cheered her up. Maybe this clothes recycling wasn't so bad. Once a good dress, always a good dress. She held her head up and smiled as she past them.

'All right, blondie, what are you smiling at? Can I buy you a half a lager?' one of them called after her.

She was really nervous by the time she reached the hotel where they were meeting. It felt so much like a first date, and she hadn't been on one of those for more than ten years. The last one had involved a quick lasagne in a cheap Italian before a medics' three-legged pub-crawl. She saw Ryan as soon as she came through the revolving door. He was leaning against the bar chatting with the barman and looked totally confident and at ease. She walked towards him. He really was very handsome: tall, athletic-looking and ever so slightly tanned. She tapped him on the shoulder and he turned around.

'Stella, hi. Honey, you look great!' He went to kiss her on the cheek and then Stella moved to kiss his other cheek and almost kissed him full on the mouth.

'Jeez, I keep forgetting about this European double-kissing thing. I'm not complaining though,' he smiled at her, 'let me get you a glass of champagne.' He beckoned the barman back over and ordered the drinks.

'So, Stella,' he said as the barman placed Stella's champagne on a paper coaster, 'tell me all about yourself. My boss tells me I need to do "due diligence" on everyone and everything at Beau Street and I'm starting with you.'

They chatted about their backgrounds and how they had both come to be doctors specialising in cosmetic surgery. He was easy to talk to, very interested in her and made it very clear that he was single.

They were led through to their table by a very pompous waiter who insisted on carrying Stella's champagne and Ryan's beer on a silver tray, which he held with one hand at head height. Ryan caught her eye and nodded towards the waiter and pulled a face. Stella laughed.

Ryan put his arm around her as they walked to the table and then pulled her chair out for her before the waiter could beat him to it.

They ordered quickly, keen to continue talking. Stella glanced at the scary prices and ordered the cheapest thing on the menu. She was petrified her credit card would be refused.

'So, did you think any more about what I said the other day about running the business?' He looked intently at her.

'I did Ryan but, like you, I'm a doctor not a businesswoman. Just because I understand the commercial side of the business doesn't mean I can run it.'

'Sure, but just because you are a doctor doesn't mean you can't run it? Look at law firms. All run by attorneys. Accountancy firms, all run by accountants. Why shouldn't you run your practice? Sure, you might need some training in how to deal with the numbers but we can fix that.'

Little do you know how much I need training in numbers, she thought, thinking of the sacred last fiver in her clutch bag.

'You understand the business, the clients, I mean patients, what they want, what sells. That's what I'm talking about,' he continued, 'as the business grows that's what we need. Someone who understands what is possible and what isn't. We need to be driven by what we, as doctors, can actually achieve and what our clients want. Some number-cruncher from a different sector can't do that but we can. You can, Stella.'

She was flattered by his belief in her. For a moment he sounded just like Ian and for a moment she felt a tinge of guilt, which she soon rationalised away. She and Ian had split up.

As their food arrived Stella asked Ryan to tell her more about his practice.

'Well currently, Stella, I spend a large amount of my time dealing with my online aftercare service.' He took a large forkful of steak and leant back, a glass of red wine in his hand.

'What does that involve?' she asked.

He finished his mouthful, dabbed his mouth with his napkin and continued.

'I offer online counselling and advice for patients who've recently had surgery. As you know some of the less professional practices let patients out of hospital far too early sometimes and even the reputable practices are sending people home with a poor understanding of what to expect for the first few weeks. I give people advice on healing times, normal swelling and bruising, excessive bleeding and sometimes infection and emergency treatment. It's quite rewarding sometimes.'

'What a great idea. Although if clinics are doing their jobs properly it shouldn't really be necessary,' she couldn't help adding.

'Well, you're right of course if you're talking about the ones that go wrong, especially the patients who get infections and haemorrhaging, but for the average Joe or Joanne it's mainly reassurance I provide. They just need to know sometimes that it's normal not to look perfect two weeks after a rhinoplasty. I get clients from all over the world, quite a lot from the UK actually.'

'Really? Why have I never heard of you?'

'Well, you know me now, Stella,' he smiled.

She smiled back, 'So apart from the online counselling what else do you do? How much involvement do you have in the business side at Equinox?'

'Stella, do we really have to talk business all night?' He put his napkin down and leant towards her, 'Why don't I get you some more wine and you can tell me more about you. Then I thought we could go to a little private members' club I know not far from here. They do great cocktails.'

He was a man very used to getting his way and after he had paid for dinner – he had insisted he could claim it back on expenses, after all he was only doing his 'due diligence' – they left the hotel and made their way to the club.

It was a beautiful Edwardian terrace from the outside with potted bay trees either side of its traditional front door. It was tardis-like inside and soon Stella and Ryan were standing at another bar drinking Long Island ice teas.

'Are you trying to get me drunk? Because if you are you are succeeding.' She felt great, she was relaxed, without a care in the world and in the company of a man she couldn't help noticing was being stared at by a lot of the women in the room.

'All part of my evil plan,' he smiled, edging his bar stool closer to hers, 'Stella you are a very attractive woman and I am hoping you might be my completion bonus if this deal happens. Come on, let's dance.' He took her hand and led her through to a small dance floor in the next room where a couple of Hooray Henrys and a leggy Eastern European woman were dancing.

He was a practised dancer and soon took her hands and brought her closer towards him as a slower track came on. Stella sighed, closed her eyes and imagined he was Ian.

CHAPTER 11

Her head was throbbing and she knew before she prised her eyelids apart that the room was too bright. She put her head back under the duvet and groaned. The Long Island iced teas had tipped her over the edge and the 'nightcap' Ryan had persuaded her she needed had been the final straw. She groaned again as she remembered him bundling her into a taxi. Thank God she hadn't gone back with him. She vaguely remembered him suggesting it. She debated whether the pain of crawling to the bathroom to get headache pills would be worth the eventual relief they might bring. She decided to go for it.

Half an hour later when the pills had kicked in she crawled out of bed, dragged herself to the kitchen and made some toast, which she nibbled at. She checked her mobile. Ryan had already texted her to see how she was. She cringed as she remembered his concerned face through the taxi window. She quickly texted him back that she was absolutely fine, totally underplaying her horrendous hangover.

It wasn't the easiest day at work and by five o'clock she was in the ladies' loo touching up her make-up. She had one more patient and then she was on her way to meet Fenella for a quick drink before a quiet, inexpensive weekend. As Stella returned to her rooms she bumped into a rather large lady who was heading in the same direction. It was her patient.

'Mrs Grundler. How are you?' she asked.

'Dr Webb, I am very well thank you.' Mrs Grundler was German and pronounced her name 'Dr Vebb', 'It is good to see you. It has been at least six months I think since I was in London.'

They reached Stella's consulting room.

'Why don't you come straight in, Mrs Grundler?' Stella opened the door.

As Mrs Grundler went in she almost sat upon one of the lawyers who was already seated in the visitor's chair. Stella remembered the young trainee lawyer, Ross something, she seemed to think he was called. He was already blushing bright red.

'Ah, Dr Webb. Your assistant showed me in. I just wanted to ask you a few questions about your medical negligence policy.'

Stella started to introduce him, 'Mrs Grundler, this is Ross he's a trainee…'

Before she could finish Mrs Grundler had interjected, 'Ah, a trainee doctor just like my son! Of course you must sit in on my treatment. I understand how you have to observe everything when you are training. It is no problem at all,' she patted Ross on the knee.

'No, it's fine really. I'm not…' Ross started to say, getting up from the chair.

'Nein. You must stay. I insist.'

Stella raised her eyebrows at Ross, now standing behind Mrs Grundler's chair.

'So, Dr Vebb, I would like the same as last time, *bitte*. Not too much above the eyebrow, I don't want to look too surprised. A little in my chin please.' Stella got the syringes and the phials of Botox ready and put her latex gloves on.

'Okay, Mrs Grundler, if you could look up towards the light for me.' Stella took a baby wipe and wiped the make-up from her forehead and chin. She took a syringe and filled it from the phial and turned towards her patient, 'Frown for me please, Mrs Grundler.' She inserted the needle swiftly into four points on her forehead. She was conscious of Ross moving behind her patient but remained focused. She inserted the needle three more times in her brow and then twice into her chin. As she inserted the needle for the final time she saw Ross sway and then thud to the floor. He had passed out.

'*Ach mein Gott!*' Mrs Grundler jumped out of her chair, 'the poor boy.' She immediately got down on all fours and crouched over him, the pinpricks of blood now obvious on her face. She slapped his cheek, not gently.

'Hello. Wake up!' she was shouting. It was hardly textbook CPR.

After putting her syringe in the sharps bin, Stella knelt down in an attempt to reach for Ross's pulse. As she did so Mrs Grundler shuffled back onto her haunches knocking Stella to one side with her massive comedy bottom. At that moment the door to the office opened and Tom Duffy walked in.

'What on earth?' His face was a picture and Stella, despite herself, almost laughed out loud. As she picked herself up, noticing that Ross now seemed to be conscious, she tried to retain her professional veneer.

'Tom, this is Mrs Grundler. One of my best patients.'

He merely raised his eyebrows.

'Is he all right?' he asked, pointing at the shell-shocked Ross who still had an eyeful of Mrs Grundler's impressive chest. Ross nodded meekly.

'Right. Stella, can I have a word when the orgy's over.' He closed the door behind him.

'Are you all right? You poor lamb. Let me help you?' Mrs Grundler was heaving herself off the floor and offering her arm to Ross. He was now sitting up with his head between his knees.

'I'm fine, really,' he said.

Mrs Grundler looked at Stella and whispered, 'I really don't think he should be a doctor.'

★★★

After ushering Mrs Grundler out and sitting Ross down at Karen's desk with a glass of water, Stella cleared up and logged off. She really needed that drink now. She checked on Ross once again before leaving. She rummaged in her bag for her five-pound note. It was still intact as Ryan had prepaid the taxi the night before and paid for all the cocktails. Fenella was waiting for her with a drink when she arrived at the funky bar with the deathtrap bar stools.

'I'm not getting down,' said Fenella who was already perched on one of the contraptions.

'Don't blame you. Right here we go,' she said as she hauled herself onto the stool next to Fenella, 'Christ, it's like we're a couple of plates being spun on top of a stick. One false move and we'll crash to the floor. Hi hon, I can't kiss you or I'll lose my balance. How's work?'

'I'm good thanks. My case has finished and I'm just reading into a new brief. Arson this time.'

Stella giggled, 'Sorry, can't help it. I always think that sounds rude. What was he doing? Arson around? Get it?'

'Get a life!' said Fenella.

'Sorry. I know it's sad. Any news from the old gang? Marcus? Amelia?' Amelia was Marcus the orthodontist's younger sister. She was a chiropodist. They had always been known as 'Foot and Mouth'.

'Marcus is good. So over me. It's embarrassing how little effect I had on him. Amelia's great too. It's her thirtieth in a few weeks and she's given me an invite for you, actually. I'll get it from my bag when we leave.' Fenella nodded towards her bag which was on the floor under the stool of doom, 'Everyone's been asking after you. No one's seen you since The Split.'

'I know. I'm sorry but I don't want to bump into Ian just yet.'

'Well, he hasn't been around either. I guess he's working his backside off in Reading. Are you okay, Stella? If you don't mind me saying so, you look like shit.'

'Only a true friend and all that...' said Stella, 'yeah, I know. Bit of an odd night last night.'

Stella spilled the beans about her evening with Ryan.

'I mean Ryan is totally gorgeous, don't get me wrong, and he made it fairly clear he was interested, well at least he did before he saw me pretty much legless and had to carry me to the taxi, but I don't know if I'm ready for anything yet.'

'That's totally understandable. It's only a couple of weeks and you were with Ian since you were in the womb practically. Take it steady, Stella. He's a work colleague too. Messy.' Fenella was shaking her head. For some reason this angered Stella.

'Christ, Fenella, I'm a single woman now. I can have a bit of fun, can't I? It's not like he's married or anything.'

'Okay, okay. I just don't want you getting hurt, that's all. You're new to this whole dating business. Take it from a seasoned professional: it's harder than it looks.'

'Yeah I'm sure you're right. Sorry, I didn't mean to jump down your throat. I'm sure you're right. Look, I'm not going to rush into anything with Ryan. Apart from anything else he lives thousands of miles away.' The friends relaxed, ordered another drink and chatted about Amelia's party. Apparently she'd booked a private room in a bar and there were about forty or so people going. Amelia had shared a house with Marcus in his final two years of dentistry and she and her friends had hung out with Stella, Ian, Marcus, Fenella and their crowd.

'Should be a laugh,' said Stella.

'Not worried about seeing Ian then?' Fenella asked. It had been Stella's first thought when Fenella mentioned the invitation.

'No. I'll be fine. We can be grown up about it. I'm certainly not going to dump all my friends just because we've split up. What are you wearing?'

'Not even thought about it yet. Why? Are you going to do one of those crash diet, crazy transformations and wear some knockout designer gear to show him what he's missing?'

'Nice idea but, A: I'm not that sad and B: I couldn't afford the clothes. I'm skint.'

'What have you been buying now?' Fenella was used to her friend's profligacy but had to admit, once Stella had filled her in, that even by her standards Stella had got herself into a bit of a pickle.

'I should have got paid today hopefully but all I can contribute tonight is this,' she said reaching for her bag so she could extract the fiver. She leant forward, felt her bottom slip and fell to the floor. 'Christ, these stools are a nightmare. Every time we come in here one of us falls off them. Can't we sue someone? Come on. You're the lawyer.' She was sitting on the floor for the second time that day, on top of both their bags, her skirt up round her thighs whilst Fenella snorted with laughter.

Their 'early doors drink' turned into an all-night session with a kebab on the way home, all at Fenella's expense. As payback she gave Stella a long lecture on the evils of credit cards, how to live within your means and how buying stuff meant buying everything on your shopping list, not your wish list. Stella took it in good grace and even reflected on how she'd always been able to do it in the days when she had no money so it shouldn't be that difficult now she was earning a decent wedge.

As her alarm went off the next morning she waited for the throbbing head and churning stomach to kick in. Nothing. Somehow she had got away without a hangover. She jumped out of bed. It was a miracle, a sign, good luck, maybe a lucky kebab. She danced to the kitchen and made a coffee. She had a Saturday ward round to do today. She felt positive for the first time in a while. She was going to get on top of her finances, pay off Mum's debt, clear her credit cards and help Tom get the sale of the business done. She even thought she might call Ryan and arrange another 'date' and this time she would go steady on the booze. She wanted to find out what her feelings really were about him and whether to take things forward with him. As she thought of him she felt a tingle of excitement. He was mega gorgeous, after all. As she got in the shower she got carried away imagining him coming with her to Amelia's party and showing him off to all her friends, including Ian.

It was a beautiful day and she strolled up to the clinic swinging her handbag.

'Morning, Fred,' she called to the doorman.

'What a lovely morning it is, Dr Webb,' he replied, 'we've got a full house this morning. Dr Cassidy is in, Mr Sutton is here and all the lawyers are here in the basement. Not the usual Saturday.'

'Is Mr Duffy in?' she asked. She remembered Tom had asked to speak to her yesterday during the fat German and the fainting solicitor debacle.

'No I don't think so,' Fred replied.

Stella had just finished her ward round and was in her rooms checking her diary for the coming week when Lloyd Cassidy put his head round her door.

'I thought I saw you, Stella. Can I borrow you for a moment?'

'Er, yes. Come in.' She beckoned him in.

'I am in theatre in ten minutes and I have a client. An actress. She has just come in unexpectedly and wants some fillers in her nasolabial folds. She is filming next week and needs them doing now. Can you help me out?' he pleaded.

'This is becoming a regular thing, Lloyd. I'm seeing Olivia Meddoes on Tuesday, don't forget.'

'Stella, I trust you. We can help each other out, can't we?' He pulled a padded envelope out of his inside pocket and put it on the table.

'What's this?' she picked up the envelope and peered inside. It was full of money.

'It's what I owe you for the other week and the money for today if you agree to do it.'

Stella thought of the conversation with Fenella last night. There must be nearly a thousand pounds in the envelope. This would definitely help kick-start her financial clean-up.

'Fine. I can do it, Lloyd. I've finished here. Come on. Introduce me to your patient.'

She put her white coat back on and followed Lloyd to his rooms.

'So how do you do it, Lloyd? You know, get all these actresses as patients. My only celebrity client was a gardener from a garden makeover show.' She was genuinely bemused.

'My reputation, I suppose. All my patients recommend me. One actress gives my details to another. I also have some contacts at a talent agency,' he said flippantly as he opened the door to his consulting room.

'Ah, Ms O'Connor, darling.' He took his patient's hand in his and then to Stella's amazement kissed her on both cheeks. He obviously knew her well. 'As Audrey has explained I am already operating this morning but as you are one of my favourite patients I think I have a solution.'

Ms O'Connor looked at him hopefully. She had barely noticed Stella who was staring at her trying to work out which TV show she recognised her from.

Lloyd introduced the two women and made it clear that Stella was almost as good a surgeon as him and that she would treat Ms O'Connor with kid gloves. The actress was clearly desperate, as she seemed so relieved that there was a solution that she kissed him again on the cheek and thanked him profusely.

'Take a seat, my darling. Dr Webb can deal with you here.' He gestured towards Stella.

'Yes that's fine. Please do sit down. I'm Dr Webb.' Stella made eye contact with the actress for the first time.

Lloyd disappeared off to do his operation and with the help of Audrey, Stella located Lloyd's drugs cabinet and, after a brief consultation, inserted the fillers into the lines between Ms O'Connor's nose and the corners of her mouth. She had clearly had the procedure several times before and barely flinched as Stella injected the filler in under her skin. She was up and reapplying her lipstick in less than ten minutes.

'Dr Webb, I'm really grateful, thanks. Look, you won't tell anyone about this will you? I don't need any "unconfirmed Harley Street reports" appearing in the celebrity mags.'

'Ms O'Connor, I can assure you that I take patient confidentiality very seriously indeed. I will give Dr Cassidy a record of today's procedure and he will keep that with his records.' She was slightly offended.

'Thanks, that's great.' She gave a thin smile and put her sunglasses on, 'I'll pay Audrey shall I?' she asked.

'Yes that will be fine. I take it Dr Cassidy has already discussed the cost with you?'

'Of course,' the actress replied.

On her way back to her rooms she made a diversion via the basement and popped into the room which the lawyers from MacArthur Warren were using as their base whilst they worked on the sale of the business. She felt quite sorry for them when she found them holed up in the windowless room surrounded by files of paper and empty coffee cups. At least her weekend started now. These guys looked like they were here for the duration. She checked on Ross's welfare. He was clearly fully recovered but mortified at the same time. She chuckled to herself as she returned to her office, where she grabbed her bag and Lloyd's padded envelope and locked up.

As she breezed out of the clinic, waving her goodbye to Fred, she remembered the cash windfall from Lloyd and decided to hail a cab. She was meeting Fenella, Amelia and Amelia's flatmate Beth for lunch near Sloane Square. She checked her watch. Great, she had plenty of time. As the cab stood in traffic Stella window-shopped. She spotted a beautiful lemon leather tote bag, a lightweight summer trench coat, and a beautiful lilac bikini in consecutive shop windows. It was the strappy blue maxi dress which broke her.

CHAPTER 12

They were sitting in a restaurant populated by legions of preppy-looking waiting staff in buttoned-down blue shirts, thin ties and neat little aprons like Stella's gran always used to wear. She had taken her new maxi dress out of its bag for the others to admire.

'Ooh, it's gorge,' said Amelia feeling the fabric.

'Fab colour. It will really suit you,' followed Beth in the ritual love-in which had to follow every purchase. Stella was sure that their responses were genuine. It was an undeniably fabulous dress and when she'd tried it on she knew she had to have it.

'It'll be perfect for my party. Did Fenella give you the invite?' Amelia asked.

'That's exactly what I thought, too. Yeah, thanks for the invitation. I can't wait.'

'How exactly did you afford it?' Fenella finally asked. 'I thought you were down to your last fiver?'

Stella had been waiting for this.

'I got paid yesterday and today I got, well, a bonus I suppose,' she didn't know how else to describe the wad of cash in her bag, 'and before you say anything else, Fen, I'm still doing everything we said, you know the credit cards, Mum's loan shark, everything. I just spent some of my bonus on the dress and that's it. I promise. Although I will buy your lunch as you paid for last night.'

She could tell Fenella wasn't totally convinced.

'So what's the gossip?' Stella directed her question at Amelia and Beth. She could do without Fenella directing her finely tuned barrister skills on her money situation in front of the others.

'Shall I mention it?' said Beth, looking at Amelia.

'Yeah. I'm sure Fenella can cope,' Amelia replied.

'What is it?' Fenella asked, taking a sip of wine.

'Marcus. He's moved on I'm afraid,' said Beth.

'Well I hardly expected him to have donned black and gone into mourning. We weren't exactly the romance of the century,' said Fenella.

'Are you sure the lady doesn't protesteth too much?' asked Beth.

'As if! Come on Beth, spill! I'm really not fussed.'

'Well, he's got a new girlfriend. He met her at some doctor/nurse/dentist/whatever do. She's a junior doctor, very pretty and apparently used to play beach volleyball for Canada. He's seen her three times in less than a week and says she has perfect teeth,' Beth blurted out.

'Whoa. He sounds besotted,' said Stella. They all nodded. Teeth were very important to Marcus.

'Yup. Well we all know that if she's got perfect teeth then she's the one,' said Fenella. 'He never stopped banging on about my protruding lateral incisors.'

'Yeah and you're not that great at beach volleyball either,' said Stella nudging her friend playfully.

'Ha bloody ha. I bet I could nail her at darts though.'

'I've never seen him like this. No offence, Fen,' Amelia chipped in.

'None taken,' said Fenella through a mouthful of wine.

'He's taking her to Mum and Dad's for lunch on Sunday,' Amelia continued.

'Christ, it took Ian and me two years to get to that stage,' Stella mused.

'Yeah and look where that got you. Maybe early enthusiasm is the way forward. We're all old enough to know our own minds now. We know within a few weeks if it's going to work with someone. We need to ruthlessly dump them and move on or marry them and procreate,' Fenella opined.

'Sounds like the way forward. Seriously, I can't afford to spend another fifteen years trying someone on for size again if I do want to have kids. Fifteen months more likely. If you add up all of our ages we're well past a hundred,' Stella said.

'More like a hundred and forty,' added Fenella.

'We can do without the maths, thanks. Anyway I'm the only one who's still the right side of thirty. Do you definitely want children then, Stella? I've still got no idea,' said Amelia as the waitress, an immaculately groomed and super polite girl, arrived to take their order.

'Yeah I'm pretty sure I do. I'm in danger of becoming one of those panicking girls heading towards her late thirties with no man and a raging body clock. I might as well get "Desperate" tattooed on my forehead,' said Stella. The waitress glanced nervously at Stella as she topped up their drinks.

'I still can't believe it about you and Ian,' said Amelia.

'Don't you start. I've been over this with Fenella. He made it quite clear he wanted a break. However much of a shock it is to you, believe me, it's been a bigger shock for me. Can we change the subject please? I came in here in a great mood. Let's get another bottle of wine and then go shoe shopping.'

'Sounds great! Count me in,' said Beth.

'Only window shopping for you though,' Fenella wagged her finger at Stella.

'Spoilsport.' Stella stuck her tongue out at her friend.

After a long, relaxed lunch they spent the rest of the afternoon retracing a well-trodden route from shoe shop to shoe concession. They tried on sandals, flip flops, wedges, stilettos, kitten heels, and anything else they could find, frustrating numerous Saturday girls in the process. Eventually Beth bought a pair of gladiator sandals and Amelia some ballet pumps whilst Fenella and Stella left empty-handed. On the tube home Stella made a mental note of a couple of pairs of high wedges she had seen which would go brilliantly with her new dress. Fenella couldn't stop her shopping online could she?

After a quiet and cheap night, in eating pasta and watching Saturday night TV, Stella woke early. She put on her gym gear and went for a quick run. It was another sunny day and she decided to spend it wisely and virtuously. After her shower she settled herself down at her 'desk'. It was really her dressing table with all her make-up and jewellery shoved away in the drawers but still it would have to do. She had gathered all her credit card statements together in one bulldog clip; she had her bank account details up on her laptop and the envelope of cash in her lap. She started with the credit cards. The damage was worse than she had thought. She was up to her spending limit on three of them and the other two weren't far behind. She took a deep breath. She dealt with the card with the highest APR first. That seemed to be the most sensible approach. She jotted down the amount of half the outstanding balance for her to transfer. Then she worked out what the minimum payments were on all the others. The total figure was almost double what was in her bank account. She drew a fierce line through the number to transfer and started again. Eventually she worked out that she had enough money to clear all the minimum balances, pay a small additional amount off the worst card and, having rifled through her drawers to find her chequebook, wrote a cheque to Neil the money lender to clear her mum's account. That left the cash in the envelope for her to live on for the month, which even after the new dress purchase should be plenty. She made the transfers and popped the cheque into an envelope and leant back in her chair and relaxed. It wasn't so bad. She was back in control. She would obviously have to stop using her credit cards and live like a monk for a bit but she was hardly in the gutter. As a celebratory gift to herself she treated herself to the cheaper of the two pairs of wedges she had been eyeing up online. She congratulated herself on using her debit card and assuaged her guilt by cutting up the two credit cards with the highest APRs.

She wondered what to do with the rest of her Sunday. These were the times when she missed Ian the most and when being single felt so single. She could do some reading for work, perhaps. She had a few academic papers she had been meaning to look at. She made a coffee and settled down on the sofa when her mobile rang. It was Ryan! Great, she had been meaning to call him but hadn't got up the courage.

'Ryan, how are you?' she asked.

'Hi Stella. I'm great thanks. Missing my favourite Brit though.' Stella giggled. 'Look, Stella, I know it's short notice but can I ask you two favours?'

'Of course, Ryan, fire away.'

'I've been invited to some industry awards ceremony on Friday. I need a plus one who is beautiful, intelligent and knows the industry.'

'Well, I can ask around for you. Lloyd Cassidy might be free.'

'I love your British humour! Obviously I mean you,' he laughed.

'I am a very busy woman, Ryan.'

'Of course you are. Do you think you could possibly find a window in your crazy schedule for me?' he teased.

'I think there might be an opening.' It sounded great. She knew about the Aesthetic Physicians awards. She was pretty sure Charles would be going. Beau Street had won best website a couple of years ago. It was at a posh London hotel and there would be champagne, a meal, dancing, the whole nine yards. It was just what she needed.

'So what was the second favour?' she asked.

'I'm in London on my own, bored out of my mind. Please could you come and entertain me? We could go for a walk along the Thames. See the sights. Ride an open-top bus. I could take you for a "pub lunch", I think they're called. I've always wanted to try one of those. Stella, please, it's almost an emergency. I'm sure I learned at Med School that boredom can be terminal.'

'Doctor, you are absolutely right. Now do exactly as I say. Make your way at once to the Embankment. I will meet you there and show you the river. It's big, wet, that kind of thing. And then I'll take you to a lovely al fresco restaurant I know where we can gradually introduce you to solids and fluids,' she replied.

'I think you may have found the cure.'

Forty-five minutes later Stella and Ryan were walking alongside the river. Stella had apologised for getting a little tipsy the other night and Ryan was teasing her.

'Hey, you weren't so bad apart from the part when your legs totally gave way and I had to carry you to your cab.'

'You liar! You so didn't!' she laughed. He looked at her and she felt the attraction spark between them.

They made their way to the restaurant Stella had recommended where they took a table facing the river and ordered a couple of beers. Stella watched Ryan from behind her sunglasses. He had an obviously handsome face and the confidence about him of a successful man. Although she guessed he wasn't much older than her, his self-assurance made her feel like she was much younger and less worldly wise. She shivered slightly as she realised he was probably a man who usually got what he wanted.

'So, Stella, tell me all about your colleagues. What are they like?' he asked leaning back in his chair.

Stella gave him the lowdown on Charles, Christopher and the other less senior doctors. She was more circumspect about Lloyd.

'Lloyd has his own very loyal following of patients. He seems to have more celebrity clients than the rest of us. I think he's developed a network of people in the entertainment industry who recommend him to each other. In some respects he is a little bit less fussy about who he treats.' She regretted it as soon as she'd said it.

'What do you mean by that, Stella?'

'I'm being a bit unfair, Ryan. Look, I'm a bit reluctant sometimes to take on the patients who show a tendency to be addicted to cosmetic surgery or the ones who have unrealistic expectations. You know the type. I'm not sure Lloyd has the same qualms that some of us have. He turns very few patients away, put it that way.'

'I know the type. That's not a problem of course as long as he's acting ethically. Is he a good practitioner?'

'As far as I know. I've seen some of his work and it looks fine. He has an awful lot of repeat patients. Look, I shouldn't have said that. It wasn't fair of me.'

'Stella, it's fine. And how's business at the moment?' he asked.

'Pretty good. No signs of any downturn. Quite the opposite really. It's a good time of year. Everyone's panicking about being "beach ready" although they would have been better off having the work done a bit earlier in the year to give them more time to heal; but a lot of patients don't think like that. They start thinking of summer holidays in the Spring, book themselves in for their tummy tucks or lipo and then get cross when I tell them they might not be fully active for six weeks.'

Ryan nodded, 'I had a woman on my post-op advice service the other day freaking out because she'd expected to be back at work after three days. Can you believe some people?'

'Heaven knows what kind of advice they were getting pre-surgery.'

'I know, Stella; there are some bad surgeons out there. That's why there's such a need for my service. It keeps me in business!' he lifted his bottle of beer up as though to toast all the dodgy doctors and then beckoned the waiter over to take their orders.

They chatted more about the business and the awards dinner next week as they ate. Ryan explained that Equinox had decided to take a table at it to raise their profile in the UK market.

'It's already raised speculation about whether we are setting up in the UK. No one seems to have thought of the possibility that we'll buy someone else, although with you on my arm some of the brighter commentators might make the connection,' he said.

'And do you mind? You know, if they do make the connection?'

'Sweetheart, I'm not obsessed about confidentiality but I guess Charles and Tom might mind. You might want to run it past them first.' He looked thoughtful. Stella realised he had a point. She would clear it with them first. God, she hoped they'd say yes.

It was another relaxed lunch. *What a great weekend this has turned out to be*, Stella thought as they got up to leave. Ryan insisted on paying, as it had been he who had begged her to rescue him from boredom. *A cheap weekend too*, she mused. *Well, apart from the dress. And the shoes.*

'Thanks so much for joining me, Stella. You saved me from British TV and room service,' he said with a mock serious face.

'You are very welcome, sir,' she smiled.

He casually put his arm around her shoulders as he walked her back to the tube. As they reached the top of the tube steps she turned to face him. She felt awkward and was just wondering whether to kiss him on the cheek when he drew her towards him. He paused for a moment and then kissed her. She melted into him and then held him to her as she kissed him back. She savoured every moment of being held. When they looked at each other she immediately felt confused and guilty.

'Do you want... ?' he began.

'Ryan, I'm really sorry I have got to go, but thank you so much for a wonderful afternoon,' she babbled before kissing him again, on the cheek this time, and disappearing down the steps of the tube. She looked back up and shouted, 'Oh and thanks for buying lunch. I'll see you at the dinner on Friday.'

As she plonked herself down on a free seat in the carriage she tried to make sense of her conflicting emotions. What must he think of her running off like that? She really liked Ryan. He was gorgeous, interesting, successful and funny. *What's not to like?* she thought. It was Ian. She couldn't help every encounter with Ryan being haunted by the ghost of Ian. It was just too soon, she decided, and totally normal. Ian had been the only man she'd kissed for fifteen years until today. Kissing Ryan was pretty momentous in itself. It almost merited a blue plaque at the top of the tube station steps. She smiled to herself. She would phone Ryan as soon as she got off the tube, apologise for rushing off and tell him how much she was looking forward to Friday. At some point she would tell him she had just come out of a long-term relationship; it would help explain her behaviour. It was strange that Ian hadn't come up in conversation with him already. Ryan had made it very clear on day one that he'd just ended a brief relationship in Chicago and was very much single. He hadn't even asked her about her relationship history.

CHAPTER 13

Stella took the tube to work for the next few days and didn't buy a newspaper, coffee or a single packet of mints on the way. She was feeling very positive about her new attitude to spending. Although she had spent a couple of hours after leaving Ryan on Sunday scouring the Internet for a cocktail dress for Friday night, she hadn't bought one. Instead she had rifled through her wardrobe and dug out a safe black dress she had worn to a medics ball with Ian. Ryan hadn't seen it and it was only a year old. *Job done*, she thought, and hung it up on her free-standing mirror so the creases could drop out.

She had just completed an early ward round when Karen caught her on the way to her office.

'Hi Stella, I've got that Mr Wallace on the phone again. Says he's seen the doctor you recommended and he's ready to go ahead with the rhinoplasty. He's asking if you've got any cancellations; which you don't. He seems very keen. Shall I book him in? You've done a consultation with him haven't you?'

Stella groaned. He was as persistent as a bad case of thrush. She had a brainwave.

'Karen, could you tell him I'll call him back personally first thing tomorrow with a date for his next appointment.'

'No problem. Just make sure you put it on the system so we don't get a double booking,' Karen replied.

She saw Tom that afternoon in his office for a catch-up on the deal. It seemed the accountants and the lawyers were about to present their first draft reports on their findings about the clinic and that the negotiations of the sale contract would start very soon.

'I will be leading the meetings on the sale agreements but I need you in the background helping me out,' Tom was saying as they both sipped at their coffees, 'I don't know how many legal agreements you've read in your life but I'm no expert and I need another pair of eyes looking at them for me. I know the lawyers will be reviewing them with their legal hats on but I need someone else with a commercial hat on to look at them. I've got to be sure the lawyers don't agree things which in reality we can't deliver.'

'Okay, Tom, I'll do my best but I think the only legal contract I have ever read is when I once skim-read all the Terms and Conditions on a software licence. I only did that because I didn't realise there was an option to skip them before installing the software on my PC.'

Tom half smiled.

'Stella, I'm serious. I really need you to focus on this. Charles is so laid back he's practically limboing and the other partners in the practice are only bothered about their share of the proceeds. If we cock this up and agree something that ties us up in liabilities we can't get out of, or obligations we can't deliver, then we're all in a mess.' Tom stood up as he spoke and went back over to his desk where he started clicking through his emails. Stella had never seen him uptight before and was surprised. Never mind Charles, she had always thought Tom was pretty chilled.

'Tom, of course I'll focus on it. I'll read whatever you need me to. Look, I'll call one of the lawyers and make sure I'm on the circulation list for all the documents they send out and I'll have a look at everything that comes through and let you know if anything jumps out at me.' She drained her coffee and got up to go.

'Thanks, Stella. That would be a help.' He looked up briefly as he continued with his emails.

'Oh and Tom. One more thing?' she asked.

'Mm,' he mumbled.

'Ryan Miller has invited me to the Aesthetic Physicians Awards dinner on Friday. Do you mind if I go?'

Tom lifted his head and looked at her.

'Has he now?' he said, grinning, 'the sly old dog. Why are you asking me, Stella? You're making me feel very old. I'm not your dad you know and I'm definitely not old enough to be either. Well, not quite anyway.'

Stella laughed nervously. Christ, this was a bit ridiculous.

'It's just that he was wondering if you'd be bothered if other industry people put two and two together and got four.'

'Stella, you really need to help me out here,' he was smiling broadly now.

'About the deal, Tom. You know. If they see me with an Equinox person they might realise there is something going on with the business.'

'Ah. I get it now. Stella, I'm relaxed about it. The only thing people will think is that you and he are dating and if you and he are okay with that then that's fine with me,' he replied, 'hang on a minute though, I thought you were living with an A&E doctor.'

'I was. Ancient history now.'

'Right you are, sorry about that. Look, just make sure you don't give away any business secrets to Ryan.'

'Such as?' Stella said.

'Mm, I don't know. Use your common sense. Look, has Ryan said anything about the deal to you? Actually this could be useful. You could be our Mata Hari. Lots of counter-espionage and honeytraps, that kind of thing.'

'Steady on, Tom. Ryan and I have had one dinner and a lunch. That's all. As far as I can tell Equinox still want to do the deal. He's even talking about who might run the business going forward.' She decided not to tell Tom that it might be her.

'Well, that's good to hear. Okay then, maybe no spying this time. Have fun at the dinner. Look out for Lloyd. He's bound to be there.'

Stella left his office, her cheeks still pink with embarrassment.

She set off to the basement to find Alex. She wasn't in the lawyers' meeting room, but Dan, the American, and Ross were both there, tapping away on their laptops.

'Afternoon, gentlemen. Hope you're still okay, Ross? Not feeling light-headed at all?' she teased.

'I'm fine. Really,' he replied.

'How can we help you, Dr Webb?' Dan asked, flashing his beautiful symmetrical teeth at her. *Wow, Marcus would like him*, she thought. She passed the message on about the circulation of the legal documents and Dan promised to action it.

'How's the work going? Uncovered any problems at all?' she asked.

'It will all be in our report,' Dan replied. Stella had expected a straight 'no'.

'So does that mean there are some problems?' she asked, suddenly concerned.

'Not necessarily, although we have found a few issues surrounding handling of complaints,' Dan expanded, 'it doesn't concern any of your patients though, Dr Webb,' he added.

'Okay, that's good to hear. Thanks. I'll look forward to reading it then.' She pulled the door closed behind her. Shit! It hadn't even crossed her mind that there would be any issues in the reports. Still, it was a big clinic. She supposed that must be normal. No business was squeaky clean. Was it?

'Fen, you did corporate law at uni didn't you?' She had decided to call Fenella and pick her legal brain.

'Yeah. Can't say it was the best two terms of my life. Why?'

'Well if someone uncovers a few issues about a business before they buy it does the purchase still go ahead usually?' she asked.

'Depends on the issues I suppose. Look, it's like buying a house, isn't it? If you find out the windows need painting and the carpets are knackered you're still going to buy it, but if the roof's falling in and it's the "location location location" for the local woodworm fraternity then you'd probably steer clear. It's all relative. If it's not too serious then the price might be negotiable I suppose. Anyway, why are you asking? Now you're feeling more in control of your money are you thinking of buying a multinational and becoming the next Richard Branson?'

'Something like that but without the beard,' Stella replied.

'Are you free for a quick flirt with danger on the bar stools from hell in a bit, then you can tell me more about your plans to take over the world?' Fenella asked.

'Sorry, working late. Filling in for a colleague. Literally. Let's catch up at the weekend. I'm out on Friday with Ryan and will need to debrief you.'

'Ooh! Maybe he'll debrief you first.'

'Shut up,' Stella laughed.

'I think you mean thanks for your help Fenella.'

'Okay, thanks for your help and see you soon.'

'Bye, hon. And don't forget to stay out of the shops,' Fenella signed off.

As Stella made her way to Lloyd's consulting room later that evening she reflected on Dan's comment. It hadn't sounded too serious. More in the flaking paint category than dry rot category. She was sure it wouldn't be an issue.

Audrey, Lloyd's assistant, was waiting for her. Audrey was about fifty, glamorous in an obvious way and had a penchant for LLG (leather, leopard print and gold). Tonight she was in a leather pencil skirt and pink satin shirt with a big pussy bow. She had gold hoop earrings on and Stella searched for the trademark leopard print. Yes, there it was. Her handbag was a large tote in faux leopard. Stella couldn't help smiling to herself. She and Karen played a game of spot the LLG and tonight she had scored a maximum three points.

Audrey was unsmiling as she greeted Stella. 'She's just called me. She'll be here in a couple of minutes. I'm going down to let her in now. Dr Cassidy's room is open for you. Here's the key to his drug cabinet.' She handed her the key and headed off towards the lifts.

Stella made her way into Lloyd's room. It was a shrine to the glory of him. There were photos of Lloyd on the golf course, at award ceremonies and giving lectures on every wall, and on a shelf were a selection of trophies he'd won for his work over the years.

Stella sat in his chair and waited for the Hollywood actress. She heard the lift arrive and the two sets of heels clicking towards Lloyd's room.

'Dr Webb. Good evening,' said Olivia thrusting out her manicured hand.

'Good evening. It's a pleasure to see you again,' Stella replied. Olivia had already sat down and was taking off a silk scarf and tucking it into her creamy leather bag, which looked so soft that Stella could imagine using it as a pillow.

'It's so disappointing to have missed Dr Cassidy again. His schedule is almost as crazy as mine. Today I think I need a little more Botox here and here.' She pointed to the area of the tiny crease lines below her eyes. 'Also a little on my elevens and on my chin.' Elevens were the two vertical frown lines at the top of her nose between her eyebrows.

'I have seen Dr Cassidy's notes from your previous Botox procedures and can see what he has done in those areas so if you are happy with what he has done for you before I will do exactly the same,' Stella replied.

'Fine,' said Olivia.

Stella surveyed her patient's face as she gently removed her make-up from the sites of the injections. She had beautiful almond-shaped eyes and fine bone structure and was still a beautiful woman. Looking at her notes it was clear that Lloyd treated her little and often, which was the secret to keeping it natural-looking. As long as she kept that up and didn't resort to anything more dramatic she would be keeping the tabloids guessing for the foreseeable future.

Stella finished the injections swiftly and efficiently and dabbed away the tiny pinpricks of blood. She pressed hard down on one of the injection sites near Olivia's eyes. It looked like a bruise might be developing.

'One more thing, Dr Webb. I mentioned to Dr Cassidy about my hands. I have been less careful about sun exposure on them than on my face and I'm afraid they are beginning to show the signs. I'm about to go on a national book tour and a US magazine recently ran a piece outing some celebrities' hands for betraying their faces. I don't need any publicity like that. I would like some fillers in them.' Olivia lay her hands out flat for Stella to inspect. As Olivia was so slim there was hardly any fat on her hands and her bones and veins were quite visible but otherwise she had perfectly normal hands for a woman in her early forties.

'Ms Meddoes, I think your hands are in good shape and don't show excessive signs of ageing. If you are really concerned there are fillers we can use which will plump out the skin slightly and reduce the appearance of tendons, joints and veins,' Stella said.

'Do it,' Olivia replied.

'Now?' Stella replied.

'Yes,' Olivia hissed.

Stella spent the next fifteen minutes injecting and massaging filler into Olivia's hands. After cleaning them thoroughly she took numerous syringes with the finest needles and injected the back of her hands over and over again. She had to give it to her, she didn't flinch once.

By the time she had finished Olivia's hands looked very pink but already noticeably improved.

As Olivia left to sort out payment with Audrey, Stella tidied up Lloyd's consulting room. Stella was rare amongst cosmetic surgeons as she hadn't had any work done herself apart from some experimentation with non-surgical procedures. She reflected on how Olivia and some of her own clients were totally *au fait* with all the latest procedures and seemed to spend as much time at their cosmetic surgeon's as they did at the hairdresser's. It must be like painting the Forth Bridge. Great for business though.

Stella waited for Audrey to return from escorting Olivia out.

'Thanks, Audrey. Was she all right?' she asked.

'Fine.'

'Great. Look, Audrey, I've got a patient I was wondering if Lloyd could see for me. As I've been helping him out a bit recently I'm sure he won't mind returning the favour. The patient has already seen me for a consultation about rhinoplasty. It's a very subtle piece of work and I'm sure Lloyd would do a wonderful job. He does have a lot more experience than me.'

Audrey looked at her through her false eyelashes, clearly suspicious of the flattery of her boss.

'When were you thinking of?' she asked, taking out an old-fashioned appointment book.

'Well, the patient is very keen to have the procedure as soon as possible,' Stella replied.

'Hmm, well Lloyd, I mean Dr Cassidy, does have a cancellation next Wednesday actually. We have enough time then I think for a rhinoplasty. What's the patient's name?'

'Wallace. Mr Wallace. I'll get Karen to give you all his details and tell Lloyd I'll be happy to chat through his history. I'll call Mr Wallace in the morning but I'm sure he'll be delighted that Lloyd can see him.'

Stella smiled to herself as she went back to her rooms. That was surely the definitive hospital pass!

***

She got home to the usual empty house and threw her coat onto the kitchen table. She had begun to get used to living alone and her standards of tidiness had definitely slipped. Her diet had suffered too. She could never be bothered to cook a proper meal for one and as she ate yet another baked potato on her lap on the sofa, she clicked on her laptop and tried to track down the handbag Olivia Meddoes had been sporting earlier in the day. It took her quite a while but Stella was adept at fashion detective work. She had lost count of the number of times she had seen an outfit in a magazine and then tracked it down online. Sometimes she would guess the designer and scroll through their latest collections. Other times she would look for the tiny credits in pictures, which sometimes referenced the clothes the model was wearing. Or she would simply start with the colour and the item and search methodically through Net-a-Porter and other fashion sites until she got a match. Stella knew her bags and she found it eventually on the website of the third designer she tried. She didn't buy it immediately. She went back to her bulldog clip of credit card statements and recalculated her repayment schedule. Then, as she remembered the envelope of cash she would get for the work she had done that evening and the extra amount she would receive for all the work on Olivia's hands, she caved in. She clicked on 'Buy' and tapped in her debit card details. It was a done deal. The impossibly soft and impractically cream bag would be hers.

CHAPTER 14

A flustered Karen confronted Stella halfway through her routine ward round. Stella was checking on the bruising on a facelift patient when Karen knocked on the door of the patient's room and signalled for her to come out. Stella excused herself from her patient.

'What's the matter?' she asked, annoyed.

'I'm really sorry to interrupt but it's Mr Duffy. He's called a meeting of all the management team. It's mega urgent. As soon as you've all finished with ward rounds and consultations you've all got to meet him in the boardroom. He told me to come and find you.'

'Okay. Thanks. I'll finish here as soon as I can and go straight up. You might have to delay my first consultation. Make some proper coffee and give them a magazine. You know the drill.' Stella spoke calmly and Karen relaxed a little.

'Fine. I'll tell him you'll be with him shortly.'

Stella was anything but calm as she hurried through the rest of the patients. She did the checks she needed to do but without the usual chit-chat and bedside banter.

What the hell was the matter? she wondered. Was it anything to do with this business Dan had hinted at?

There was a definite atmosphere in the boardroom. Tom was pacing up and down in one corner and barely looked up from his phone. Charles Sutton had his serious face on and Christopher gave Stella a nervous smile as she sat down next to him and raised his eyebrows and shrugged his shoulders in a manner which suggested he had no idea what was going on either.

'Right, everyone's here,' said Tom, putting his phone into his jacket pocket, 'let's get on with it.'

'Lloyd isn't here yet,' Stella said.

'He's not coming,' Tom replied, grim-faced.

Christ, what on earth had happened? she wondered.

'There's no easy way of saying this but I have had some shocking news from the accountants and the lawyers. Basically they have uncovered malpractice, fraud and a secret "out of hours" clinic. Lloyd seems to be at the epicentre of it all. I had a most unpleasant session with him earlier on. It is highly likely he will be getting his marching orders.'

Charles had clearly been briefed and had known what was coming but Christopher and Stella stared back in disbelief.

'Tom, what on earth do you mean? What has the man been doing?' Christopher asked.

'It seems he has been running a clinic mainly for celebrities. It takes place out of hours and he has been co-opting in theatre staff to help him. At the moment it seems they have just treated it all as overtime and know nothing about what else has been going on. Though woe betide anyone else who is in on it,' Tom said through gritted teeth, 'Lloyd has been treating patients under false names to give them anonymity, and the worst of it is that he hasn't been declaring all his income. The figures in the records he has kept, which frankly are flimsy to say the least, record our normal list price for procedures but he has been charging the patients way over the odds. He justifies it by telling the patients it is for a confidential out-of-hours clinic, and then he's been pocketing the difference. He gets them all to pay in cash so there is no paper trail. The accountants reckon Lloyd has personally been making tens of thousands of pounds from the racket.'

Christopher was flabbergasted.

'The slimy charlatan,' he spluttered, 'never liked the man. How long as this been going on?'

'No one really knows but it could be years. It's not just the fraud though. The lawyers reckon there could be all sorts of other issues. We could be uninsured for the work he has done, there are possible regulatory issues surrounding his record-keeping and on top of that there will be bad publicity if he is hauled up in front of the General Medical Council. Oh, and the lawyers have uncovered evidence that he hasn't been handling his complaints properly. There is an actress threatening to go to the papers about a breast augmentation that has gone horribly wrong. I've got to broker some kind of deal with her to shut her up. The whole thing is a nightmare.'

'What are the implications for the deal?' Christopher asked, clearly hoping to wash his hands of Beau Street once and for all.

'Not good. Charles and I have already spoken to Lawson Green. The advisers said we should be totally straight with Equinox.'

'Quite right too,' muttered Charles, nodding.

'Equinox are obviously shocked and surprised and have concerns about any ongoing liabilities. The other problem is that Lloyd was our most successful doctor in terms of fee income. If he goes, and if I have my way he will, then we lose a very significant income stream which of course then has a massive impact on what they might be prepared to pay for Beau Street. That's assuming of course that they still want to buy us. And even if they do, their bargaining strength is now far superior to ours and the lawyers reckon they will use this whole fiasco and the fact we seem to have let it go on for so long as a stick to beat us with all the way through any negotiations. The whole thing is a disaster.'

Stella listened to everything in silence. It all made sense now. Lloyd's celebrity clients. The fact that very few of them were ever mentioned at management board meetings. Olivia being booked in under her original name. The envelope full of cash. The out-of-hours work. She felt a rising sense of panic. If the deal was scuppered that would be then end of her dreams of a big fat payout and there would be no more envelopes of cash from Lloyd to help her out. He hadn't even paid her yet for the work on Olivia on Tuesday.

'So what can we do?' Christopher was asking.

'Not much. Keep your heads down. Work hard and keep quiet about it. We need to contain the scandal as much as we can. We can't play it down to Equinox but if we can be seen to do the right thing, which in my book is sacking Lloyd and demonstrating that none of the rest of us are involved in anything remotely dodgy, then that's something. I'm getting the advisers to uncover everything and we can present it all to Equinox. We can't be seen to be hiding anything. We need to do a *mea culpa* and grovel like mad. I'm assuming none of you had any idea what was going on?'

'Absolutely not!' Charles responded.

'Of course not,' added Christopher.

Stella just shook her head. She couldn't be quite as emphatic as the other two but she was as shocked as them that Lloyd had been pocketing money and defrauding the business. She walked back to her office in a daze.

After dealing with her consultations she decided to go out to grab a sandwich. She hadn't made a packed lunch that morning and she needed some air. She walked past Fred the doorman who was as chirpy as ever.

'Unseasonal good weather we are having.'

She smiled at him and walked to a large sandwich bar at the end of the road. She grabbed a salad and some juice and sat at a corner table. What would she do if the deal didn't happen? She understood the numbers only too well and she knew that Lloyd on his own brought in more than two of the other doctors put together. His patients were the best type too. Repeat business was always easier to maintain than drumming up new work. If Lloyd left where would his patients go? Would he be able to practise again? And what about her? If she was honest her job had always been a bit about the thrill of the chase. She had spent years aiming for and striving to be a consultant. Now she had got there she wasn't sure if she wanted to do it for the rest of her life. She didn't get a huge amount of job satisfaction from doing boob jobs and cosmetic work. It was only the prospect of the deal which had excited her in recent weeks. Life would be so much easier if she had a vocation, she thought. Ian had never questioned his job for one second. He'd still be saving lives in his seventies.

Her phone was vibrating persistently. She had ignored it hoping it would go to voicemail but the caller wouldn't give up. They'd redialled her number three times. She sighed and fished it out of her bag. Oh God, it was Lloyd. What on earth did he want? Tom hadn't said whether or not they should speak to him. She hesitated then picked up.

'Stella, it's Lloyd. I need to speak to you. Where are you?'

Did he know she knew?

'Ah hi, Lloyd. I'm just grabbing a spot of lunch actually. I'm not at the clinic.'

'Neither am I. Where are you?'

'I'm at the sandwich shop on the corner.'

'Perfect. Don't leave. I need to talk to you. I'll be there very soon.'

He hung up. Stella didn't know what to do. Was he going to confide in her and come clean or deny it all? Or maybe he just wanted her to do some more work for her. She contemplated calling Tom to see if there was some sort of party line she should follow but decided against it. She would just leave Lloyd to do the talking. She had a slim hope that the whole thing had been a terrible misunderstanding and he would have a plausible explanation for everything.

Lloyd arrived a couple of minutes later. Stella wondered where he'd been hanging out if he hadn't been at the clinic.

'Stella. Thanks for waiting for me.' He pulled a chair up to her table and flicked the hair from his eyes. He was as tanned and dapper as usual but with an unfamiliar air of panic about him.

'Have you heard? What they have said about me? What they have done?' he said, clearly outraged.

Again Stella didn't know what to say.

'Well, Tom has spoken to me.'

'And what has he said? Is he going to fire me? Do you believe him? Those damned accountants. Stella, you know I do work outside normal office hours. What's the big deal in that, heh? So what? It's what my patients want. And so what if I don't always use their names? I know who they are. Audrey and I have systems so we can identify who they really are. You British. I don't understand it. So picky picky picky.' As he spoke his hand gestures were becoming more and more extravagant. Stella let him continue.

'And this precious deal. Hah, without me there is no business, so what are Equinox going to buy?'

'Lloyd, there are other doctors at the clinic you know. You do have a successful practice but so do the rest of us.' Lloyd suddenly stared at her.

'Stella, you have a business brain just like me. Like I said the other day we are very alike. Do you want the deal to happen? Do you? You are much younger than me. I expect several hundred thousand pounds would make a huge difference to you.'

'Lloyd, of course it would. It would transform my life.'

'Listen to me, Stella. If you help me out of my predicament then the deal would be much more likely to happen.'

'What do you mean? How can I help you?' What was he getting at? How can you help someone out of fraud?

Lloyd leant closer towards her. 'Stella, they only have very limited evidence on me. The only thing they can really make stick is the fact that yes, on one or two occasions I didn't declare the full amount of what I charged the client and I took the extra money. But Stella, so what? I am not your average surgeon. I deserve more than the list price for my work. My clients are much more demanding. You've met some of them. You have seen how attentive you have to be. They want work doing any hour of the day or night and on short notice. If you say that the extra money went to you for helping me out then that would really help. That would explain the extra mark-up on the list price and we could say there had been a misunderstanding. You had thought I would put it through my books and I had thought you would declare it. I'll take the blame for that bit. Please, Stella, what do you think?'

She was appalled that he was trying to drag her into his sordid mess.

'What do you mean? I don't understand. Are you saying we lie and say we worked on patients together?'

'No, not lie. It's a fib that's all. You have helped me out with patients haven't you? Only recently. We just say you helped me out regularly and we charged the client a little more for extra consultant time. You took the extra cash and I made a mistake on the record-keeping. Please, Stella. I'll make it worth your while, financially I mean.' He had it all worked out.

'Lloyd, I'm sorry but I can't do that.'

'Why? Please Stella, do you want the deal to happen or not?'

'Because it would mean lying to Tom, the advisers, my colleagues, everyone. That's not what happened. What you did was wrong, Lloyd. You defrauded the business.'

'And what about the deal?' his voice was quieter now.

'Look, I want the deal to happen, believe me, but I

can't lie and cheat my way into making it happen. What you did was wrong.'

'Are you sure about this because it doesn't look that good for you anyhow.'

'What do you mean?'

'Stella, you did help me out. You did work for me at my so-called "secret surgery". You took cash from me. I've got records of it. There would be more than one interpretation of what you've been doing. It could look bad for you too.'

He head was closer to hers now and his tone was decidedly less friendly.

'Lloyd, are you threatening me?' Her heart was hammering away.

'Stella, I'm just saying that you have taken a large envelope of cash from me. You have worked on a couple of patients including a Hollywood actress. I charged Olivia more than list price for her work so most people would assume you knew that as you actually did the work. You referred a patient back to me, Mr Wallace. To an outsider it looks like we work very closely together. It doesn't look good for you either.'

'But you know the truth, Lloyd. I was just helping you out.'

'Well, help me out now then.' He spat out the words, all pretence now gone.

'I can't. Not the way you want me to.'

'Stella, it's quite simple. You say you helped me and the mark-up was a straightforward payment for additional consultant time and Audrey and I messed up our record-keeping. We apologise for the rest, the record-keeping, the false names, all of that. I stay at the business, the deal happens and you and I are a lot richer. Or I tell Tom and Charles that not only was I taking money from the business but that you were in on it too. I show them the patient records for Olivia and the records for the cash payment. It really won't look good for you. Then we both lose our jobs. Is that really what you want?'

She was horrified. She had barely registered the shock of Lloyd's fraud but to discover that he was prepared to take her down with him was something else.

'So basically you are blackmailing me.'

'Such an unpleasant word, Stella,' he was getting up from the table, 'let's just say I'm trying to persuade you to do the best thing for the business. You and I both know that without me this business is nothing. The Americans won't buy Beau Street without me. Think about it, Stella. You have my number.' He turned away and strode out of the cafe.

Stella stared at him as he left without a backward glance. She had always found him a bit smarmy but had never thought Lloyd capable of this. To commit fraud and then threaten to implicate her was bad enough but the worst thing was that she was momentarily tempted to go along with his suggestion. But she couldn't. Could she?

Stella couldn't sleep that night. She had no doubt at all that the right thing was to stick to her guns and refuse to go along with Lloyd's suggestion, but on her own at three in the morning a nagging doubt permeated her thoughts. He hadn't hurt anyone. His work was fine. It was just a money thing and if he paid it back to the business then where was the damage? If the deal didn't happen then it would be years before she could sort out her finances and her life. She wasn't really fooling herself about her debt. It would take months of frugal living before she could pay it off and much longer to save up a deposit for a house. Did she really want to throw away the prospect of the deal of her life happening? It was when she thought of what Ian would have said to her that she finally fell asleep.

CHAPTER 15

As Stella got out of the shower she grabbed her watch from the bathroom windowsill. It was six twenty. She was meeting Ryan in little more than an hour's time. The excitement of her night out with him had been soured by the revelations about Lloyd. She hadn't spoken to Ryan since the scandal had broken and had no idea if that was a good sign or not.

She stepped into the black dress which despite its week hanging up on her mirror was still creased. She cursed under her breath. She didn't have time to get out the iron, it would have to do. She struggled to zip herself into it and found another reason to miss Ian. After hurriedly applying her 'evening look' make-up which basically involved her daytime look with slightly more dramatic eyes, she slipped on her heels, grabbed a sparkly clutch bag and left. She didn't have enough time for public transport so hailed a cab. How on earth did you save money living in London, she wondered? Unless you became a Trappist monk, it was impossible.

She arrived at the hotel and was directed by a posse of surgically enhanced 'hostesses' to the bar where Ryan had suggested they meet. The girls were in full-length low-cut satin ballgowns in a variety of bright colours with 'Miss World' white sashes emblazoned with the name of the awards' sponsor. She couldn't help inspecting their cleavages with professional interest and noted without surprise that they had all opted for the less natural spherical implants. Sometimes she felt like the only real person in a cartoon world.

She took a glass of complimentary champagne from one of the hostesses and took a seat near the bar. Ryan hadn't arrived yet. She fished out a compact from her bag and inspected her make-up again, conscious that her preparation for the evening had been hurried and feeling a bit underdressed compared to the hostesses.

'You look absolutely stunning.' She looked up to see Ryan smiling at her. Flustered, she put away the mirror and stood up. They exchanged pecks on the cheek and sat down.

'You really look fabulous. I made the right choice. Lloyd couldn't have carried off that dress,' Ryan joked. Stella smiled nervously at the mention of Lloyd's name.

'So, here's the brief for tonight. We are on a table hosted by a laser company who really want Equinox's business so they will be all over me like a bad case of fleas. We eat, we sit through the awards, applaud politely and then get away somewhere else as soon as it is safe to leave.' He grabbed a glass of champagne from a passing Amazonian-like hostess as he spoke.

'Sounds good to me,' Stella replied. They drank, flirted and chatted before being ushered to their table by yet another of the ubiquitous girls. He had said nothing about Lloyd. Stella was beginning to wonder if Lawson had told him.

A tall man was approaching them, his arms spread wide as though to greet them.

'This is our host,' Ryan whispered, 'he likes to talk.'

'Ryan, how good to see you. So glad you could make it this evening. It promises to be an exceptional night,' the man pumped Ryan's hand and patted him enthusiastically on the back, 'and who is your lovely guest?'

'Fraser, this is Stella Webb, one of the consultants at the Beau Street clinic. Stella, meet Fraser McBride. Fraser is the managing director of Laser Cosmeceuticals.'

'Delighted to meet you, Stella,' he was pumping her arm now, 'come and meet everyone else on our table.'

After a round of loud and detailed introductions to Fraser's colleagues and other guests Ryan and Stella took their seats at the table. Stella was positioned between Fraser and Ryan, and Fraser was already doing his sales pitch on his business and its products.

'Stella, you must have heard of our business. We're up for Best Product tonight. We manufacture the highest quality ablative and non-ablative lasers out there at the moment. All the top clinics in the States are using us now. We also have one of the best CO_2 lasers for skin tag and wart removal. Whatever you need in the laser department, we can supply it. I should really come and pay you a visit at Beau Street. I'm sure we could do great business and I can talk you through all the technical details.' Stella pretended to look interested and didn't admit to him that she rarely used laser treatment for anything other than the occasional mole removal.

'You okay?' Ryan asked her when Fraser's sales pitch finally ran out of steam and he turned his attention to the wine waiter, 'I'm feeling a bit jealous of old Fraser the Laser dominating you.'

'No need, believe me. That man can bore for Scotland. I had no idea there were so many lasers out there. Did you see him demonstrating his laser pen?'

'I know. I'm sorry, but as the most beautiful woman in the room by some margin he was bound to want to be next to you,' he whispered.

'Ah Stella, I just remembered I didn't tell you about our Fraxel lasers.' Fraser leant towards Stella and started another monologue. Stella listened and nodded again occasionally glancing towards Ryan who was trying to contain his laughter.

After the meal had finished Ryan and Stella escaped to the bar. The awards ceremony was about to begin and Fraser was beside himself.

'If he asks me again if he's going to win I'm going to get his laser pen and shine it into his eyes. Let's get a cocktail. Can I trust you with a mojito? I'm not getting

Long Island ice teas again. Then I would like you to tell me what you know about a certain Lloyd Cassidy.'

He ordered the drinks and then shuffled closer to her.

'So I've been hearing what a naughty boy Dr Cassidy has been. Did you know about it?'

'I knew he did some work out of hours.' She decided it was best to be circumspect until she had told Lloyd she wasn't going to play along with his blackmail.

'Sounds like a lot more than that. He has been taking a lot of cash out of the business. Lawson freaked when we told him. He wanted to pull the deal but I think we can contain it. Don't you?'

'Well, it is only one doctor.'

'Precisely. I think I've calmed Lawson down and at the moment we still want to go ahead. I'll do what I can for you, Stella, but I can't give any guarantees. If Lawson gets a hint that this is anything more than one rogue trader the whole thing will be off. I've told Tom he needs to fire Cassidy and handle all of the complaints as soon as possible. That just leaves us with a hole in the numbers to fill.'

'What do you mean complaints?'

'Oh a couple of people have had problems post op and Cassidy hasn't dealt with them properly. It seems the more famous you are the better his aftercare is, if you know what I mean. Some of the actresses who are lower down the food chain have been getting a raw deal from him.'

'Well I'd be happy to work on any rectification work if it's necessary.'

'Great. You do know this will have a big impact on what we will pay for the business?' he said.

'Er yes, I suppose so. But what if we get a new doctor in to replace Lloyd?'

'Well, I guess that would make a difference. But who are you going to get on a few weeks' notice? It would have to be someone with a client following to match Cassidy's.'

As their drinks arrived Stella excused herself and made her way to the ladies' washroom. She mulled over what Ryan had said. It did sound as though he was doing his best to keep the deal on track but she was getting concerned about all the comments about 'price'. As long as her several thousand didn't dwindle to nothing, but then again it would be hardly be the end of the world if she took home say two hundred thousand instead of four hundred thousand. Frankly, any number ending in a few noughts would be great at the moment. As she opened her clutch bag to reapply her lipstick she instinctively checked her phone. There were five missed calls from Michelle and a text message all in capital letters which screamed at her: 'CALL ME ASAP. LOAN SHARK BEEN ROUND. ALL HELL BROKEN LOOSE.'

Shit, what on earth had happened? She had paid Neil. She'd sent the cheque at the weekend. She left the washrooms and made her way to the reception area of the hotel away from the guests and the hostesses at the dinner. She found a seat in a quiet corner and dialled Michelle's number, biting her nails as she waited for her to pick up.

'Stella. You've finally called. Where the hell have you been?' her sister shouted.

'Steady on, Shell. I'm at a big awards do. I only just checked my phone.'

'Well, lucky old you. Whilst I'm here dealing with both my parents having breakdowns. Me Dad's in pieces, Stella. Pieces. I nearly called an ambulance an hour ago.'

'An ambulance? What on earth for? What the hell's going on?'

'Well, your man Neil and his big bully boy boss turned up here didn't they, threatening all sorts of charming things. They doorstepped Mam, barged in and then started getting heavy with Dad.'

'Why? Shell, I paid the man, I sent a cheque. He should have had it at the beginning of the week.'

'Oh yeah, he got the cheque all right but it bounced. Stella what's going on? It's the beginning of the month. Even I don't run out of money until the last week of the month? Mam is devastated. She thought Dad would never get to know. Dad is livid. He says he feels dirty and ashamed. Said Mam had broken one of his moral codes. You know what he's like about debt and holding his head up round here. The worst thing is he can't believe Mam kept it from him. Mam hasn't stopped crying. She's been in their bedroom for ages now. God, it's a nightmare.'

Stella put her head in her hand and held the phone close to her ear so she could hear the awful things her sister was telling her. The waves of shame washed over her as she remembered first the maxi dress, then the shoes and then the bag. Any one of those items was more than the amount of her mum's debt. She had thought she was so clever using her debit card, failing to register the effect that would have on her bank balance after transferring all the cash to clear the credit card payment. She hadn't even paid into her account what was left of Lloyd's cash. She just hadn't got round to it.

'Shell, I'm so sorry. How's Dad now?' she managed to say without crying.

'A bit better but I was really scared for a bit. I thought he was having a heart attack. His blood pressure went through the roof. Mam used that monitor you bought them. He's just sat down now. He spent the past hour scraping together all the cash in the house to get rid of Neil and his boss. It wasn't enough to pay it all off but Neil managed to persuade his boss to go.'

'I'm so, so sorry.'

'Yeah, so you said. Look, Sis, I know it's Mam's debt not yours but she thought you had it covered. That's the thing. Dad can't believe your cheque bounced. Says he's never had a cheque bounce in his life and he's on benefits. Stella, seriously, what's going on? Tell me it's a mistake please.'

'It's not, that's just the thing. It isn't,' she was crying now, 'I'm in a mess, Shell. It's totally my fault. I think I've got an addiction.'

'Christ, it's not drugs is it? I did wonder what with all that access you must get to medicines and stuff. Stella, tell me it's not drugs.'

'No, it's not drugs,' she smiled despite herself, she supposed the situation could have been worse, 'just, you know, stuff.'

'What kind of stuff? Is that a street name for something? Share it with me, I'm not exactly down with the kids up here.'

'Oh, shoes, clothes, bags, cars, you name it really. Ever since I've had a decent wage I've blown it. Don't ask me why. I'm sure a psychologist would have a field day. Used to drive Ian mad. Probably one of the reasons he left me.' She was crying again.

'You stupid, stupid cow. Please don't try and make me feel sorry for you because I'm still too angry but Stella, seriously, sort yourself out. You have got everything and Mam and Dad have basically got nothing. In fact all they have got is you. They never shut up about you, bragging to everyone they meet. You're the opening topic of conversation at bingo, the butcher's, the bus station, you name it. If they haven't got you then they've got nothing. Look I've got to go, Mam's just come out of her bedroom. I'll try and sort out the money.'

'Can't I speak to her?'

'Not a good idea. Bye.' Michelle hung up. Stella put her head in both hands. What a total mess. She tried to work out how much of Lloyd's money she had left. Maybe she could drive home tomorrow and give it to her mum but the thought of her father's disappointed face haunted her. She looked at her watch. She would fix her make-up and make her excuses to Ryan.

As she got up she sensed someone looking at her. She turned to her left and saw Lloyd Cassidy. He was now striding towards her.

'Hello there, I thought it was you. Why are you here?' he asked.

'I'm at the awards dinner.'

'Who did you come with?' he interrogated. Stella was irritated yet again by his total failure to acknowledge that she too was a successful cosmetic surgeon and might be considered worthy of an invitation to an industry event.

'I'm a guest of Ryan Miller from Equinox and I really should be getting back,' she replied.

'Just one second.' He grabbed her arm. She shook him away.

'Lloyd. Leave me alone.'

'Not until you tell me what you have decided. Are you going to help me out?'

'If you mean am I going to go along with your cock and bull story and lie to my colleagues and a load of professionals, who probably know more about what goes on at our business than we do, then no. I won't. You can do your worst, Lloyd. If you really feel the need to take me down with you then go for it.'

He looked stunned initially and then just smiled.

'If that is what you want, Stella. So be it. You know how to reach me if you change your mind.' With that he did up the button on his tuxedo, straightened his back and strode back towards the ballroom.

Stella found Ryan back at the table where Fraser the Laser was showing off his trophy. She congratulated Fraser and made her excuses to Ryan. She could sense his annoyance but there was nothing he could say. She told him she had received some bad news and he seemed to go along with it. He muttered something about an early start for a cricket match the next day, put her into a cab and left the dinner at the same time.

★★★

The next morning she was up at six and on the road by six thirty. All she had with her was her handbag and Lloyd's envelope. She hadn't even taken the cash out of it. The envelope had sat in her kitchen and she had been dipping into it for petty cash. Most of the money was still there and there was definitely enough to settle the debt even with a bit more compound interest. She phoned Neil from a service station a couple of hours later whilst picking up a box of Quality Street for her dad.

'Okay, Neil, how much is left after last night?'

'What? Oh Stella. Hi. How are you?'

'Cut the small talk, Neil. How much is left to pay? I'm driving up now to sort this thing once and for all.'

'Look I'm really sorry about last night. I tried to stop my boss but he insisted on going round. It was the bounced cheque. He hates bounced cheques. They always tip him over the edge.'

'Look I'm sorry about the cheque too but there was no need to upset my parents like that. You should have come straight to me like we agreed. Come on, how much do I have to pay?'

He gave her the figure. It was less than she expected. Stella was surprised by how much money her dad had managed to scrape together the previous evening. Neil kept apologising over again.

'Please apologise to your parents for me too. They're good people. My dad'll kill me when he finds out,' he said.

'Neil, I'll be with you in about an hour and a half. And Neil, do me a favour, get a new job. Loan shark doesn't suit you.'

'Believe me, Stella, I'd love to but what with the wedding coming up I've got no choice. There's nothing else out there for a lanky lad with sticking out ears and two GCSEs.'

CHAPTER 16

Stella jumped as the ballad on her car radio switched to the shrill ring tone of her speakerphone. It was Lloyd.

'Good morning, Stella. Hope I haven't interrupted anything?'

'Er, no, Lloyd. I'm in the car actually.'

'Did you enjoy your evening with Dr Miller? You two seem to be getting along very well.' He overemphasised the last two words.

'Yes, thank you. Come on. Cut to the chase, Lloyd.'

'I hope you haven't been spending any of that money I gave you, Stella,' there was a silence, 'because you know it just implicates you even more. Although I suppose if your mother is in financial difficulties, perhaps you have?'

Stella felt the colour rise in her cheeks and her hands go sticky on the wheel. How did he know about her mum?

'What are you talking about?' she said, in as calm a voice as she could muster.

'I couldn't help overhearing your conversation in the foyer last night. I have to say though, I'm surprised that a successful surgeon like you can't help her own mother with some small money problems. Look, Stella, I can help you. All you need to do is agree that you provided additional consultant support to certain clients. I'll take the rap for all the paperwork irregularities and sort you out with a nice thank you bonus. That would solve all your problems, wouldn't it? Otherwise, if you spend that money I gave you, it will look like you've been getting, what do you call them, "backhanders" from me. That cash came straight from Olivia and I'm sure she and Audrey would both confirm they saw me hand it straight to you. My clients and staff are *very* loyal to me, you know. Think about it. You've got till tomorrow night,' he snarled and hung up.

Stella wiped her palms on her jeans. Her mind was racing with a jumble of conflicting thoughts. A part of her screamed, 'Do it, go along with him. Where's the harm? No patients have suffered. If they wanted to pay more for their treatment for secrecy, what's the problem? If Lloyd gave her a share of the upside, her immediate financial woes would be dealt with; if she helped him brush off the allegations against him he would stay, the deal would happen and everything would go back to normal. But the gnawing doubt which had been with her since she had first grasped the brown envelope of cash from him was eating away at her like a persistent piranha. Everyone smelled a rat when envelopes of cash were involved. That money was outside of the business.

It hadn't gone through any books. It was wrong. What Lloyd had done was wrong. She couldn't let herself be implicated any more. She wasn't that type of person. She might not be as straight-laced as her father. In fact she definitely wasn't. She certainly wasn't afraid of debt or credit cards. But she knew it would continue to eat away at her if she took Lloyd's offer. Did she want to end up as sleazy and crooked as him? She thought of her dad and then Ian. She could imagine both their reactions, if they had any inkling of what she had momentarily considered doing.

She glanced at the envelope and let out a sigh. If she couldn't use that money then how would she pay off Neil? She had an hour to come up with a plan.

Stella pulled up outside the small 1970s semi. The irony of turning up to do a deal with a loan shark in her flash car and expensive clothes wasn't lost on her. Neil was at the window in the front room looking out for her and opened the door as she walked up the narrow pathway through the front yard.

'Morning, Stella,' he smiled, a little sheepishly she thought.

'Hi, Neil.'

He motioned her inside and directed her to the front room where she sat down on a shiny black faux leather sofa.

'Look, I'm so sorry about the bounced cheque but you have to understand that you cannot go around harassing my parents again,' she began.

'Seriously, that wasn't down to me, Stella. It was me boss. Like I said, he hates bounced cheques. Says they're an insult to his intelligence.'

'So, if I sort payment of the outstanding amount, you'll go away, right?'

'Well, yeah, like I said last time. But the figure I gave you earlier is wrong. See I spoke to the boss and there's an additional admin fee to cover the visit yesterday and a daily interest amount, it's changing every day.' He at least had the decency to look embarrassed.

After a debate about the outrageous rate of compound interest, Stella pinned him down to a weekly amount she could pay to get rid of the debt in two months. She was embarrassed not to be able to clear it there and then, and Neil was clearly surprised that she'd even asked about weekly repayments.

'But look, Neil, you need to understand that this is my loan now, not my mum's, okay? Any problems, you come to me not her. I'll do a weekly bank transfer to you and if my cash flow improves, I'll call you for a total to clear it in one go.'

'Right you are. Look, there is another way you could clear it. If you do something to me, I could make it go away.'

Stella was horrified.

'No nothing like that,' he blurted, 'God, no. No, I meant surgery. Plastic surgery.'

'Neil, what are you on about?' She was relieved it wasn't a sordid payment in kind he was suggesting.

'Look, if you pin me ears back, I'll sort your mam's debt. One hundred per cent.'

'Seriously?'

'Yeah, for real.'

The meeting was getting more surreal by the second but actually, why not? She could do the operation with a student present. Maybe claim it was a training session or something. Or even get an NHS referral. His ears were pretty shocking. She was sure they could run an argument he was suffering psychological damage.

'Leave it with me, Neil. I might be able to sort something. In the meantime, I'll sort the weekly payment till you hear from me. But if Mum and Dad hear from you again there is no deal. I'll call you about the surgery.' She got up and he followed her to the door.

'Okay, Stella, thanks so much. I'll wait for your call then. Great to see you,' he called, as she hurried to a car.

She wasn't sure if the next stop on her journey was going to be any better.

As she knocked on the door of her parents' house, she was acutely aware of the contrast in fortunes since her last visit, when she had been the golden girl who'd thrown them and their friends a fabulous party. Her mum let her in.

'Hi, Mam.' Stella gave her a hug and was touched to feel the same strength of hug as usual.

'Hello, pet. You shouldn't have come all this way you know.'

'Of course I should. I'm so sorry about the cheque,' Stella mumbled still holding her mum's small soft body to hers. She bit her lip to stop the tears coming. *Christ, stop feeling sorry for yourself.*

'Is that our Stella?' her dad called from the living room.

Her dad was as forgiving and welcoming as her mum. Stella looked for the disappointment in his eyes but could only find the genuine pleasure and pride she always found there. Her mum bustled off to the kitchen to make a pot of tea. Her dad was the one looking embarrassed.

'I'm sorry that you've been dragged into this, Stella. It shouldn't have happened and I wish you knew nothing about it. Your mam got herself in a bit of a pickle and I don't blame her for that. Although, why she didn't tell me I'll never know. And why she went to those lowlifes…' He shook his head, 'I have never been in debt in my life apart from the mortgage, which I budgeted carefully. And I hate that.'

She knew he did. Her childhood had been defined by 'The Mortgage' once they'd bought the house. It was the excuse for all manner of deprivations. She would never forget missing a school trip to France in Year 7 because of 'The Mortgage'. She had never minded particularly. It was just the way it was.

'Thanks for trying to sort it out for us, Stella, but it's our problem. You need to have a word with your bank though. Bouncing your cheque like that. It's an outrage.

With your wage and all. What were they playing at? They should compensate you for the stigma. Was it because cheques are old-fashioned now do you think?'

Michelle had obviously kept her mouth shut and she couldn't bring herself to come clean. He'd had enough disappointment and stress in the past twenty-four hours.

'Oh yeah. Don't worry, I gave them a piece of my mind,' she said unconvincingly.

Her mum brought the tray of tea in and placed it on the footstool in front of her dad.

'I've been to see Neil before I came here,' she continued, 'it's all sorted out now. He said that you've paid most of it off with that money Dad got together yesterday and I've sorted out the rest which was additional charges because of the bounced cheque which was my, I mean the bank's, fault.'

'Are you sure?' her mum asked, 'I'm sure that Neil said there were hundreds to pay. Which I don't understand, as it was more than I borrowed in the first place.'

'Oh he got it wrong. He's useless with numbers, that Neil. Always was at school. Rubbish loan shark if you ask me.' Her father was stirring his tea thoughtfully.

'Is that right? Like I said, this is our problem. I'm not having you bailing us out. Fair enough if the bank sorts out the extra charges which are their fault for bouncing your cheque by mistake. I'm not taking your cash though, Stella.' Her dad was looking her straight in the eye. She looked straight back.

'Yes, Dad. It's sorted. Gone away. Over.'

The relief in the room was palpable. She just hoped she'd got away with it and that Neil never breathed a word of their deal.

'I'm so sorry you've been involved in this, love,' her mum said, 'I'm truly ashamed.'

'Mam, it's fine. One of those things. You two are the most sensible, careful people I know but we all slip up sometimes.' She couldn't believe she was saying this. She felt such a hypocrite.

'Anyway where's Michelle?'

'Working. Saturday's her busiest day in the shop,' said her dad.

Stella was back on the road heading south again by lunchtime. She gave herself the biggest talking to on the journey home after a detour via Michelle's travel agent shop, which had involved the humiliation of borrowing her petrol money home, some grateful thanks for her not telling their parents about her financial situation, and a promise that she would, in Michelle's words, 'sort her bloody life out'.

That evening she dug out the blue maxi dress and the receipt. That could go back on Monday. She packaged up the beautiful baby-soft handbag after one more session modelling it in front of the mirror and emailed the supplier to explain she was returning it. She also put the wedges back in their box and did the same. That lot totalled more than five times her mum's debt.

The next morning Fenella arrived with a black velvet dustsheet and her phone in her hand. Stella had called her from the car yesterday and told her everything.

'Right, I am here to fix you, Ms Webb. Let's get your life back on track. I'm going through that bloody Aladdin's cave of a wardrobe of yours and I'm putting your bank balance back in the black. Grab this,' she handed Stella a giant takeaway coffee, 'it's too early for wine but that may come later,' she pulled a bottle of Sauvignon Blanc out of her handbag, 'chuck this in the fridge.'

The two of them set to work. Fenella cleared a corner of Stella's bedroom and draped the black velvet sheet over an armchair, which she moved through from the living room. She put all the bedroom lights on and grabbed an anglepoise lamp that Ian had used for his studying and directed its beam at the chair.

'This is my studio,' she declared, 'where is my first item? What about this?' she pointed at a designer bag on the floor of the wardrobe that had cost Stella a fortune a couple of years previously but which was barely marked.

'Ah, I love that. No!' Stella squealed.

'I have never seen you with it apart from when you first bought it and kept showing off, as you were one of the first people in the UK to have it because you'd been on some stupid waiting list. Seriously, when did you last use it?'

'Well…'

'See? You've got to be ruthless. You know what they say: if you haven't worn something in the past three months, then you never will. It's taking up valuable space and is a wasting asset. This is cash tied up in an inanimate object. Let it go!' Fenella grabbed the bag, gave it a quick dust, arranged it on the sheet and started clicking away with her phone. Within five minutes it was listed on a resale site and had received its first bid.

And so it continued, three bags, five pairs of shoes and a necklace still in its original packaging. Then they moved onto the clothes.

'Right, let's start with the things I've never worn,' said Stella who was now enjoying the clear-out, 'look for the labels.'

'Bloody hell, Stella, there's loads in here. How can you have so much stuff you don't even wear? Look at this!' Fenella held up a long halternecked midnight-blue evening dress with the labels attached, 'I mean, this is beautiful but it's the third ballgown I've come across. How many do you need? Are you moonlighting as a high-class escort or something?'

'Oh God yeah, it's lovely isn't it? Should have worn that to the awards do the other night but I totally forgot about it. That was that time Ian got called out all night and I stayed up and watched the Oscars. I was googling all the dresses and this was a "looky likey" some designer knocked up overnight. I had it three days later but the moment had passed by then.'

'Seriously? You need to stop the impulse buy. That's your issue. It's like emotional eating.'

'At least I don't get fat.'

'Yeah and neither does your bank balance. Talking of Ian, I was with Amelia yesterday. She's seen him recently. Had a bit of a heart to heart actually.'

'Who did? You and her?'

'No. She did. With Ian.'

'Really? What did he say? Did he talk about me?'

'That's pretty much all he talked about, apparently. Oh and his new job, which is apparently going really well. On track and all that. He'll be a consultant before you know it, it seems.'

'Less about the job and more about me please,' said Stella, as she displayed the blue gown to be photographed.

'Well, he still worships you, that seemed pretty clear, but he couldn't see a future. Said he wasn't sure about your commitment. Didn't think you were ready to settle down with him. Something about you not wanting to buy a place with him.'

'What! That's a crock! She's got that totally wrong.'

'Whoah! Don't shoot the messenger! That's definitely what she said he said. I think it was the deposit that did it. You did tell him then that you hadn't saved it?'

'No. No I didn't. I always implied I had. Shit. He must have found out I didn't have a penny. How did he find out?'

Fenella shrugged and photographed the ballgown. 'No idea,' she said as the flash lit up the room.

Stella sank onto the bed. 'Shit, so that was it. I never knew what triggered it. I thought he didn't want to settle. Thought he wanted a clean break. To go to Reading without me in tow and focus on his career. But all the time it was my bloody incompetence with money. Can't you see? I've caused the break-up with all this,' she cast her arm around the room at the clothes, bags, shoes and other 'stuff', 'this could have been my deposit. Christ, Fenella, I've been such a fool.'

'Are you saying you want to get back with him? What about that Ryan fella?'

'I think I am, Fen. Oh, I'm not sure. But it was always weird, the break-up. I just thought he'd had enough. I was trying to be grown up and dignified but no, I didn't want to split. That very morning I'd thought I might be pregnant and in my head, I'd been planning our lives together. It was a shock I can tell you. But he wouldn't have me back, would he?' She looked at Fenella hopefully. Fenella sat down on the bed and put her arm round her.

'Hon, I have no idea but he's obviously still mad about you. You need to think carefully before you rush into anything. You seemed pretty keen on that American a few days ago. I think you need to focus on your finances first. If you do decide to get back with him then at least your house is in order, your debts are under control and you can show him you've made an effort to at least put yourself in a position to save up for a deposit. I'm sure it's not about the money for him, more about your intentions. He obviously thought you had no genuine wish to buy a place with him. Rather than the truth, which is that you have CSD.'

'What's that?'

'Compulsive Shopping Disorder. Come on, let's crack on with this and then we can open that bottle of wine. Sunday rules apply. You can drink any time after midday, you know. I'm sure I read that somewhere.'

They spent the rest of the day photographing and listing items on resale sites. Stella was both pleased and horrified by the amount she might raise even at modest estimates. The only item she refused to list was a beautiful strappy dress she had bought the previous summer and which she had totally forgotten about. It was a bit creased as it had been stuffed in its bag in the back of the wardrobe. It would be perfect for Amelia's party, which was now taking on a new significance.

As she lay in bed that evening she mulled over the issue of Lloyd. She knew what she would do tomorrow. For the first time in days she slept soundly.

CHAPTER 17

Stella arrived early at the clinic and smiled as she breezed past Fred at the main entrance.

'Lovely morning again, Dr Webb.

'Yes, isn't it?' she replied as she looked back.

Fred took his chance, 'Er, Dr Webb, I wonder if I can have a word when you have a moment. Something personal.'

Stella's smile faded and she immediately corrected herself, 'Er, yes, of course Fred. Does it need to be now? I'm in a bit of a hurry this morning.' There was a meeting of all the partners in thirty minutes and she wanted to do some prep. She was certain it would all be about Lloyd.

'No, no of course.' Fred put his hands up defensively, 'any time. No rush at all. Just a bit of professional advice, that's all.'

'How about I catch up with you later? When does your shift end?'

'Not till six thirty, Dr Webb. Bob's on nights this week.'

'Why don't you come to my consulting room then? You know where I am don't you?'

'Yes of course. That would be lovely. Wonderful. Thank you very much. Much appreciated.'

Stella smiled again and set off before he started grovelling. *No wonder Equinox want to buy us*, she thought, *there must be a cosmetic surgery boom if folk like Neil the loan shark and Fred the doorman wanted work doing. Who next?* she wondered. *Her dad?*

For once Stella had beaten Karen into work. She unlocked the door to her consulting room and turned on the coffee machine. As she waited for the machine to rumble into action she reflected on where she had got to the previous evening. The literal and figurative clear-out of her hoard of excess baggage had been as cathartic as all the declutter lifestyle gurus claimed. Everything did seem clearer now and she had been horrified that she had even flirted with the idea of going along with Lloyd's suggestion.

Charles Sutton had called the meeting for all the partners at eight thirty. Stella made her way down the corridor to his office and bumped into Tom on the way. He was grim-faced.

'Morning. Can't say I've been looking forward to today. Charles and I are scheduled to see Lloyd later. I need to give you some of the legal documents to look at. They're focusing on the warranties and the disclosure letter now and I'd like you to manage that for us. It was Ryan's suggestion actually.'

Stella had no idea what he was talking about but nodded. Ryan obviously thought she could handle it. She'd call him later. She felt a familiar flutter at the mention of his name and realised that her feelings for both Ryan and Ian were as confused as ever.

They entered Charles' office after a cursory knock and found Charles and Christopher waiting for them. The only partner missing was Lloyd.

'Good morning gentlemen, Stella.' Charles nodded at the men and then at Stella. He clearly still struggled with the concept of a female doctor. He was such a dinosaur.

'Take a seat,' Charles said.

They settled down around a circular highly-polished table and Charles launched into a very dignified but surprisingly impassioned speech about how Lloyd had let them all down and deceived them dreadfully. Charles obviously felt Lloyd had broken every code of morality and etiquette by his behaviour.

'I have taken legal advice and really feel we have no alternative but to ask him to leave the partnership. If he refuses we should expel him. The partnership deed is clear on the matter.'

'For the record I must say that the man has behaved appallingly and dishonestly and must not be allowed to bring the name of Beau Street into disrepute but, will this have a big impact on the deal? I know you say Equinox are still talking about going ahead but will this affect the price they will pay?' Christopher asked.

Stella interjected, 'I was speaking with Ryan Miller the other evening and he indicated that they would go ahead without Lloyd but his departure could make a big impact on the numbers. I think that means the price.'

Tom nodded and added, 'We're lucky the deal isn't off but I think if we lose Lloyd we can save it but at a reduced sale price.'

'I suggested to Ryan that if we brought in another doctor with an established reputation and a good following we might be able to replace Lloyd without a change in price and he didn't dismiss it out of hand,' Stella countered.

'That's not going to be easy to achieve in the time frame we have,' said Charles, 'can I just ask if we are all agreed that we need to ask Lloyd to leave?'

It seemed that they all were.

'What if he won't go quietly?' Stella asked, acutely conscious that so far Lloyd didn't seem to be taking his exposure lying down.

'If he wants a fight he can have one,' said Tom, 'we can throw the book at him. We've got the fraud, the record keeping, not to mention the negligence claim. I've got some C-list actress threatening to go to the papers after the shocking aftercare he gave her. In fact I need someone to agree to do some rectification work on her.'

'I'd be more than happy to sort that out for her. Refer her to me, Tom.'

'Thanks Stella, I appreciate that.'

Stella continued, 'And can I just say that I think we need to be sensible and not antagonise Lloyd any more than we need to. I think he could get nasty and harm us if he generates any publicity. We need to handle this carefully. We need him out of the business but we don't need to ruin him. If we do that then he has nothing to lose and could make life difficult. We need to let him leave in a manner that allows him to continue to practise somewhere else.'

'Stella, I agree, reluctantly though. I think we need to give him the opportunity to make good any potential fraud he's committed and leave with a semblance of dignity, although frankly that man doesn't deserve it. If it wasn't for the sale of the business I would throw the book at him,' Christopher added.

'Well, that's settled then. Tom and I will meet with Lloyd shortly and explain the views of his partners. In the meantime I understand that Tom and Stella have a lot of work to do to keep the deal on track. If I get any inkling of a significant change in the price the Americans will pay, I will of course let you all know.' With that it was apparent that Charles considered the meeting at an end and they filed out of his office one by one.

Karen was waiting with her appointment book in hand as Stella returned to her office.

'Everything okay?'

Stella sat down.

'I hope so but I might as well tell you that Lloyd has been up to no good. We're all hoping it doesn't affect the sale of the business.'

Karen didn't look surprised. 'Slippery as an eel, that one. Can't get a straight answer out of Audrey either. Thinks she's something special, that one. Personally I think she looks like a hooker.'

Stella smiled. Karen wasn't great at holding back her views on anyone.

'So how's Benji doing?' she asked.

Karen's face lit up, 'he's doing great. We've decided to apply for the private school. For a bursary if possible. No idea how we'll afford it otherwise. And his football is going great. He's been scouted for Reading FC and Leyton Orient. He's got trials coming up and regular training.'

Stella made a mental note to ask about staff bonuses. If the partners were all going to make a ton of money out of the deal then surely the staff should get a share of it too.

'That's fantastic news. Now do you fancy some overtime if you need money for school fees and football boots?'

'Sure, if I can fit it round Benji's football. Of course I do. But why? Our paperwork is bang up to date.'

'It's the sale of the clinic. Looks like Tom and I are running this deal.' Stella didn't say that Charles and Christopher were already halfway out of the door and had no interest in the fine details of the transaction, 'There's going to be loads of paperwork and stuff. To be honest I've got no idea what it is I'm supposed to be doing. I suppose I should ask the lawyers or Ryan,' she said to herself as much as to Karen, 'anyway, I'll let you know what I need and when. Okay, what's on the agenda today?'

Karen talked her through her morning schedule of a nose job and an eyelift followed by a ward round and some consultations and non-surgical patients. She should be able to find a window in the schedule to talk to the lawyers.

Later that morning in between surgeries Stella checked her phone. A text. From Tom.

'He's gone. Spitting mad – both of us! Didn't go quietly.'

Stella pursed her lips and put her phone back in her bag. Had Lloyd said anything? Two hours and a straightforward eyelift later, Stella decided to take the initiative and call Lloyd. He picked up immediately.

'I expect you know what they've done to me,' he didn't sound quite as hostile as she'd expected.

'Yes. I do. Can you meet me at the sandwich place again? Fifteen minutes?'

Stella grabbed her bag and hurried out of the building.

Lloyd was already at a table when she reached the café and signalled to the coffee he'd already bought for her.

'Look, let's dispense with the pleasantries shall we? However you look at it you've been fiddling the business, not keeping proper records, using false names, in fact carrying on in an unprofessional, probably unethical, practice. I'm not questioning the quality of your work, Lloyd,' she saw the outrage on his face and tried to pander to his ego a little to avoid him exploding, 'you're a talented cosmetic surgeon and I'm sure you want to carry on working. But we both know that I knew nothing about what you were up to. Maybe the envelope of cash should have set an alarm bell ringing, and the business of Olivia Meddoes' name, but it wasn't a false name, just her real name, so there was probably nothing wrong there. I haven't spent that cash by the way.' He raised an eyebrow and smirked. She continued crossing her fingers under the table at the fib, 'The other partners were livid this morning and wanted to hang you out to dry. I persuaded them to let you go with minimal fuss. If Karen, Audrey and I straighten up your paperwork you should be able to set up again somewhere. You've got a loyal client base. You said so yourself. But you need the sale of the clinic to go through too. If it doesn't happen because of you causing trouble can you imagine how angry all the partners will be? Charles won't be able to retire. Christopher loses his nest egg and Tom and I will still be saddled with mortgages and debts. That's when they'll go nuclear. Call the police in, the GMC. The works. You'll never work again even if you're cleared. Your clients will be petrified by the publicity. You know how much they like their privacy.'

There was a moment's silence.

'And you accused *me* of blackmail, Stella,' he said.

'This isn't blackmail. It's a promise. And you made this mess, not me. Lloyd, I'm fighting your corner to get you out of the business as cleanly as possible. Piss me off and I'm sorry, I don't care about your future. Who are they really going to believe? You with your sleazy practice, which the lawyers are exposing more and more of on a daily basis, or squeaky-clean Stella with Karen's impeccable record-keeping.'

Lloyd stared at her, still smirking slightly but not as arrogantly as usual. Stella could detect a nervousness about him she'd never seen before and his left foot was tapping away manically under the table.

'Clever girl, Stella. Okay, it's a fair cop. I will go quietly, officer,' he said with an unpleasant sneer, 'I don't care about you and stupid Beau Street. I just care about my practice. I won't make trouble for you if you can make sure I get a smooth exit. No big fanfare. No bad publicity for my clients or me. But don't fool yourself, Stella. You're not Miss Perfect. You and me are alike. The only difference is for you it is *all* about the money. I am an artist too.' With that he got up and casually glided out of the café.

As Stella made her way back to the clinic she reflected on Lloyd's parting shot. What was wrong with it being about the money? She was professional. She cared about her patients. Well, most of them. It was the same debate she used to have with Ian. If she was a lawyer no one would criticise her if her motivation was money. Why was being a doctor different? As long as she did her job well. She shook her head. Unless you come from a home with threadbare carpets, the spectre of unemployment and where the only ambition was to escape from a particularly bad council estate then you couldn't comment, in her opinion.

She checked her watch. There was enough time to see the lawyers and find out what on earth it was she was meant to be doing. She found Alex, Ross and Dan huddled away in their basement surrounded by files of paper.

'So what is it I'm supposed to be doing? Something to do with warranties I think,' she asked Alex.

'Right, well Tom has said he wants you in charge of reviewing the warranties and doing the disclosure exercise,' Alex replied.

'Come again? Over my head I'm afraid,' Stella theatrically whisked her hand over the top of her head.

Alex smiled.

'Okay, let's start at the very beginning.'

'A very good place to start,' Dan chipped in.

'Oh my God, we're not going to start singing are we!' Stella laughed and the others joined her.

'A warranty is, if you like, a promise that a particular statement of fact is true and can be relied on. So if Beau Street gives a warranty that it has had no clinical negligence cases in the past three years then Equinox can rely on that. But if they find out there was a case then they can bring a warranty claim against you for any loss they suffer as a result,' Alex explained.

'Okay. I get that. So what warranties do we have to give about the clinic?'

'At the moment, this lot,' Alex replied as she leafed through several pages of the legal document in front of her.

'You're kidding!'

'No. They ask for warranties about the finances, the staff, the property, the clinic's tax affairs, litigation. The list goes on. It's my job to try and limit them and cut them down and this isn't the final draft, but yes it's perfectly normal to have pages and pages of them.'

'Okay, so where do I come in?'

'You need to understand the warranties that the business is giving and be clear that it can give them. But you also need to do a disclosure exercise.'

'You've lost me again there. Can we go back to the very beginning again?'

'Disclosures are made against the warranties so, going back to my example of the warranty about clinical negligence cases, if you know there has been a case or a potential case then you have to disclose it to negate that warranty.'

'Okay, so I can promise we have had no claims in the past three years and then go "Ta Dah" actually we did have a claim two years ago as Stella Webb was sued for a million pounds because she did a shoddy facelift.'

'Yes. Sort of. You basically need to go through every warranty carefully and make sure you tell Equinox of anything you know which could be a breach of that warranty. If they already know about something then they can't bring a claim against you. Obviously they've done loads of due diligence about the clinic but this is another way to flush out information from you.'

'Got it. Sounds like a lot of work,' Stella said, half to herself.

'To be honest there's usually more than one person who would handle a disclosure exercise. We will help you as much as we can and Dan has already started on it using all the information we have about the clinic,' Alex replied.

'Oh and can I have a copy of the presentation you gave them? They've asked you to warrant that,' Dan asked.

'Of course, I'll ask Karen to dig it out. I might have another look at it too actually. And can I take a copy of the warranties so I can start reading through them and thinking about what you need to know?'

'Already done. Here's the latest draft of the warranties and a copy of Dan's draft disclosure letter. I'll email them too.' Alex handed her two stapled sheaves of paper.

'Happy reading,' Dan said.

'Thanks. I think. Shouldn't have any trouble sleeping tonight!' Stella got up to leave.

Later, as Stella's last patient left her consulting room, there was a knock on the door at the same time as her phone started ringing.

'Come in,' she called as she picked up her phone.

'Dr Webb,' she said to the caller as Fred came into the room. She motioned for him to sit down as she pointed to the phone.

'Ah, doctor, I wonder if you could help me?' It was Ryan. She couldn't help smiling.

'Let me see what I can do.'

'I am suffering from neglect.'

'Sounds serious,' she replied.

'It is. There's a beautiful woman I need to see. Without her I am lost, lonely, pathetic.'

Stella suppressed a giggle.

'Look, don't leave me hanging. Are you free for dinner? Drinks at my hotel at seven thirty?'

'I'm so sorry, Ryan, but I'm not. I'm already busy this evening,' she heard herself say.

'Bummer. My condition will get worse you know. Are you at least free for a quick business meeting tomorrow? There are a few deal issues I need to chat through.'

'Sure. Tomorrow at four?'

'It's a date.'

'It's a business meeting! Look, I'm sorry about tonight.'

Stella finished the call with a tinge of regret but proud of her new-found determination to sort her life out. Tonight she had the joy of reading the warranties.

'Fred. Sorry about that. Now what can I do for you?'

Fred looked nervous and embarrassed. A textbook patient really.

'Well, Dr Webb, I'm sure you know I'm keen on meteorology,' he began.

'Er, yes.' Where was this going?

'It's been my passion for years. I've done lots of courses you know. I've got all the kit.'

'I'm sure you're very well qualified, Fred, and you always give me plenty of warning about when to bring an umbrella in. But how can I help you?'

'Well there's this local cable channel. Looking for a weatherman. I've applied and I've got an interview in a fortnight. I know my stuff. I could do the job standing on my head but it's my age, doctor. These TV people are ageist. Everyone knows that. I'm sixty-one and I look it. I know I do. My wife would kill me if she knew I was here but is there anything you can do, doctor? Make me "screen friendly" and look ten years younger?'

'Fred, there are always things I can do. For you I'd probably recommend an eye lift, maybe some Botox and fillers or perhaps a full facelift depending on what you want to spend, but you need to be absolutely sure. I regularly treat patients who want to compete at work in today's youth culture. I understand you want to optimise your chances but really do you want to work somewhere where they value your looks more than your skills?'

Stella was asking this question more often.

'I know, doctor. You're right. But I really want the job. Weather is my life.'

'Look Fred, why don't you go along to the interview and see how you get on. I can't do anything much before then anyway. Some Botox and fillers perhaps.'

'I don't want any poisons injecting. I was thinking something more drastic. I really don't like the idea of it and like I say my wife'll go mad if I spend any of our savings on it '

'Well that's another reason to wait I think.'

'I suppose you're right,' he nodded, 'if I'm in the running for the job after the interview maybe I could see you then. I can always tell them I'm prepared to have something done if they need me to.'

'Fred, I would just go in there and impress them with your knowledge. Save your money for something else.'

'Right you are. Thank you for your time, doctor.' He got up.

'Stella. Call me Stella please.'

'You'll need an umbrella tomorrow, doctor. Light rain forecast first thing.'

CHAPTER 18

Stella poured a glass of wine and settled on the sofa with the papers that Dan had given her. She had a feeling of mounting panic as she read. It was like revising for her GCSEs when she'd discovered that her shambolic English teacher had taught her class the wrong text for eighteen months.

There were large chunks of the legal wording she didn't understand. The section on tax was especially incomprehensible. She knew nothing about corporate tax. Surely Tom could look at that? And the clinic? She had no idea about the lease on the building. She might have a copy of it somewhere but she had no idea if it had a 'change of control' clause in it. She didn't know what a change of control clause was. Then there were long sections on the employees, any potential claims they had about the business, environmental liabilities, intellectual property; it just went on. She might as well be reading the small print on a software licence.

Then she turned to Dan's draft disclosure letter. She swiftly concluded that he knew a lot more about the business than she did. She managed to jot down a couple of thoughts but really it was hopeless. The most worrying thing was her presentation. The Americans wanted her and the other partners to promise that everything she'd put in the presentation document was true and accurate. She cringed as she remembered how she'd put it together. She'd got her information on industry trends from a few articles she'd stumbled across online and made some bits of it up. Some of her forecasts had been based on the trends section of a fashion magazine. She'd been told to big up the business and that's what she'd done. Now she was being asked to promise it was all a hundred per cent true. Then she remembered what Alex had said about limiting the warranties by disclosing stuff. Maybe she could make some disclosures and say that there were bits of the presentation were wrong, or at least show where she'd got some of her facts and figures from and say something about not being able to guarantee the accuracy of the original sources. Was it too late to call Alex?

After another half an hour of trying to subtly disclose the fact that her presentation was a collection of unauthenticated statistics and ambitious claims, she decided to call her.

'Alex, I'm so sorry to bother you at this hour but I've got a few questions about the warranties.'

'Not a problem, Stella. I'm still here,' Alex replied.

'Where?' Stella asked.

'At Beau Street.'

'Gosh you guys work hard. It's half past nine!'

'It's always like this on a deal. So how can I help you?'

Stella explained her predicament.

'So you see I was totally in "sales mode" when I did the presentation and I think I overdid it a bit. There's no way I can warrant that document is a hundred per cent true and accurate.'

'Okay. Well I understand that sometimes budgeting can change and that sales pitches can be a bit optimistic but can't we just go through the presentation page by page and disclose where we think it's a bit wide of the mark?' Alex replied.

'But that's exactly what I've been trying to do and basically I might as well disclose that the whole presentation is a pack of lies.'

'I'm sure it's not as bad as that. Come on, you must have got industry statistics and your forecasts from somewhere? What were your sources?'

Stella proceeded to explain how Ryan had asked her to 'sell' the business and how she'd based her projections about the growth of the cosmetic surgery sector on some statistics she had found online, 'To be honest Alex, a lot of it was guestimating. I'm not saying that the basic premise was wrong but that I might have exaggerated a bit. Well, a lot, actually.'

'Well we have two options. We either disclose like mad, which will just annoy them, or we come clean. They might have asked you to warrant the presentation to flush this out. Maybe they suspected it was all a bit too good to be true and wanted to see who would blink first. The other thing of course is all the business with Dr Cassidy. Whatever you said in the presentation will have changed now anyway. Without Dr Cassidy's earnings the income for the business is inevitably going to be down, until a replacement doctor is hired.'

'So when you say "come clean", I basically admit that I've overhyped the figures.'

'Yes.'

'Great! Can't wait for that conversation.'

'Let me know how it goes, Stella, as I'll need to amend the documents. There is also the chance it could negatively affect the price Equinox will pay but I know they're looking at that already because of the Cassidy affair.'

After a night of odd dreams, featuring giant PowerPoint slides repeatedly attacking her, Stella jumped off the bus near the clinic into a puddle. Cursing as she remembered Fred's warning about 'light rain', she dodged her way along the pavement trying to take refuge under shop awnings and doorways. She reached the door of the clinic and shook the excess water from her hair like a dog after a swim.

'Morning, Dr Webb. I did warn you about the rain, didn't I?' Fred was wagging his finger at her theatrically.

'No one likes a Know It All,' she mustered a smile, 'but I can't deny your weather forecasting skills.'

Fred beamed back at her, 'I'm at the top of my game at the moment, what with the job interview coming up.'

As Stella strode to her consulting rooms she suddenly changed course and headed towards Tom's office. Alex had been right. She needed to come clean about the presentation. She knocked and Tom called her in.

'Stella, I can't say this is good news but it isn't a total surprise,' Tom responded, after she breathlessly poured out her concerns about the warranties and disclosures about her presentation, 'perhaps I should have given you more guidance. But I had to keep quiet during your presentation myself. I had no idea where you'd got most of your information but at the time we wanted to clinch the deal and your presentation certainly helped us do that. The problem now is that it's all about price. We're basically giving them a bigger stick to beat us with if we do a "mea culpa" and tell them the presentation was a work of fiction. Leave it with me, Stella. I'm going to see if we can delete the warranty and laugh the whole thing off as a bit of sales puffery. Everyone knows there's always a bit of exaggeration in a sales pitch. We've got bigger concerns really, namely how we fill the gap that Lloyd leaves. There is a tiny chance that Alex, the lawyer, might have come up with a solution to that.'

'What's that?' Stella was intrigued.

'Have you ever come across a doctor called Rob Sweeney?'

She shook her head.

'There is a chance he could be the next Lloyd Cassidy.'

'Christ, I hope not.'

'In a good way,' said Tom, 'if that's possible. Anyway, he's a mate of mine. Met him at the rugby. There's an outside chance he might move to Beau Street. He would help drum up more business for us and he already has a strong established practice. It's a long shot at the moment but it's one I'm actively pursuing.'

'I'm seeing Ryan this afternoon by the way,' Stella said.

'Work or play?' said Tom smirking.

'Work. A hundred per cent.' She was regretting her previous joking with Tom about Ryan.

'Well, don't mention Rob Sweeney to him. That's a very long way from being a done deal at the moment. And if you can come up with any other solutions to plug the hole in the figures, let me know. Don't mention the presentation at the moment. That's a headache we can deal with at a later date.'

***

As Ryan sat down in her office later that afternoon, Stella couldn't help admiring his beautifully-cut suit and the languid ease with which he crossed his legs and put his elbows behind his head.

'So Stella. How are the two of us going to keep this show on the road? We need this deal on track, so I can spend as much time in the UK as possible,' he was as flirtatious as ever but there was gravity to his tone, 'this Cassidy business isn't great and I'm having to really work on my CEO to keep him engaged. I don't imagine this will help either.' As he spoke, Ryan took his phone from his pocket and passed it to Stella. The screen showed the front page of a London evening newspaper. Halfway down was an article about a soap actress.

'I'm sorry, Ryan, I don't understand?'

'It's an exposé on this woman's cosmetic surgery. It links her to Beau Street. It's pretty clear she hasn't consented to the piece. I imagine she's mega pissed about this. Whether it's true or not.'

Stella frowned as she scrolled through the article on Ryan's smartphone. If it was true, someone was leaking patient data to the media.

'Who would leak information about Beau Street's patients?' Ryan asked. She knew they were both thinking the same thing: Lloyd.

'But why would he do that? He wanted to leave quietly so he could set up somewhere else. Why would he jeopardise that and his precious celebrity clients' privacy? He was obsessed about that. It was the whole rationale for his secret surgery,' said Stella.

'Not quite, Stella. As I understand it, the main reason for that was so he could skim his own cut off the top. Anyway, this leak needs plugging. Fast. Equinox hates bad publicity. The other issue is the revenue. I was chatting to Meredith from Clinton Wahlberg at that cricket game and with Cassidy out, the number-crunchers don't like it.'

'We know, Ryan. We're as aware of that as you are and we are working now to minimise the impact. We're exploring a couple of options.'

'Good to hear it. Give Tom a push will you? We need a plan before my CEO comes over. He's not going to fly over for meetings unless he thinks there's a genuine chance this will happen and frankly, I'm not moving to the UK to run a business that's in turnaround.'

Stella stared at him.

'You? Run the business? I thought you said…' her voice trailed off.

'Yeah, sure, honey. Didn't I tell you? Great plan don't you think? I run it. Then I'm your boss. It looks great from where I'm sitting. I know I said you might do it but this way we get to see more of each other. I'm ready for a move and we're gonna need you operating and consulting. We need your income more than ever now Cassidy's gone.'

He had a point. The business couldn't afford to lose her time to management 'stuff' and now she'd had a closer look at some of the business issues, she was less confident about being cut out for it. She wasn't sure how she felt about working for Ryan.

He was leaning towards her with his hands outstretched.

'Come on, Stella, that's enough talk about the deal. What about you? You're gorgeous, intelligent, got that crazy accent and you're soon to be rich. I really want to get to know you better. When can I see you again?'

She was flattered. He was undeniably hot. He was also successful, understood her job, and probably, as her mother would say, not short of a bob or two.

Ryan's phone rang before Stella had a chance to answer him.

'Sorry Stella, I need to get this. It's the bank.' He got up from his chair as he took the call, giving her an apologetic shrug, 'Meredith, hi. How can I help?'

Stella pretended to check her emails as Ryan paced and chatted with the banker. As he signed off, there was an awkwardness in his usually smooth banter she'd never encountered before, 'Yes okay, Meredith. Of course. I will have to firm up that commitment at another time.' As he finished the call, he abruptly made his goodbyes and left.

Before Stella could dwell on the oddness of his behaviour, Karen knocked on her door and seeing that Ryan had left, charged in, a look of panic etched on her face.

'It's Benji,' she panted, 'he's had an accident.'

'Calm down, Karen, tell me what happened.'

'He's been knocked over. By a bike.' Stella visibly relaxed at the word bike, 'but Stella, that's just it. It wasn't a kid on a bike but some big guy doing about fifty miles an hour. He's on his way to hospital now. His coach just called me. I need to go, Stella, I'm sorry. He's miles away in Reading.'

'Don't apologise. Of course you've got to go. Come on, let's get your stuff.' Stella ushered her out of her office, as Karen continued babbling.

'He's at his soccer academy. I've no idea how it happened. Knocked over by a speeding bike. That's what his coach said. But he sounded serious. I don't think it's just bumps and bruises.' At this she burst into tears.

Stella went into doctor mode.

'Look, he'll be fine. I'm calling you a cab to the station. It's not far at all on the train. Do you know which hospital he's in?'

As Karen replied, the name of the hospital immediately resonated with Stella. It was where Ian worked.

'I know someone in A&E there. I'll call them and tell them to look out for Benji. Don't worry.'

After bundling Karen into a cab with Fred fussing about her, Stella phoned Ian. His phone went through to answerphone. She left a rambling message about Benji and Karen. She hoped he was working. She couldn't imagine anyone who would be a safer pair of hands for Karen's son.

★★★

As she left the clinic that evening, she picked up a free newspaper from the rack near her bus stop. She read the article about the soap actress more slowly this time. It was obvious someone had given the journalist some detailed information. The allegations about her procedures were more than vague conjectures. Tom had been livid when she'd told him. He was instigating an internal investigation into the leak and at the moment the main names in the frame were Lloyd and Audrey.

224

As she boarded the bus, her phone rang. It was Ian. She wedged the phone under her chin, as she scanned her payment card.

'Hi. How are you?'

'I'm fine. Look I got your message. I didn't pick it up until after Benji arrived. He's taken a real tumble but I think he's going to be fine.'

'Have you seen him then?' Stella asked.

'Yeah, I took over his care from one of my colleagues, Max. Left arm fracture and a head injury. Nasty one though. Bloody cyclist was unrepentant apparently. Cycling through a public park at speed. Benji didn't stand a chance. Lovely boy, isn't he? I've just left him and his mum.'

'He's great and a really talented footballer. Thanks, Ian. It will have made a big difference to Karen, I'm sure. She was in a bit of a state when she left here.'

'She seems okay now. She's focusing all her anger on the cyclist. He's in here too with some bruising and a broken finger. I've had to make sure they're at separate ends of the unit! She was threatening to hire one of those injury lawyers and sue the pants off him when I left her.'

Stella laughed, 'I wouldn't want to get on the wrong side of Karen and hurting her son is certainly one way to do that!'

Ian laughed and then there was a short silence.

'Well, I guess that's that. Good to talk to you,' he said.

'Yeah and you.'

'Okay. Bye then,' he said.

'Yeah bye, Ian. And thanks again. I really appreciate it.'

CHAPTER **19**

Stella sat in her flat staring at her laptop screen. The sun was shining through the window gently heating the side of her face but it did little to stem the cold reality that was facing her. Her bank account was empty. Again.

She perused the page of her standing orders. Three in the last month had been returned due to insufficient funds. She had been about to set up a weekly payment to Neil, the 'wing nut' loan shark, to finally settle this damn debt but what if that bounced? She couldn't manage making sure she had enough money every month, let alone every week. And the last thing she wanted was them turning up on the doorstep again. That would finish her dad. True, it wasn't exactly the largest amount of money but it needed to be sorted. If she could just find a way to pay the rest in one go and be shot of it.

She sat back on the sofa and rested her head against the large rear cushion. A couple of spider-like cracks were creeping their way across the ceiling between the neat rows of twinkling downlighters. Yet another thing that she didn't have the money to sort out. God, she needed this deal to happen. Stella spent a happy few minutes dreaming about a world after a lovely influx of cash; a world with no money worries, without robbing Peter to pay Paul every month, without credit cards maxed to the limit. She sighed and returned to the task in hand: what to do about this debt? She sat rubbing her chin, her bottom lip absentmindedly jutting in and out, as she searched for a solution. And then she remembered her conversation with Neil about his ears. That was it! She could pin back his ears for him in return for the debt being written off. He'd still have to pay the costs for the other people involved, like the nurses and the theatre time. But if she didn't charge for her time, that would give him a pretty hefty discount, certainly against any other price he could get elsewhere. And then at least the issue would go away. She picked up her phone.

'Yeah,' Neil sounded half asleep. Stella looked at her watch; nine fifteen on a Saturday morning probably was a bit early for those working in the grey economy.

'Neil, it's Stella Webb.'

'All right, Stella. Need to borrow some money?' Stella smiled to herself, he never missed a heartbeat.

'No thanks. I was ringing about settling my mum's debt.'

'Yeah, we've been through this, you're paying me weekly. Don't tell me you can't even do that now?'

'I'd like to propose something else. I know you want to have your ears pinned back, so how about I do that for you free of charge? You'd have to pay something, as

I would need to book other people to help, and some theatre time, but I wouldn't charge you and I am the most expensive bit of the treatment. In return for you forgetting all about this debt, obviously.'

'How much less?' He sounded dubious.

'Well, our standard price for a straightforward pinnaplasty is two thousand five hundred pounds. But if I don't charge you, it will cost about nine hundred. You'll never find a price as low as that anywhere else. Or if you do, you should run a mile! That more than offsets everything I owe you. But I'd need your word…' she paused, his word wasn't worth anything, '… something in writing that says the debt has been settled.'

'That is cheap. I have looked at prices already and most are around the two grand mark. I really want it done. As I said before, I'm getting married soon and the other half really wants loads of photos and a video, the works. And my ears look loads worse since me hair fell out and I had the rest all shaved off. I look like an egg with massive jug ears now. It'd be awesome to get them back to how they should be. I'm trying to get in shape too, you know, going to the gym a bit more and all that.'

It wasn't just women who stressed about their wedding day. Neil seemed just as keen to 'look perfect' as most of the girls she knew.

'So is that a yes?' Stella asked.

'How long does it take to get over it?'

'You can normally go home on the day of the operation and you would have bandages on your ears for a week.

You'll have stitches and some bruising behind your ears but most of that will be gone within four weeks. When's your wedding?'

'Three months away.'

'Oh, you'll be fine for that. You should be totally healed by then.'

'All right, let's do it. I want to get on with it, mind. How soon can you fit me in?'

Stella paused and picked up her laptop.

'Let me just have a look at what I've got on.'

The operation would only take a couple of hours, so she was sure she could find a slot pretty quickly. She needed to do all the pre-op checks but some of those she could do on the phone now.

'How about next Wednesday? And I can run through a questionnaire with you now, so that will save some time.'

They agreed a time and Stella opened up a standard medical questionnaire on her laptop and began running through the questions.

'Any history of chest pains, heart attack or palpitations?'

'Not if you don't count the heart attack I had when me mam caught me with a load of girlie mags when I was about fourteen,' he laughed loudly.

'Are you on any forms of medication?'

'Nope. Fit as a butcher's dog I am.'

And so the list went on. His answers to the smoking and drinking section left a bit to be desired but no more than half the other patients she met.

'So what is it you hope to achieve from the operation? We would like to make sure that your expectations are realistic.'

'Er, ears that don't stick out. What else is there?' Neil sounded confused by the question. Stella could see his point but she had to make sure that she had talked him through all the risks.

'I just want you to know that we can't guarantee that your ears will be exactly the same. You need to think of them as sisters, rather than twins. And there is a possibility that they can move again in the future, as the skin relaxes. Although I have to say that has never happened yet with one of my patients.' Stella silently congratulated herself. Whatever people might think about the merits or otherwise of her job, she was damn good at it.

'Yeah, yeah, got all that. Are we done?'

'Nearly. We just need to talk about the anaesthetic. We can do this procedure under local or general anaesthetic. The benefit of a local anaesthetic is that there is less risk and you will feel less groggy on the day but you will have to stay very still during the operation, which can take up to two hours. We lay you on your front, using a bed with a hole around your face, so although you will be comfortable, some patients do find it a bit claustrophobic for that length of time. If we use a general anaesthetic, then I would do the appointment in the morning, to give you time to recover and still go home the same day. The risks of modern general anaesthetics are very low, particularly for someone young and fit like you, but they still need to be borne in mind.'

'General, definitely. There's no way I want to be awake. I'm a right old fidget, even when I'm watching telly. So local would be a nightmare.'

'Okay. I will book it in as a general anaesthetic then. No problem.'

Stella finished off running through the questionnaire, gave Neil the directions on how to find the clinic and then emailed Karen with all the details, so that she could book everything in for next week. That was a job well done. One thing off her plate at least.

She checked her online resale account where several pairs of shoes and bags were still waiting for bids. Disappointingly, none were at the asking price and she wasn't going to drop the price any further; they were already on at a steal. She would just have to focus her efforts on getting the Equinox offer over the line. But there were so many things still to sort out that could derail it: her exaggerated figures, Lloyd leaving, the whole press leaks thing, never mind a load of warranties that she didn't really understand that would probably land her in prison if she didn't get them right. Her earlier dreams of a life on Easy Street suddenly seemed rather a long way away.

The next day, Stella glanced at her watch as she jumped off the bus. She had a consultation in half an hour and wanted to try and catch Dan and discuss the wretched warranties before then.

'Morning, Dr Webb. A glorious day for it.' Fred seemed in a positive mood.

'Morning, Fred. Any news on that opportunity we discussed?' she said, tapping the side of her nose with her finger and winking.

'It went as well as can be expected,' he replied, and then under his breath, 'I think they were impressed by my knowledge. One of the other candidates didn't even know what a barotropic system was. Unbelievable!' he shook his head, 'they were all a lot younger than me though.'

'Fred, if they want a meteorologist then you're their man. Let me know when you find out.' She patted him on the arm and continued into the building.

The phone was ringing as she walked in. She dropped her bag on the floor and leant over her desk to grab the handset. It was Ian.

'Hi, Ian. How are you?' She sat down and started removing her jacket, the phone nestled under her chin as she pulled her arm through the sleeve.

'Great thanks. Look, Stella, have you time for a quick word about Benji?'

'Yeah sure. How is he? Look, thanks for keeping an eye out for him. I really appreciate that.'

'Well, I wish I'd been a bit more involved in his care to be honest,' Ian replied.

Stella positioned her jacket onto the back of the chair and leant forward, 'Why? Ian, is something the matter?'

'No. Don't panic. Nothing serious. Benji will be fine. His arm's in a cast now. It's his face I'm a bit worried about. I think I told you he'd banged his head. His helmet saved him from any serious injury but he must have landed on a stone or something as he's got quite a lot of damage on his cheek near his eye. He sustained a nasty cut which we had to stitch.'

'Poor Benji. No permanent damage though?'

'Well, that's the reason for the call. Stella, could I ask a favour?'

'Of course. But what can I do?'

'A new junior doctor did the stitching last night. It's fine, Stella, but you know what some first attempts at stitching are like. Put it this way, that guy won't be getting a job sewing posh frocks for a fashion designer anytime soon. It would be fine if it was somewhere else on the body but it's Benji's face. He doesn't need a massive Action Man scar for the rest of his life. It will fade obviously but it's not very even and I'm worried he might end up with a bit of a seam. You're amazing at stitching. Always have been. And you do such fabulous cosmetic work. Do you think you could take a look? Maybe redo it? It would have to be today before it starts to heal.'

Stella felt her cheeks redden. She was flattered. She knew that Ian had rated her skills at medical school but he'd rarely spoken about her work like this before.

'Ian, I'd be delighted to. You know I would. You were the one doing me a favour looking out for Benji in the first place. I'll call Karen and tell her to bring him in. Can you get his notes to me?'

'Thanks so much, Stella. You're a star.'

'Well they didn't call me Stella for nothing!' she laughed.

'Doh. Should have seen that one coming! I'll get you his notes. That's really good of you. Thanks.'

'No problem. So, how's things going in Reading?'

'Okay thanks. Well, more than okay. Pretty good really. Getting loads of experience and pretty much running the team here, as the main A&E Consultant is involved in some government initiative at the moment so isn't on the ground as much. Yeah, it's going well. Thanks for asking. And you? How are you ?'

She gave him a brief lowdown on the deal, being sure not to mention Ryan.

'That's good to hear. I really hope it happens for you. The deal that is. You deserve it.'

There was an awkward pause.

'I'd better get going, Ian. See you soon. Amelia's thirtieth maybe?'

'God. I'd totally forgotten about that. Need to check my shifts but yeah, hopefully see you then.'

Stella was disappointed. It hadn't even crossed her mind that Ian might not be at the party and realised how much she'd been looking forward to seeing him again.

She called Karen and suggested she bring Benji in later that afternoon so she could take a look at his stitches. Karen was gushing in her thanks.

Karen's temporary replacement poked her head around the door to announce her first patient. 'Mr Wallace is here for you, Dr Webb.'

Stella hadn't recognised the name but as his well-groomed immaculate head appeared around the door she inwardly groaned. It was the SIMON again. Back to badger her for totally unnecessary surgery.

Thirty minutes later, after moaning on his part about Dr Cassidy's sudden disappearance and more futile attempts to counsel him on her part, he had left. Lloyd had been apparently more than happy to perform the nose job. *No surprises there*, she thought. And the annoying little surgery pimp Albert Cheung had apparently also had absolutely no problem in persuading him to have eye surgery, laser removal of armpit hair and Botox in his hair-free armpits to stop sweating. The only problem for Mr Wallace was that now Lloyd had left he had no one willing to perform the work. Reluctantly Stella had agreed to the armpit work but on condition he continued to see the psychologist she had recommended. She reasoned that at least she would do the work properly. He could get the laser and Botox work done at most beauty salons anyway. It was the surgery that she was worried about. He could end up being the classic case of the person no one recognised anymore at the age of forty if he carried on down that path.

She had a short break before her next patient and took the opportunity to seek out the lawyers. They were beavering away as usual in the basement room where they had been holed up for what seemed like weeks now.

'Morning, guys. You lot are a permanent fixture round here these days,' she said as she entered the gloomy windowless room.

Alex, Dan and Ross looked up from their paperwork. Ross immediately blushed when he saw the doctor he had so recently prostrated himself in front of.

She sat down and proceeded to explain that there was just no way they could warrant her previous sales presentation.

'To be honest it was over the top and far too ambitious when I gave it, but now with Lloyd going it is pretty much a work of fiction. What I was wondering was, if this Rob guy is going to join the team and if we're going to have to reformulate the sales figures and business plan, then surely we need to produce a totally new plan? If I put that together with the rest of the team then perhaps we could warrant that and just ditch the old one. What do you think?' she directed her question to Alex.

'You're right, things have moved on a lot and it's not difficult to argue the old sales presentation is obsolete although obviously the core business hasn't changed. From what I understand it looks likely that Rob Sweeney is going to join the team and I suppose you know about the potential TV deal?'

It was apparent from the bemused look on Stella's face that she had absolutely no idea what Alex was talking about.

'I'm sorry, I assumed you knew? This was part of the rationale for Rob joining Beau Street? We came up with the idea of a reality show at the clinic filming surgery on celebrities. Not A-listers, of course.'

'Of course,' said Stella. This was getting more bizarre by the moment.

'There's interest from a respectable TV company and it won't be prurient or shallow. It would give the clinic great coverage, celebrity endorsement and good publicity. Apparently Equinox were involved in a similar programme in the States. Dan and I have done some digging about that and we've got some stats on how their sales went up after the show. It could be great for business if managed well.'

Stella took in what Alex was saying. She smiled wryly when she thought how gutted Lloyd would be when he heard about it. It would have been right up his street. He loved blowing his own trumpet, and to be on TV! That would have been his dream. A sudden thought struck her.

'They wouldn't expect me to appear on camera would they?'

'No. That's why Rob is coming on board. Have you met him?'

'Er, no,' said Stella, wondering why the lawyer seemed to know more about her business than she did.

'I was at uni with him. Anyway I suppose you would say he has the face for TV and by all accounts already has an established practice as a cosmetic surgeon.'

'Right, well that's a relief. So he'll do all the TV stuff? I'll need some more info on all of this and I'll want to have a proper chat with the rest of the team here. I can see the advantages but some of the more established partners might need some convincing, although from what I hear most of them are planning to disappear as soon as they get their payout from the deal.'

Stella mulled over the conversation with Alex all afternoon. Tom had mentioned Rob Sweeney to her but she was a bit annoyed that no one had run the TV idea past her. She wasn't convinced it was necessarily the right way forward but couldn't argue with the fact it would give them publicity. The danger was that it would scare off the celebrities and members of the public who wanted to keep their surgery a secret. Despite the number of people now flaunting their latest 'work' on social media there were still a significant number of her clients who didn't even tell their partners they were getting things tweaked and augmented. She wasn't too sure how they would feel about rocking up to a clinic with a camera crew outside.

CHAPTER 20

As soon as Benji walked into the room Stella could see why Ian had called her. He had a deep facial wound just below his right eye and the stitching was less than ideal. The stiches were large and continuous. She would have preferred smaller interrupted stitches to minimise scarring. She directed him to the bed neatly covered in paper towel and adjusted the backrest so he was slightly reclined. She examined him carefully. She would have to remove the existing stitches carefully. The wound was still fresh but she was confident she could significantly improve the outcome for the boy.

She explained to Karen and Benji what she needed to do and Karen brought a chair up to hold Benji's hand as Stella administered the local anaesthetic.

Karen was chatting away throughout the procedure.

'We saw him you know, the cyclist. All I wanted was an apology for Benji but no, nothing. Didn't even acknowledge us. I was livid. I could tell the doctors didn't like him either. I'm seriously thinking about making one of those claims for compensation. Benji can't train for his football and how's he supposed to sit his scholarship with his arm in a cast? And then there's me. Time off work and all the hassle.'

'Karen, you can have the time off as compassionate leave. I've already told you that.' Stella secured the bead to the final stich.

'Thanks, Stella. I just don't know who to talk to about a claim. I don't want to go to one of those law firms on the TV. Someone local I want. Someone I can trust. I don't even know what a claim would be worth.'

'I could have a chat with my mate Fenella. She's a barrister but she'll know who to go to.'

'Would you mind? That would be great. Thanks so much and thanks for sorting this out,' she said peering at the new, much smaller, neater stitches on Benji's cheek.

'Thanks, Dr Webb,' Benji muttered as he climbed down from the bed.

'I'll see you next week to get those stitches out, okay? Karen make sure you bring him in,' said Stella.

'Thanks so much, Stella. You're a star.'

Stella smiled to herself as she remembered Ian's same words earlier that day.

As Karen and Benji left Stella packed her things away and called Ian to update him.

'I knew you could do a miles better job. Thanks again,' Ian said after Stella explained what she'd done, 'as I said earlier I couldn't think of anyone better to rectify it. By the way I've checked my rota and I'm definitely going to Amelia's party so I'll see you then.'

The day was getting even better. Stella called Fenella on her way home and agreed to meet up to discuss Karen and Benji's case. She knew some good personal injury lawyers she could discuss the case with.

She walked out of the building that evening feeling a brief flutter of excitement and pride. Her head was momentarily turned by a beautiful white trench coat in a shop window but she resisted the temptation to stop and stare or worse, go in and try it on. This was the new Stella. Top surgeon, businesswoman and friend. She was genuinely excited by the prospect of getting the deal back on track. She was determined that it would happen. She had been so immersed in the issues with Lloyd, her mum's debt and the flirtation with Ryan that she had almost forgotten that she could be on the brink of making a serious amount of cash. As she thought of Ryan again she realised that her feelings for him were still unresolved. She needed to see him one more time in a social setting to determine whether there was anything more than flirtation between them. He had never made it clear whether he was interested in anything more than a quick fling and she was pretty sure she didn't want a quick fling. She was more and more certain that she wanted a proper relationship. Like the one she'd had with Ian.

That evening as she sat in bed in her joggers and T-shirt, she checked the resale sites again. The bids were increasing on the handbag but nothing else was moving. Stella hoped that there would be a frantic last-minute bidding war for the rest of her stuff but she wasn't holding out any hope. At least if she did the op for Neil she could finally put the loan shark debacle to bed.

She flicked through her emails and spotted an email from a company she had vaguely heard of before. She clicked on the email expecting it to be spam but soon realised it was from the TV company Alex had been talking about earlier. She and Tom had been copied in on an email to Rob Sweeney. She moved closer to her laptop. The email described the format of the programme. As Alex had said it didn't seem trashy at all; more like a documentary. They clearly wanted Rob to feature as the surgeon. Tom had sent a follow-up email to her attaching Rob's CV. He certainly had all the credentials and if his CV was to be believed already had a successful practice and established client base and was running the non-surgical side of his current clinic's business. Tom had met and interviewed him apparently and seemed keen to hire him. Tom had finished his email with the following:

'So it would be my recommendation to hire Rob Sweeney. I think we'll have to do the TV show too though, if Equinox agrees with it, as I think that's one of the main reasons he's prepared to move. Please could you produce a new sales pitch/business plan incorporating projections for the TV income, Rob's practice and the potential impact on future sales? The lawyers and accountants can help you with the detail. I'll send some confidential details of Rob's current annual gross fees. It needs to be a tighter document which we can verify and warrant. No crazy projections this time please or unsubstantiated claims.'

Christ. This was going to take some time and research. What sort of document would they want? She realised she had never actually read a business plan. She could do with a template to use as a starting point. She got off the bed and paced the room. She could do this. She just needed to be more methodical this time. It would be like writing her dissertation at uni again. She needed to quote sources, verify claims and be methodical. Maybe Ryan could help?

She checked her watch. It would be the afternoon in the US. Or was he still in the UK? She couldn't remember what his movements were but she dialled his number anyway. She continued pacing the room willing him to pick up. She really wanted to hear his voice and not just for professional reasons.

He didn't pick up. It went to voicemail. She left a message and threw her phone on the bed. She read Tom's email again. Maybe she would be better contacting the lawyers and accountants? She emailed Alex Fisher and Rachel Altman requesting details of the figures for the impact of the US reality show, a template for a business plan and a request that they review her first draft. How difficult could this be?

★★★

Stella swung her handbag as she strolled towards the restaurant where she was meeting Fenella for lunch. It was a beautiful sunny day and she had had a productive morning making a start on the business plan. Rachel had sent her a template and she was gradually and carefully constructing a growth plan for the business. Even without Lloyd's income stream it was showing positive numbers. Tom had sent her through Rob's figures. She had added them to the projections but had been careful to add a caveat that they were not verified. She arrived at the café and sat down at an outside table enjoying the opportunity to put her face up to the sun. As a cosmetic surgeon she knew of the damage of sun-ravaged skin but couldn't resist a little intake of vitamin D.

'Yo Stella!' Fenella called as she sprinted towards her.

Stella took her face away from the sun and smiled and waved at her friend. Fenella plonked herself down after giving her a hug and planting a big kiss on her cheek. Stella smiled. Fenella was like an overgrown puppy sometimes.

'So what's new with you, hon? Any juicy celebrity stories? I saw an article in the paper the other day about your clinic. Who spilled the beans on that one then?'

Stella frowned. She'd forgotten about the leak. She must discuss that with Tom. It just didn't seem likely that it would be Lloyd or Audrey. What would be in it for them?

'No. I've got no idea who leaked it. And no, no more gossip. Working on the deal mainly. I'm just praying that it will go through and generate me some serious cash. It's hard work though. Bloody lawyers and accountants. Bane of my life at the moment. How are you anyway? How's the love life?'

'Same as ever. Disastrous online dating experience last week. You know, the usual. Claimed to be a six-foot professional in his twenties. More like five foot, darts professional. He was in his twenties though. About twenty-two stone, I reckon.'

Stella laughed.

'Anyway enough about me. How's your gorgeous American? Have you got to first base yet?'

'Nah. All gone a bit quiet really. He was all over me at one point and now he's not returning my calls. I left him a message last night and not heard from him since. I'm not sure he was right though.'

'Right for what? He was rich and gorgeous. That ticks two pretty important boxes in my book.'

'Yeah, but Fenella I'm thirty-six. I don't want flings and one-night stands. I want Mr Right and we need to think about babies fairly soon. That's if we want them. Do you?' Stella realised that she and Fenella had never really discussed this issue.

'Honestly?'

'Yep,' said Stella.

'Yeah I do. But it's been all about my career and having fun for me. It's when you suddenly realise you're in your mid thirties and then all these scary articles are everywhere about your fertility dropping off a cliff. I don't know. I've just been head in the sand about the whole thing. And anyway I don't want to be one of those people who forms a plan and then follows it with military precision. Meeting the man of your dreams and falling in love and having babies isn't supposed to be like that is it?'

'I don't know, Fenella, I really don't. I've gone from thinking I'm pregnant with a long-term partner to flirting with an American businessman in less than a month. But I know I've always assumed I'd be a mum at some point.'

Their food arrived and they both unwrapped their napkins and started eating.

'So what's this personal injury case all about. Fill me in,' said Fenella.

Stella proceeded to tell her the saga of Benji and the cyclist and his injuries.

'I think Karen just wants to know if she could bring a claim and roughly how much she might be able to expect as a payout.'

'Well, it's not my area as you know but my gut reaction is that she's probably in with a chance. I could speak to Ian and maybe the other doctor who treated him and get a clearer evidential picture of his injuries. Benji or his teacher could give a statement about the actual accident and I could take all that to a PI lawyer I know. I assume we have the cyclist's name?'

'Oh yeah. Karen was adamant about that. She's got her head screwed on. Would you mind? That would be a great help. Would you mind going to Reading to do that? You know, meet the doctor and Ian?'

'Not a problem. Coincidentally I've got a hearing there the day after tomorrow so I'll just call Ian and sort it out.'

'Thanks, Fenella. That's brilliant. Karen will be really grateful. Lunch is on me.'

'Er, no I don't think so. You're skint remember. I'd assumed I'd be paying.'

'Shit yes. I'd totally forgotten.'

'That's your problem. Especially when you're in a designer shoe shop.'

When Stella returned to the clinic the temp intercepted her to tell her that Tom had been looking for her. She headed straight to his office.

CHAPTER 21

Neil was sitting in the reception at Beau Street pretending to read a glossy lifestyle magazine when Stella come down to greet him. He looked up nervously as she approached and held out her hand.

'Hello Neil, good to see you again.'

As he stood up, Stella noticed his tight white T-shirt and aftershave. Dressing up for surgery? Such a change from the scruffy, couldn't-care-less boy she'd known at school.

'Have you been away? You look like you've picked up a nice tan.'

'Nah, no money for that. Just been using the girlfriend's sunbed she hired. Both of us fancy a bit of a tan for the wedding, so thought we'd give it a go.'

'They are really bad for your skin, you know,' Stella frowned, 'you really shouldn't use them often, if at all really.'

'I use all the creams they say, and all that. We'll be fine. Can I go home today?'

'Yes, assuming you feel okay when you come round. Is someone picking you up?'

'Yeah, my girlfriend's down with me, staying at a mate's.'

Neil followed Stella up into the lift and down the many corridors of the Beau Street clinic until she found the room that he had been allocated.

'So, this is where you will be staying today. One of the team will be along soon to check you in, do all the necessary paperwork and then Ahmed, our anaesthetist, will be along to meet you and just run through a few things. He will also give you some medication to help prepare you for surgery. We are due to start in about an hour, so make yourself comfortable and I will see you soon.'

Stella made her way back to her office, where Karen was waiting for her with details of the rest of her patients for that day.

'So, after your pinnoplasty, you have Mrs Longburn's facelift and then just your Botox clinic. Five patients are booked in for that so far, although one other is trying to rearrange a meeting to get here before you finish. She has a big party this weekend, and is desperate for a bit of a "pick-me-up" as she put it. No doubt she'll come running in with five minutes to spare!'

'Who is it?'

Karen looked at her notes, 'Sandra Druick. I think you have seen her quite a few times?'

Stella nodded, 'That's okay. I'm in no rush tonight. If she calls, tell her I'll see her when she gets here, within reason.' Stella thought about the work she had to do on the deal warranties, 'I've got a load of paperwork to do tonight anyway.'

'You're too good to your patients,' said Karen shaking her head.

'That's why they keep coming back.'

When Stella arrived at the operating theatre, Neil was already there. He was sitting upright, sideways on the bed, talking to Ahmed who was holding a face mask. Amy, the scrub nurse, was busying herself unpacking various instruments from their crackly sterile packaging and laying them in neat lines on a wheelie table next to the bed.

'So, once you are lying down on the bed, with your face through the hole, I will gently pull the face mask over your mouth and nose like this…' Ahmed held the mask against Neil's face, 'and then count slowly to ten. You'll be asleep before I get there. About seven is the norm.' He smiled gently at Neil, who just nodded, his eyes darting around the room as if trying to get his bearings.

'Okay, shall we get going?' Stella looked at Neil. He took a deep breath.

'Guess so.'

It took a few minutes to get Neil fixed up to the various drips and machines that would monitor him during the operation. Once that was complete, Amy helped Neil lie down on the bed and put his face through the hole.

'So, would you like a full massage or just back and shoulders?' said Amy. It was the standard joke for patients in this position.

'Either, providing it comes with extras,' said Neil, in a muffled voice.

'Cheeky,' said Amy. She and Stella smiled at each other.

Ahmed placed the mask over Neil's face, opened the tap to the gas and started counting.

It took Stella about forty-five minutes to complete the first ear.

'Very neat,' said Amy, admiring the curved row of tiny stitches behind Neil's ear. Stella measured the distance from the edge of Neil's ear to his head at several points and drafted a quick sketch, adding each measurement to the drawing as she went.

'Right, that gives us what we need to start the next ear,' said Stella.

She had just moved across to the other side of the bed when the blood pressure monitor next to Ahmed started to beep. He looked at it anxiously.

'Okay?' asked Stella.

'His pressure just dropped, which is odd. Let me just stabilise him.' Ahmed adjusted the dials on the front of the machine.

After a few seconds, the beeping stopped.

'What caused that?' Stella asked.

'I'm not sure. Let's just wait a few minutes and see he's okay before we carry on.'

Stella nodded, 'Amy, you'd better record that we are in monitoring mode and take readings every fifteen seconds for the next five minutes.'

They sat quietly watching the blood pressure monitor and after a couple of minutes, the alarm sounded again.

'Shit, dropping again and fast this time.'

Stella took one look at the readings and hit auto-pilot.

'Right, let's abort. Ahmed bring him round. Amy, clean up the site and get a bandage on pronto. This doesn't make sense. He's fit and well, no history of heart or blood pressure problems.' She shook her head; something wasn't right.

'Still dropping,' said Ahmed, 'I'm starting fluids.'

Ahmed hooked up a bag of saline fluids and linked it to the drip in the back of Neil's hand.

Stella picked up the phone on the wall of the operating theatre.

'This is Stella Webb in theatre three. We have a patient with severe anaesthetic hypotension and we need an ambulance straight away. The team need to be prepared for a cardiac crisis.'

She turned to Ahmed, 'Heart rate?'

'Also low. We need to get his legs in the air.'

Ahmed worked quickly to free the mask and looked at his watch. Stella and Amy carefully turned Neil onto his back.

'Mask back on. Amy, note absence for fourteen seconds as patient was turned to facilitate elevation posture.'

Amy picked up a large foam support cushion and placed it under Neil's legs. They all looked at the blood pressure monitor.

'A bit better, but we're still in cardiac arrest territory,' said Ahmed.

'Right, let's stand by with the defibrillator until the ambulance crew gets here.'

After what seemed like the longest seven minutes of Stella's life, the ambulance crew arrived and took over. She stepped back to the side of the operating theatre and watched as Ahmed briefed them on what had gone on. She felt dizzy and slightly sick. This had never happened to her before. Never. Of course it was always a possibility that something could go wrong but it was normally things like the risk of infection or that people weren't happy with the results.

Had she missed something? Was it her fault? All she could do was pray that Neil would be okay, as they moved him onto a wheeled stretcher and rushed him out of the building. It made her think about Ian, working in A&E. God, it must be stressful dealing with that level of crisis all the time. She decided to ring him.

'Hi, it's me, can you talk for a minute?'

'Sure, what's up?'

'Oh Ian, I've just had a patient go hypotension on me during a pinnoplasty. He just crashed and I mean really crashed, you know, cardiac territory. He's on his way to A&E now and I'm really worried I've missed something.' She fought back the tears.

'I'm sure you haven't. What sort of patient?'

'A young man, in his early thirties, fit and well. No previous medical issues. Just a real shock.'

'Did he look well today? You know, not pallid or under the weather?'

'No, I don't think so. Mind you, had a good tan from using a sunbed, the vain idiot. He wants to be in shape for his wedding, so he's been working out, getting a tan and now his ears pinned. You know the type, tight white T-shirt brigade.'

As she finished the sentence, alarm bells started to go off in her head.

'Shit, Ian, what if he's been taking steroids?'

'Well, that would definitely explain it. We come across that in A&E a lot. And it's really common that they don't tell you. Most of the steroids are illegal, so they worry about getting into trouble and they have no idea how long they stay in the body for. You'd better get on to the A&E team and tell them to run some tests. If they can find out what's in his system quickly, then it will be much easier to deal with.'

'Do you think he might have permanent damage?'

'How long was he low for?'

'At least fifteen minutes. We had him a bit more stable by the time the ambulance crew arrived. But he could have had a heart attack on the way and be dead by now, for all I know.'

'If it is steroids, then he should be okay, as it is a temporary effect caused by the anaesthetic, rather than some underlying medical problem. And it sounds like you did exactly the right thing. Were you mid op? Is there a risk of secondary infection?'

'No, fortunately I had just finished one ear. It was all stitched and ready to go.'

'So you'd only done one?'

Stella paused, 'yeah, that's not great either, is it? I hadn't really focused on that.'

'Well, that's easily fixable,' said Ian pragmatically, 'assuming he's not dead, of course.'

Stella managed a half smile, 'yes, assuming he's not dead. Thanks Ian. I'd better ring the hospital and tell them to check for steroids. I'll let you know what happens.'

***

Neil had been transferred to a large teaching hospital that was a ten-minute drive from Beau Street. It was a huge, modern building with a new state-of-the-art accident and emergency department. Stella was on her way to meet the consultant who had treated Neil, for a post-operative review meeting. Despite the fact that she was sure she had done nothing wrong, she felt nervous.

A tall, tired-looking doctor about her age stood up as she entered the small consulting room. The surfaces were covered in paper and files, punctuated with the occasional coffee cup. He held out his hand.

'Gregg Brooks.'

'Hi Gregg. Stella Webb. How is he?'

'Recovering. No lasting damage we hope and you were right, we found Anadrol and Clenbuterol in his blood tests.'

A wave of relief swept over Stella.

'Was that the cause of the hypotension?'

'Yup, could have easily killed him. Why people take this stuff and then don't tell us I never know. Did you bring his files?'

Stella nodded and took Neil's pre-operative paperwork, including the questionnaire they had done over the phone from her bag. Gregg took it from her and started reading.

'There's nothing on it. He didn't mention anything beforehand,' said Stella.

'I'm sure that's right but you know what it's like, it's just procedure when we get transfers in from a private clinic. Do you have the pre-op blood pressure readings?'

Stella leant over and found the correct pages in the file.

'Yes, here see. All normal.'

'Over what period had you known the patient? Were there any signs of rapid muscular build-up?'

'I saw him a few weeks before the operation and looking back, he did look a bit bigger when he came in for surgery. But not so much that I noticed anything out of the ordinary. It was only when I was trying to work out the problem that a few pointers came together that led me to wonder if he'd been taking steroids.'

'Well, it was a good spot. And it looks like you've done everything okay ahead of time. Just a classic case of inaccurate patient disclosure, I think. No need for us to send it upstairs.'

'That's great, thanks. It did give me a bit of a shock. Not something we see every day at Beau Street.'

'We see it far too much, sadly,' said Gregg, shaking his head, 'drugs of all sorts playing merry hell with our diagnosis. It's a right minefield when patients don't tell us everything.'

'I'm going to go and see Neil if that's okay?' Stella asked.

Gregg wrote a room number down on a piece of paper and handed it to her.

'Sure. You'll find him here.'

Stella made her way to Neil's recovery room. He looked pale and very tired.

'How are you feeling?'

'Shit.' He stared blankly at her.

'Why didn't you tell me you were taking steroids? Didn't it occur to you that it might be relevant? You could have died.'

'It was just a few shakes that the guys gave me at the gym. I didn't even really know what was in them. Yeah, I knew that they would help make me bulk up quicker but no one ever actually said they were steroids. No one said very much about anything. We just took them.'

Stella felt a bit sorry for him. He really had no idea.

'Still, at least I got my ears done. When does this bloody bandage come off? Feels like I'm wearing a crash helmet.'

He doesn't know, thought Stella. Why would he? No one had removed his bandages since he'd been in.

They'd been in full-on life-saving mode, not patient-management mode.

'I'm really sorry, Neil, but I didn't get to finish your operation. Your blood pressure dropped to really dangerous levels part way through, so we had to stop and bring you round.'

'What did you get done?'

'Just one ear, I'm afraid.'

'One ear?' he looked at her incredulously, 'what, you only did one of them? And the other is still sticking out?'

'Yes, that's right. I did completely finish the first ear, so I'm not expecting any problems. It should just heal normally.'

'What the bloody hell use is that? I'm going to look even more stupid now, with one ear in and one ear out. A right freak show. When can you do the other?'

'Well, that depends on how quickly you recover from this episode and how long it takes for the steroids to leave your system. We can't risk another general anaesthetic until we are sure you are up to it.'

'That could be ages. What about the wedding?'

'Oh I am sure we can sort it out before that. Perhaps we could use a local anaesthetic this time?'

'Could we do that sooner?'

'Yes, probably.'

Neil looked totally crestfallen.

'I'm really sorry, Neil. It could have been so much worse. At least there has been no permanent damage.'

'Apart from the fact that once these bandages come off, I'll be a laughing stock.'

'You must get this in perspective. You could have had a heart attack or a stroke or ended up with brain damage. You didn't tell us about dangerous and illegal drugs that you'd been taking and that was a big mistake. At least you're here for us to put it right.'

Neil didn't say anything. Stella figured he wasn't the humble pie type, so decided to leave it at that.

'Look, I think you will be going home in a day or so. You'll then need to come back and see me in a week, so I can take those bandages off and check your stitches. We'll run some blood tests and I'll talk to the anaesthetist and we'll see what we can sort out.'

★★★

As Stella was brushing her teeth that evening there was a loud knock at her door.

Who on earth was that? she wondered as she went to check the peephole on her front door. She noticed the slightly nervous feeling that was more prevalent now that Ian wasn't living with her.

'It's only me. Let me in.'

It was Fenella, slightly the worse for wear. Stella let her in and she stumbled into her hallway, a mass of bags, hair and outstretched arms.

'Give me a hug, gorgeous. How are you?' she mumbled as she embraced her friend.

Stella giggled.

'What are you like? It's a bloody weekday night. Aren't you in court tomorrow?'

'Yep. Look I'm not that bad. I'm high on life.'

'Mm, right. Let me get you a cup of tea.' Stella directed her friend to the kitchen where she plonked herself on a bar stool.

'Seriously I'm not that bad, I just wanted to update you on a few things on my way home. I got the statements for Karen. Open and shut case I reckon. I saw Ian. Lovely guy. Why did you let him go again?'

'Yeah thanks for that,' Stella popped teabags into two mugs and avoided Fenella's stare.

'I mean it must be something about doctors. The other doctor, you know the one that treated Benji. Max, that's his name. I got his statement too. Oh my God, Stella, he was so hot. Absolutely bloody gorgeous. Maybe a bit younger than me but we're not in cougar territory.'

'Fenella, what are you like!'

'Anyway, I've got his number. He might be coming to Amelia's party with Ian so obvs I am definitely coming to that gig now.'

Stella smiled. At least it sounded like Ian would be at the party.

'So I've passed all the statements onto my mate Tim and he's going to handle the personal injury claim for Karen. He reckons he should be able to get a few grand for her.'

'That's great news. Karen will be seriously pleased with that.'

'It was worth it! Can't wait for Saturday now!'

Neither can I, thought Stella. Ryan was becoming a distant memory and Ian was dominating her thoughts. Fenella was right. Why had she let him go so easily?

CHAPTER 22

Stella hadn't stressed so much about getting ready for a night out since her uni prom. She'd had a facial, a blow dry and had her brows done. She had toyed with a few potential purchases but had stuck with the dress she'd earmarked for tonight. She had modelled all her shoes and bags in various combinations and had FaceTimed Fenella for second opinions. As she waited for Fenella to jump in the cab, she reflected on how odd it was that she was so obsessed about impressing a man who had seen her at her very worst. Poor Ian had watched her vomiting on many occasions, seen her with her worst hangovers and witnessed her having unpleasant medical procedures to ensure she didn't have fertility issues and yet she was now staring at herself in the cab driver's rear-view mirror overanalysing her eyebrows.

'Hi Fen. Wow, you look fab.' Stella checked out Fenella's prominent cleavage as she climbed into the taxi.

'Thought I'd max out my assets for Max! Not too much, do you think?' Fenella displayed a sliver of insecurity.

'No! You look amazing and for once not a prim lawyer. What about me? Are my brows too Scouse brow?'

'Darling, you look stunning. I told you earlier. Really. I love your dress and your hair. Everything. You've made a real effort. Must have had some time on your hands. Or are you trying to pull? Or rub Ian's face in it. Maybe literally.' Fen laughed at her own joke until the penny dropped, 'Oh my God. That's it, isn't it? You're after Ian. Hooray!'

'Don't you dare tell anyone.'

The cab pulled up at a Hamptons-inspired restaurant framed by fake violet wisteria. They made their way in and were directed by the doorman to a staircase leading to the upstairs private room.

They weren't the first guests and the bar was already swarming. The room was festooned with bright pink bunting and balloons and the DJ was already on the decks. They honed in on Beth who was at the bar ordering cocktails.

'Hi ladies! You both look amazing. Thanks so much for coming.' Amelia, who was wearing a tiara and draped in a silk sash proclaiming her birthday, intercepted them and kissed them enthusiastically. She had clearly already been celebrating hard.

'Happy birthday! Welcome to your thirties. Here you go, gorgeous. This is from me and Stella. Don't lose it.' Fenella passed over an envelope containing a voucher for a spa experience which she had insisted on paying for, 'are Ian and Max here yet?' Fenella checked out the room.

'Thanks ladies. That's so kind. Don't think Ian's here yet and who's Max?' Amelia responded. As Fenella filled her in on her target man, Stella shuffled in at the bar next to Beth. She ordered two mojitos and then, as an afterthought, two shots of tequila.

After chatting to Beth and Marcus, who seemed to demonstrate some regret at breaking up with Fenella after observing her impressive boobs, Fenella and Stella drifted to the end of the bar where they sipped their cocktails and watched the party take off.

'So, how's the finances looking? Any good online sales?'

'Thanks so much for paying for Amelia's present. I will pay you back, Fen. They're not great to be honest but things should be looking up. As long as the sale of the business goes through. I've sold a handbag which will basically fund tonight for me and I've relisted some of the other stuff but with lower minimum prices. To be honest I'll be glad to get rid of all the stuff and declutter a bit.'

Fenella wasn't listening. Stella noticed her distraction and watched her gaze settle on a nervous, dark-haired man at the top of the stairs. He was scanning the room for a familiar face and smiled when his eyes locked on Fenella's.

'So that's Max?'

'Yes,' Fenella squeaked.

He came straight over to them and Fenella didn't take her eyes off him as she introduced him to Stella.

'Lovely to meet you. I understand you work with Ian Maynard,' said Stella.

'Yeah, he's my boss. Great guy. How do you know him?' Max replied.

'Oh, I was at uni with him. We go back a long way. Actually I thought he was coming with you tonight?'

'He was but he got tied up at work so I came on my own. I was hoping to see you again.' He was back staring at Fenella.

Stella made her excuses and escaped to the Ladies. She was conscious she was already a gooseberry. Fenella was right. He was hot.

The evening progressed, the drinking increased and the music ramped up. Fenella and Max were glued to each other so Stella gravitated to Beth and her crowd and worked her way through the cocktail menu. She danced, laughed and sang but couldn't suppress the empty feeling in the pit of her stomach.

She glanced at her phone and although it wasn't even midnight, decided to order a cab.

She tapped Fenella on the shoulder and explained that she was leaving. Fenella hugged her tightly and said she'd call her at some point tomorrow. She was clearly having a very different night to Stella's and she couldn't hide her delight at being with Max.

Stella made her way downstairs and waited outside under the flowing wisteria. At least her hangover wouldn't be too bad and she could do some work tomorrow. She couldn't stop the tears as they started to well up. She had subconsciously pinned so much hope on tonight. Her phone buzzed to confirm her cab was almost there. As she put her two forefingers under her eyes to blot her tears, she spotted the taxi screech around the corner and pull up. She reached for the door as it opened towards her and Ian stepped out.

They stared at each other in surprise and confusion.

As Ian fumbled for cash to pay the driver, Stella's tears returned.

'Hey, Stell. What's wrong? Are you okay?'

He momentarily held back and then instinctively held his arms out. She fell into them and hugged him.

'I've missed you, so much. I thought you'd be here. I've had some cocktails. And some shots. I'm sorry.' Her sobs punctuated her words.

'It's okay. I'm here now. Shhh.' He hugged her back.

Another taxi pulled up alongside them and beeped its horn.

'That's my cab,' she mumbled into his chest.

'You're leaving? Already? I've just legged it all the way from Reading to see you.'

'Really? To see me?' She looked up at him.

The stressed-out cab driver sounded the horn again.

'We could go back to yours?' Ian raised his shoulders quizzically.

'You mean ours?'

They both smiled. Ian held her hand and they got into the taxi.

It was a quiet journey but the hand-holding was constant and Stella smiled as she thought of her concerns about her eyebrows on the way there. Now it was the state of her mascara which was on her mind. The tears just continued. She felt like all the worries, stress and concerns of the past few months were pouring out of her.

Ian was as stoical as ever but the tenderness in his eyes was paramount.

It was weird arriving back at the house together and when they closed the door behind them Ian expelled the biggest sigh and pulled her towards him again.

'How the hell did we split up? How did that happen? I'm so, so sorry. Sod my job. I don't care where I work. I'm not me without you. The last month or so has been awful.'

Stella gazed at him. Was he asking to get back together?

'Ian, why did you suggest the split? Really?'

He knelt down on to the floor and put his head in his hands.

'I don't know. I really don't. I think it was my ego? I just wanted to get the big job and be the breadwinner and I was conscious that my agenda was holding back your hopes for children and a family. I think I was re-enacting my dad's life. God, I don't know. All I do know is I have felt lost without you. We're a team. Or we were. Stella, I'll bin my job and come back here. That's if you'll have me? You haven't met anyone else have you?' He looked at her suddenly, fear in his eyes.

Ryan's face momentarily flashed before her but she batted that image away immediately. If anything, Ryan had been a blessing. The ultimate proof that grass isn't greener. Stella joined Ian on the floor.

'Don't leave your job. From what I hear you're acing it and will get promoted soon. Then you can come back to London. We can make this work. If we're a couple again we can go back and forth. Reading isn't far at all and you could commute from here. Which I suppose means I could commute from Reading to Beau Street. We can make it work.'

'So do you want to get together again. Really?'

'Yeah I do. And I'm sorry about the house deposit. I know you know about it. I lied to you about that. It's my turn to be sorry.'

'I'll be honest, Stella, that was the red light for me. I just thought you didn't want to settle down with me. But then I was confused as you always seemed to want kids. I don't know why I made Reading such a big deal. My colleague Max lives in London and commutes to Reading daily. But Stella, I don't want to hold you back.'

'Ian for the last time you've never held me back! It doesn't matter if I earn more than you for a bit or if you're not a consultant yet. Really. It's about us. We're not competing. Like you say, we're a team.'

As she spoke, he cupped her face in his hands and drew her towards him. As they kissed, she felt a surge of happiness and a sense of belonging.

They chatted most of the night about the break-up, Stella's spending and her attempts to rein it in, Ian's subtle jealousy of Stella's possible potential wealth and his slight obsession with getting the title 'consultant'. It was the ultimate cathartic therapy session which ended with them lying in bed staring at each other with the same wonder that they felt on their first date.

CHAPTER 23

As she strode towards Beau Street Stella noticed the spring in her step and the feeling of normality which had returned with Ian. He had moved straight back in. They had spent Sunday driving to Reading to pick up some of his stuff and had reached the conclusion that he would live back in London but would stay at his flat in Reading whenever he was on call or on a late shift. Stella had agreed to do overnights in Reading whenever it suited her work commitments and whenever Ian had a particularly tough schedule. They went for a celebratory Mexican last night and true to form Stella was feeling a bit nauseous this morning although she smiled to herself when she ruled out the possibility of pregnancy. As a trained doctor she knew the symptoms took more than twenty-four hours to manifest.

As seemed to be the usual form these days she had just been summoned by Tom for an early meeting before the day's surgery and consultations. She knocked and entered his office and was greeted by a man who looked like it was ten o'clock on a Friday night rather than eight o'clock on a Monday morning.

'Hi, Stella. Take a seat.'

Tom proceeded to download the whole story about the leaks about the clinic to the media. Despite initial thoughts that Lloyd and maybe Audrey had been behind the leaks it had become apparent that the last thing Lloyd had wanted was for his celebrity clients to be splashed all over mainstream media. Confidentiality for him was key. Hence his dodgy out-of-hours clinic. All the roads were leading to Albert Cheung, apparently, Lloyd's favourite referrer of patients and the man who'd triggered the SIMON into seeking even more ridiculous work from Stella.

'Well, I have to say I did have my suspicions about him,' Stella commented.

'Well, I met with him earlier and he tried to run the line that he may have indiscreetly dropped something into a conversation with a friend of his who's a tabloid journalist but I didn't believe him. We have found more evidence that he had lists of Lloyd's clients. Those that were the most famous and those that had had the most obscure and potentially interesting procedures performed on them. I told him I was going to get the police involved and that's when he caved. Even his Botoxed face showed fear at that threat. He confessed that he had been feeding all the stories to his journalist friend. No doubt for a good backhander. Anyway, I fired him. He's out of here.'

Stella took it all in. It was rather shocking but, in a way, unsurprising. She had never thought a fellow doctor, nurse or medical practitioner of any calling would disclose a patient's details. Even Lloyd.

'Tom. Well done. You did the right thing. At least we have some closure now. From the perspective of the deal, that's surely a good thing?'

'Yes. I suppose you're right. We can do another "mea culpa" and move on now. As you know we have the important all-party meeting coming up with the lawyers and Equinox next week. Lawson Green the CEO is coming from the States, and their US lawyer. I'm just hoping that we can plug the gap that Lloyd has left, draw a line under the media leaks and secure the deal. Hopefully your sales plan will help with that.'

'It's a good sign that they're coming, surely?' Stella asked, 'They wouldn't travel for a meeting unless there was a prospect of the deal happening, would they?'

'Indeed. That's what Alex, Meredith and Rachel are saying too.'

'Any news on the potential TV show? Will that really swing it do you think? And is that Rob Sweeney definitely joining us?'

'It's all happening, Stella. To be honest it's Alex the lawyer who's all over it. I just hope they don't balk at the idea but as Alex pointed out, Equinox worked on a similar show in the US and it had a massive impact on revenues for the clinic which featured in it. I'll forward her latest emails to you. Your presentation next week needs to include a section assuming Rob is joining us, the TV show is happening and its potential impact on income going forward.'

'Am I presenting then?'

'Yes. Of course. Alex is presenting and so are you. Then there'll be a Q and A session with all the Beau Street partners in the room as well as the Equinox crowd. Ryan's going to be there too. Is that okay?'

'It's fine.'

'Oh, and one more thing before you go. When we went through Albert's emails, we found the name of one of your clients too. A Mr Wallace. A YouTuber, apparently?'

'What! How did he have his details? I had no idea he was famous.'

'No idea. Sorry I didn't ask him that. It's quite obvious though that he's about as discreet as his own cosmetic tweaks.'

★★★

Stella arrived back at her office fuming from her meeting with Tom. Yes, they had identified Albert as the source of the leak from Lloyd's office, but how had they found out about Mr Wallace? Albert didn't have access to her records. He must have seen someone coming in or out, or something like that. Maybe Karen would have an idea.

'Morning Karen. How are you?'

Karen looked up from her desk, smiled and nodded.

'I heard from Fenella that Benji's claim is going well,' Stella continued, 'he could well be in line for a few thousand in compensation. So that's good news, hey?'

'Oh, it's great news! It will make such a difference,' said Karen looking relieved, 'shall we go through your diary for the day?'

'Yes in a minute but I wanted to ask you about something first. You know the leaks to the press? Well, I've been talking to Tom about it and we've identified the source as Albert Cheung.'

'Oh,' said Karen looking surprised.

'Yes, bit of a shock all round. But the odd thing is he seemed to know about one of my patients as well. I'm wondering if he's seen something. Have you seen him hanging about or asking any odd questions?'

'No. I hardly ever see Albert. Not much reason for our paths to cross.'

'Hmm, okay. If you do think of anything, make sure you let me know won't you?'

Karen nodded but Stella could see that she was feeling uncomfortable.

'What is it Karen? If you know something, you must tell me.'

Karen looked down at the floor.

'Karen?'

Karen started to speak and then stopped. Stella could see that she was getting tearful. She grabbed a chair and sat down in front of Karen.

'Okay, c'mon tell me,' she said softly, 'I won't be cross if you've made a mistake. These things happen. We just need to get to the bottom of it and make sure that it can't happen again. These leaks are putting the deal at risk, never mind the reputation of the practice.'

Karen looked up at Stella and began to cry. Large teardrops ran down her checks and dropped on to her lap.

'Oh Stella. You've been so kind to me. Everything you've done for Benji, redoing his stitches, all the support you've given me. I can't believe how awful I've been.' Karen put her head in her hands.

'I'm sure it's nothing that can't be sorted out,' said Stella taking Karen's hands and holding them in hers, 'just start at the beginning and tell me what's happened.'

Karen took a deep breath.

'You know how it's been for me and Benji. Things have been really tight, for years now. And I so wanted to help him with his football but it's so expensive: the kit, boots, trips. It's never-ending. I was at Sarah's leaving do, you know the young girl in accounts, who's going back to college to become a nurse?'

Stella nodded, not at all sure where this was all going.

'Well, Albert was there and we got talking. I was telling him how short of money I was and how great it was to have a night out where someone else was paying for a few drinks. And he said he knew a way to get me some good money, and quick. Just by getting a few details of a patient.'

Stella looked horrified.

'Karen, no!'

'Stella, I'm so sorry. He said that mostly the press know that these celebs have had the work done anyway. They just need a nod that the story is true so that they can run it. I didn't give them any details. All I had to do was confirm they'd been a patient and they gave me two thousand pounds, just like that. No questions. Honestly, I only did it for Benji. You have no idea what difference that money made for us.'

'Of course they pay for it. It means that they won't be sued for getting the story wrong. That makes a massive difference to them. These stories are worth a fortune if they know that the celebrity can't fight back. I can't believe you did that!'

Stella got up and paced around the room in disbelief.

'That is the most fundamental rule of our clinic. We never give out patient details. Of any sort. Under any circumstances. You know that. Shit, Karen, this is really serious.'

'I know,' said Karen, crying quietly, 'I feel terrible.'

'And so you should! I trusted you completely. And in one stupid act, you've thrown that all away.'

'What are you going to do?'

'I have no idea,' said Stella.

And she really didn't. How could Karen have done that? It was unforgivable. Of course, Stella knew what it was like to be short of money. And yes, she'd done extra work with Lloyd. But once she knew how he'd got the money, she hadn't been able to bring herself to use it, which reminded her that she really must give that envelope to Tom and make sure it got paid in.

'Please let me make it right somehow,' Karen begged.

'I don't think you can,' said Stella, 'it's done now, the genie has left the bottle. We can't undo the fact that you have breached our patient confidentiality and have been paid for it. It wasn't an administrative error or anything. You did it deliberately. That's a serious breach of your contract and cause for a straight dismissal.'

Karen looked distraught.

'Look, let me sleep on it. I can see how upset you are and I do know what's it's like to be short of money,' said Stella without thinking.

'Do you? Do you really? You with your flash car and lovely clothes and all that. You have no idea what it's like to be me.'

Karen seemed angry. Stella tried not to get angry too. That wouldn't help.

'Karen, it wasn't always like that, okay?'

And it isn't even like that now, thought Stella.

Stella left the office, still reeling from Karen's bombshell. She had promised to sleep on it but she wasn't sure that would make any difference. She had two choices: forget that Karen ever told her or report it. And she didn't like either of them. She felt the need to talk to Ian about it. He was bound to have something to say. And she was right when she confided in him later that evening.

'That's an absolute bloody disgrace! She needs to go and quick smart too, before she can do any more damage.'

'Oh, I don't think she'll do it again now,' said Stella, 'she was so upset about it.'

'I bet she was. And if she knows that she's going to be fired, then her only hope of any more money is to get hold of a load more names to sell. She's probably in the office now, downloading all your client files.'

Stella hadn't thought about that. Surely Karen wouldn't do that? Mind you, Stella would have bet her house on the fact that Karen was as honest as the day is long, and she'd got that all wrong.

'Can you see any other options? Full apology, training course, public flogging?' Stella was clutching at straws now.

'What does your HR policy say?' Ian asked.

'Fired. Do not pass go, do not collect £200. But I thought maybe, if I argued extraneous circumstances, then we could make an exception.'

'What extraneous circumstances? I ran out of money, so I sold some patient data? I hardly think that would cut it. Also, you need to think about your reputation in all of this. How would your fellow partners feel about you trying to argue her corner? It would almost certainly undermine what they think of you.'

Stella knew Ian was right; she had no choice. Karen would have to go. And if she wanted to be Chief Medical Officer, as Tom had suggested, this was probably just the start of some very difficult decision-making. She shook her head and rubbed her fingers across her eyebrows to try and relieve some of the tension from the heavy frown she'd had across her face for the last ten minutes.

'Yes, I guess you are right. I was just hoping beyond hope that maybe you could come up with something. I just feel so bad for her. We're very close you know. You can't work with someone for that long and not care about what happens to them. It feels like I've lived every drama and triumph with her and Benji. And now with his accident and everything. Well, the timing's just terrible.'

'I know it must be hard and of course you care. But this time it's not your problem to solve,' said Ian.

CHAPTER 24

Stella arrived at work the next day with a heavy heart. Ian's words were still on a loop in her head. Surely Karen wouldn't have done anything silly, like steal more data overnight? And if she had, how would Stella know? Perhaps she should have had her locked out last night? Anyway, it was too late now and she had to act fast. But she was dreading it. And for once, her daily encounter with Fred didn't help either. He looked decidedly downcast as she passed him.

'Hi Fred,' she said, trying to sound cheerier than she felt.

'Morning, Miss Stella, not such a good one for me today, I'm afraid. Didn't get the weatherman job. Told you I was too old. Some whippersnapper of a lad got it. Bet he only knows half as much as I do.' He sighed and shrugged his shoulders.

'I'm really sorry about that, Fred,' said Stella, she didn't know what else to say.

'Not your fault,' said Fred, 'ah well, maybe next time.' He forced a smile.

'Yes, I'm sure the next one is yours,' said Stella, copying Fred's false positivity.

When she got to her office, she was relieved to see that Karen hadn't arrived yet. It gave her a few minutes to gather her thoughts. She rang Charles Sutton and gave him the news.

'Charles, it's Stella. How are you?'

'Under the cosh, as usual. Is it a quick one?'

Charles listened in silence, as Stella explained Karen's confession.

'As if we haven't got enough bloody problems, what with Lloyd Cassidy and trying to get this deal done. Well, I completely agree with you. She's out and pronto. I guess we can at least say that it's all part and parcel of the same issue. I don't want Equinox worrying that the entire place is crawling with dishonest no-gooders. Can you deal with it for me? I mean HR will do all the paperwork, but can you do the exit meeting?'

'Yes, I plan to,' said Stella, 'I think it's best that it comes from me anyway. She's worked for me for years. I'm so disappointed!'

'Yes, well, nothing will surprise me anymore. Money does funny things to people, you know, Stella. Always has, always will.'

Stella hung up reflecting on those words. Had she let money change her? She thought about her 'ambitious' sales presentation and vowed to do better next time. This time it would be accurate, no flannel, exactly what she thought Beau Street could achieve. Her train of thought was interrupted by Karen opening the door. She looked terrible.

'Karen, come in,' said Stella, gesturing to the chair usually reserved for her patients.

'Now, I have had a chance to think …' started Stella.

Karen stopped her mid-sentence.

'Please let me say something first. I really need to say this to you. I've been thinking about it all night and, well, I've written a few things down.' She got a folded envelope out of her handbag, covered in scribbled notes. Stella looked at them with bemusement.

'Okay, you go first.'

Karen gave a little cough, like she was about to start a formal speech and started reading from her notes.

'Dear Stella. I just want to say how very sorry I am. You have done so much for me and Benji and for that I am so very grateful. I am very ashamed of what I have done but I love my boy and would do anything for him. That's what made me do it. Not for myself, I didn't spend a penny on myself. I'm not a bad person you know, I just made a mistake. And if you can forgive me that mistake, I promise I will make it right. I will be the best, most hard-working, most loyal employee that Beau Street has ever known. Please just give me another chance. Please Stella.'

She finally looked up, her large brown eyes pleading with Stella to find a way out. To find a way for her to keep her job. Stella felt sick to her stomach. This was even worse than she'd imagined.

'I'm so sorry, Karen. There isn't another way. I've spoken to Charles Sutton and we are agreed that we have no choice but to terminate your employment with immediate effect. You have to clear your desk and leave, I'm afraid. HR will be in touch with your termination letter, final pay and so forth.'

'What right now? I've only just arrived. Don't I get notice or anything?'

Stella shook her head, 'No, I'm sorry. For gross misconduct matters, particularly concerning patient data, our policy is that your access to our systems and the office is immediately withdrawn. I'll need to get Fred to come and stay with you, whilst you pack up your desk. I'm so sorry, Karen, you left me no choice.'

'Oh God!' Karen let out a loud, rather alarming wail. She put her head in her hands and cried, her large shoulders bobbing up and down with each juddering sob.

'What am I going to do, what am I going to do?' Karen moaned, rocking backwards and forwards in the chair.

Stella picked up the phone to Fred and asked him to come up, quickly. She didn't need a scene.

'Look, Karen, I know this is really difficult for you and for me. There is one potential opportunity I can think of for you. I know Lloyd is planning to move on and set up his practice somewhere else. He could really do with someone with your level of experience and the fact you know this business inside out already.

And I think you'll find he has a slightly more flexible approach,' Stella smiled ruefully, 'look, here's his mobile number. Why don't you get in touch with him?'

Stella handed the number over and gave her an awkward hug as Fred knocked gently on the door.

Twenty minutes later, Karen had gone and a temporary secretary was sitting at her desk. Karen had been a huge part of Stella's daily life, but like a hand coming out of a bucket of water, the space she left behind was soon filled. Stella felt numb. She knew that she had done the right thing but she felt absolutely terrible about it. She'd never forget Karen's broken expression. Telling herself that it was Karen's own fault just didn't seem to help.

Anna, her new temporary secretary, interrupted her train of thought and for once she was more than grateful. She needed to stay busy.

'Your next appointment is for a pinnaplasty under local anaesthetic. Just one ear, does that sound right?' Anna asked.

'Yes, that's right,' said Stella.

'One ear, that's quite unusual,' said Anna.

'Yes, it's a long story,' said Stella smiling ruefully to herself.

It was almost a pleasant sight to see Neil shuffle his way awkwardly into her office. He had a grey and orange striped beanie pulled firmly down over both ears, despite the fact that it was a warm day.

'Neil, how have you been? I'm so pleased that we can finally finish your operation. How is your good ear?'

'Healed thanks, Doc. But I tell you, it's been a nightmare waiting for this one to be done. I've had a beanie on for ages now. Even in the gym. Couldn't let anyone see me like this, well, apart from my girlfriend. And she practically wet herself when she first saw me!'

Stella gently removed his beanie to examine his ears. The right one popped out of the beanie like a jack-in-the-box while the other sat back beautifully against his head. He was right, he looked ridiculous. Fortunately for him the bruising morning she'd had already stifled any temptation to laugh.

'That looks excellent,' said Stella, carefully examining the neat-looking scar behind Neil's 'good' ear, 'can I see your blood tests?'

Neil had agreed to have weekly blood tests to show that he was free from steroids as part of the deal, so that Stella could do the other ear as soon as possible.

'Okay, that all looks great. Now, I know we have talked about the local anaesthetic before, but just to make sure that everything is clear. It will probably take me around forty-five minutes to do your second ear. And it is very normal that we use a local anaesthetic for adults, so I am very used to doing it this way. You will be able to feel me pulling and tugging a little bit, but you won't feel any pain. We will lay you on your front as we did before and you will be able to talk to me if you want. Although many patients prefer to try and drift off to sleep.'

'I don't think I'll be able to sleep.' Neil looked doubtful.

'Well don't worry either way, just try and relax. Now please follow me.'

Stella opened the door and led Neil to the treatment room.

'We'll be in here today.'

'This one looks even more like a massage room,' said Neil, grinning at the bed covered with towels that had an oval gap in one end where his face would go. Amy, one of Beau Street's scrub nurses, was already in the room, setting out Stella's instruments.

'Not that dissimilar actually,' said Stella smiling, 'you remember Amy? She was the nurse that helped us last time.'

'Yeah, sort of. It's all a bit of a blur actually.'

'Right, if you'd like to get yourself into this gown. There's a bathroom just through that door. You can keep your T-shirt and underwear on.'

'Sure about that?' Neil winked at Stella.

Just his way of dealing with his nerves, thought Stella. Or at least she hoped that was the case.

Once they were ready to start, Neil got onto the bed and lay down with his face over the gap that allowed him to breathe.

'This is a bit snug.'

He wriggled his face around trying to get comfortable and then sat up.

'Oh, I don't like that. I feel like I can't breathe.'

'Here, let me use a different towel, something thinner,' said Amy, reaching for a couple of white muslin-style cloths that were stored in neat piles in the cupboards at the end of the bed. She placed one on either side of the hole in the bed, tucking the overhang through the hole and underneath into a neat elasticated strap to hold them out of the way.

'That should give you a bit more space,' she said.

Neil lay back down again and put his face over the hole.

'Yeah, bit better I guess,' he said doubtfully, 'how long do I have to stay like this again?'

'About forty-five minutes,' said Stella, 'just try and relax. It will fly by. Shall we put some music on?'

'Yeah, all right,' said Neil.

Amy started a playlist of soft, lilting music and the sounds of pan pipes and birdsong soon filled the room. It was clearly not Neil's style of music.

'What's that crap?'

'It's meant to relax you, Neil,' said Stella.

'Only if you're dead,' said Neil, 'can't we have something, you know, a bit more funky?'

Stella and Amy exchanged glances and Amy changed the playlist to one of chart hits that they usually reserved for staff parties.

'Yeah, that's better,' said Neil, shuffling his shoulders from side to side in time to the music.

'Neil, if this is going to work, you must keep still. Otherwise I might end up cutting in the wrong place!'

Neil stiffened on the bed and said nothing else.

'Right, I am about to start the local anaesthetic, with a series of small injections around your ear. You will feel a few sharp pricks, but hopefully nothing too uncomfortable,' said Stella.

'I know quite a few sharp pricks,' said Neil in a muffled voice, causing both Stella and Amy to laugh.

Amy cleaned the area around Neil's remaining prominent ear and Stella began administering the first local anaesthetic injection. As the needle went in, Neil nearly jumped out of his skin. His head jerked upwards from the bed, hitting Stella's hand and nearly knocking the syringe out of her hand. It wasn't a good start.

'I don't feel well,' he said. 'I feel a bit dizzy.'

Amy and Stella helped him sit up. He had gone very pale and he was breathing quite fast.

'I don't think I can do this,' he said, 'my arms have gone all tingly and I can't breathe properly. And my heart's kicking off like a Saturday night outside the Bluebell. I feel shit.'

'I think you're just getting yourself a bit panicked,' said Stella calmly, trying not to look at her watch, 'being face down does take a bit of getting used to. Just take a few minutes to try and calm down. Amy, could you get Neil a glass of water, please?'

Neil sat sideways on the bed for a few minutes sipping his glass of water, whilst Stella and Amy 'busied' themselves, so that he was not the focus of attention.

'Ready to try again?' Stella asked.

Neil nodded but as soon as his face touched the bed, he bounced straight back up.

'No, it's no good. It makes me feel trapped having my face stuck in that bloody hole.'

'How about I give you a sedative, to calm you down a bit,' said Stella, looking at Amy who nodded in agreement. She had to get this operation done somehow; she couldn't just leave him looking like a car with its one door left open.

'Can I still go home today, if you do that?'

Stella nodded, 'Yes, you might take a little longer to feel ready to leave but probably only a couple of hours' difference at the most.'

'All right, go for it,' said Neil.

Stella gave Neil a mild sedative in liquid form. He gulped it down in one go declaring that he 'had had worse' and after another five or so minutes, this time sitting in a normal chair so he couldn't fall over, he started to look a bit drowsy.

'Good stuff this,' he said smiling, his head cocked slightly to one side, 'can I buy some to take home?'

Much to Stella's relief, he was finally able to lie face down on the bed and stay still and within a few minutes of her starting the operation, he had fallen asleep. She worked as quickly as she could, cutting behind his ear to reveal the ear cartilage. She then removed a neat sliver of the cartilage and a curved strip of excess skin, before stitching the incision back together. As she started to stitch, she was careful to match the distance from the back of his ear to his head with that of the other ear, taking a little more or little less skin as she went, so that the two ears would be as symmetrical as possible. She prided herself on the accuracy of her stitching and even resorted to using a ruler to check the distances behind each ear, much to Amy's amusement.

'Sorry,' said Stella, not sorry at all, 'once a perfectionist, always a perfectionist.'

'That's okay,' said Amy, nodding in approval, 'it's good to see. And I'm sure he's going to be very happy with the results.'

CHAPTER 25

It was a bright and sunny Saturday, perfect for an afternoon lazing in the park or a long lunch with Ian but sadly, that was not at all the sort of day Stella had planned. She had a revised sales presentation to do and this time, she was determined to get it right: Lloyd out, TV show in, most definitely credible and something that the whole management team would be happy to warrant. Over the last week, she had spent quite a few hours searching for different types of top quality published reports and independent data that could help support her forecasts. Quality sources, not random websites and dodgy statistics like last time; she knew that now. Her inbox was full of 'note to self' emails with all sorts of links and attachments that needed some serious organising. She had also recorded several US cosmetic surgery and makeover shows, to give her some inspiration for portraying Beau Street's show. It all seemed a bit overwhelming, although on the plus side at least she was getting a chance to redo it without having to come clean that her first attempt had been a bit of a fairy tale.

She decided to start by mocking up an outline of the presentation, a road map for her to work through. Then she would print out and organise her sources, with a few breaks watching TV in between. That sounded like a sensible plan, just as soon as she'd had breakfast; after all, she needed plenty of sustenance for a busy day ahead. After several slices of toast and jam and a large cup of coffee presented by Ian her barista, Stella got to work. She started by scrutinising several of the reports that she had found. She was particularly interested in the report from the British Association of Plastic Surgeons on the most popular procedures in the UK. Breast augmentation was the most popular procedure for women, as it had been for some years, but breast reduction had risen to third; it seems no one is happy. And breast reduction had also risen to be the third most popular procedure for men, after eyelids and nose jobs. Moobs were obviously so last century.

Stella tracked the trends in the UK national statistics over the last few years against Beau Street's own sales and then used that to help support the forecasts she had prepared for the next few years. They were a pretty good reflection of the UK picture across all of the top procedures. Plus Beau Street offered many of the more leading-edge procedures, such as thread facelifts and the lunchtime boob job using injections, which kept the enquiries coming in. And combining forces with Equinox was really going to help here. It would give them first-hand access to all the newest procedures being developed in the US and somewhere for their people to train. It was an exciting prospect. Stella tried her best to incorporate some of that sense of excitement and possibility in her presentation, liberally using words like 'forefront' and 'pacey' to describe her vision for the business.

She then turned her mind to the TV show. Despite Beau Street's great growth prospects, there was still the gap left by Lloyd to fill and the TV show seemed a perfect solution. It would provide revenue directly by selling the show to various TV and online channels but if done well, it also had the potential to boost the reputation of Beau Street and significantly increase patient numbers. A real win–win. But that meant a quality show that showed safe and successful procedures. Stella wondered what the other TV shows she had recorded were like. It was not the sort of show she'd ever normally watch, not when you'd been doing the real thing all day. She went and sat down by the television and started the first of the shows. It was a US show called *The Big Reveal*, where individuals were given a full cosmetic surgery makeover unbeknown to partners, friends or family and then the results are 'revealed' at a surprise party. Stella didn't like the concept from the outset. She always urged her patients to discuss their surgery plans with loved ones, particularly their partners. It was an important part of the decision-making process and helped to ensure that they were making the decision for the right reasons. Surprising them with it seemed like a dreadful idea. The first case was a young woman aged about twenty-five who wanted a smaller nose. She had always hated her large, slightly crooked nose and was super excited about surprising her boyfriend, Tod, with her new look.

'He's gonna just love it,' she drawled, smiling sideways at the camera.

Stella watched on and after pretending to take her mother away for a couple of weeks, the young woman was whisked into surgery. The surgeon performed a perfectly acceptable rhinoplasty and the results were revealed two weeks later to a seemingly thrilled boyfriend. *Okay, maybe it wasn't such a bad show after all*, thought Stella. But then they started the next case: a woman in her forties who wanted to look at least ten years younger. She was dressed to the nines in a very unflattering, skin-tight mini-dress and skyscraper heels. She told the presenters all about her numerous failed relationships, how looking younger would help her meet people in bars and then, worryingly, showed them a picture of a lingerie model that she wanted to look like.

'Totally unrealistic expectations,' said Stella, shaking her head at the television.

But the presenters clearly didn't agree. They went through a mind-blowing list of procedures that left Stella staring in astonishment.

'Well, we can remove this excess skin from your eyelids and give you a brow lift. Then by combining that with a lower facelift and cheek implants, we can create a much younger and more rounded look for you. We would also recommend a chemical peel to help freshen your skin and Botox around your eyes and mouth. In terms of your body, you would benefit from liposuction to the back of your arms, tummy and thighs and a breast lift. You don't need breast implants as you have plenty of volume,' said the surgeon cupping the woman's ample, but rather sagging breasts, 'they just need to sit a bit higher. And I guess we could look at a tummy tuck.'

'That's bloody ridiculous,' said Stella to herself. That was exactly the sort of show that Beau Street didn't want to make.

Stella started the next show she had recorded, hoping for something a bit more inspirational. The next one was called *Make Me Over* and was more of a holistic makeover show that included personal trainers, stylists and dieticians, as well as the odd nip and tuck to complete the look. Not quite what Stella had in mind. And she already knew that the last show she had recorded wasn't going to be either. Billed as 'extreme and shocking', Stella nearly didn't bother to watch it. However, she decided it was important to understand the whole gambit of shows being produced, so she could position Beau Street's show right at the top end. But after twenty minutes of watching a mother and daughter having matching labia reductions, so that their 'lady gardens looked nice and neat', a man having horns implanted to look like a lizard and someone trying to turn themselves into a living doll, Stella switched off. She'd just have to work it out for herself.

Stella worked solidly for the next two hours drafting an outline of how the Beau Street show would work. She was pretty pleased with her working title of 'Under The Skin' and it was much more focused on giving patients a realistic behind-the-scenes view of what it was like to undergo surgery, rather than shock tactics. She made it clear that consultations would be filmed showing surgeons explaining the risks and benefits of each procedure and in some cases, turning people away who were deemed unsuitable. Recovery times would be shown in a realistic light and patients, in return for a sizeable discount, would be followed all the way through their journey. Yes, there would be drama and human interest stories, but in a way that showed Beau Street in its best light.

Stella was back at Beau Street running through her presentation for the umpteenth time when her phone rang. It was Ryan.

'Hey Stella, how's the sales pitch going? I hear you're going to be centre stage at the all-party meeting on Friday. Looking forward to hearing what your new plans are.'

'The presentation's going well, thanks. Just looking at it right now actually. Tom tells me that you've changed your mind about coming here to run the business?'

'Yeah, that's right. We've been talking through things over here and Lawson wasn't too happy about me going. Seems he thinks I'm pretty key to the set-up here in Chicago.'

'I thought you said Lawson was happy with the idea?'

'Well, er, he was but then when he started talking to the rest of the management over here, I guess they changed his mind.'

Stella wasn't convinced. She was sure there was more to it than that. But Ryan was such a slippery charmer, who knew what was really going on in his head?

'I see,' said Stella.

'But I understand that they have you in the frame for Chief Medical Officer and I have to say, Stella, I'm supporting that all the way. I think you'd be great and I'm going to make sure I say as much on Friday.'

'Thank you, that's very kind. It came as a bit of a sideways offer and it seems a bit terrifying but I'm going to work hard and see how things turn out. What do you think about me doing a business qualification, like an MBA or something?'

'I think that's a great idea. Not sure you need to do the whole shooting match, as you have a pretty good understanding of the business already and we wouldn't want you out of the business for too long. There are some really good intensive short management courses that take weeks, rather than months, I think. One of those would be great. Maybe if you look into it and send me some budgets.'

Budgets? She hadn't really thought about Equinox needing to agree it. But in a post-deal world, she guessed there would be a whole load of new approval processes to get used to.

Today was the big day that her whole week had been building up to. She had done a dry run of her presentation with Ian last night and he had seemed genuinely impressed by it. Stella arrived at the Beau Street boardroom and peered through the small glass panel at the side of the door. Charles Sutton and Tom Duffy were sitting on one side of the table and the Equinox team of Lawson Green, Ryan, Brenda Martinez, their in-house counsel and another lawyer-type man were sitting on the other side. Stella knocked and entered the room.

'Ah Stella, come in,' said Charles gesturing to a chair next to him, 'we're just finishing up here.'

'How's it going?' Stella asked.

'Yes, very well,' said Ryan, 'we're just about agreed on all the main commercial terms of the deal now. We just need to get happy with your new business plan, make sure that it supports the price we are offering and then we can let the lawyers get on with the rest.'

'No pressure then,' said Stella jokingly, trying not to show how nervous she felt.

'We will be asking the management team to give us a warranty on this presentation, obviously. That they believe it is achievable, balanced, you know, the standard stuff,' said Brenda Martinez dryly.

'Obviously,' echoed Stella.

Tom nodded at Stella to start and she handed out hard copies of her carefully prepared presentation to the assembled audience.

'So I'd like to start by giving you an overview of what I am going to cover today. Firstly, I'm going to give you a canter through our sales history, trends in procedures, pricing and a few facts and stats by each doctor. And then I will take you through the adjustments we are making to the business plan to reflect those that are leaving,' Stella nodded towards Charles, 'for good reasons such as retirement and for not-so-good reasons, such as Lloyd Cassidy.'

Stella looked directly at Lawson Green and lowered her voice, 'I just wanted to apologise again for the appalling lack of judgement and integrity shown by one of our doctors and add my own personal assurance that it is not reflective of any other part of our practice.'

Lawson smiled and nodded to acknowledge her apology.

'I have then produced a sales forecast for the next three years,' she continued, 'that I have talked through and agreed with each of my colleagues, which is fully supported by independent industry data and our own track record. I am confident that our business plan is robust, realistic and well thought through.'

The Equinox team nodded in approval at these last words. Stella knew that was what they wanted and she was determined to show she could deliver. The rest of the presentation seemed to fly by and Stella's hard work and preparation had clearly paid off. The responses she received were mainly nods and smiles apart from a few challenging questions from Equinox's lawyers which she felt she had managed to put to bed.

'Very impressive,' said Lawson Green. 'I can see our two businesses working very well together.'

'Yes, very smart presentation,' Ryan agreed. 'And I think we all know that Stella has been offered the role of Chief Medical Officer in the new set-up. And I, for one, am very keen that she takes it.'

'Oh, I'm sure she will. Although to be fair we do need to at least give her a job description before we start putting her on the spot to accept it,' said Charles, raising his eyebrows in a fatherly way at Stella.

'Thank you and I am very pleased and flattered to be asked. You're right, we need to define what the role involves but I can guarantee that you have my full commitment. What I do know is that I am excited to be part of the future, as our two businesses come together.'

Wow, hopefully a large payout as well as a promotion. As Stella left the office later that evening, she bumped into Alex who was lugging out more paperwork from the basement office.

'That went well didn't it?' Stella asked.

'Certainly did. Looking like the deal will be completed in the next few days,' Alex responded.

'Really? You think so?'

'In my experience once the key issues are resolved, which they certainly seem to be, then there might be a little dance around the final price but then we head into the completion meeting. Ninety per cent of all the legal documents are there now and although the price isn't finalised, everyone is aware of the ballpark. Be warned though. Completion meetings can last forever. I went into one on a Thursday once and came out on a Saturday.'

'Wow. Really? Well I'll get myself a packed lunch sorted for that!'

Alex flagged down a cab and Fred came over and helped her and her piles of files into it.

'Thanks, Fred. See you again in the next day or so, Stella.'

'She's a lovely lady. Sounds like her work here is nearly done,' Fred raised his eyebrows at Stella.

'I couldn't possibly say, Fred, but between me and you I don't think we'll have a basement full of lawyers for much longer. Anyway, how are you doing?' she asked.

'I'm fine. Had some good news actually. About the weatherman job,' Fred beamed.

'Did you get it after all?'

'No. I still don't have the face for TV. However, I do have the face for radio apparently. They've asked me to do some weekend weather slots on the local radio channel.' He was clearly ecstatic.

'Fred I'm so pleased. That's fantastic news and very well deserved. That doesn't mean you're leaving Beau Street does it?' Stella was already in Chief Medical Officer mode. Would they need to hire a new security guy?

'No, Dr Webb, don't worry. It's only at the weekend and worst-case scenario I might need to drop one shift a week.'

'Phew. We don't want to lose you, Fred.'

CHAPTER 26

Stella was intrigued by Ian's for once very secretive approach to the weekend ahead. He had told her to pack for a night out and to prepare for a long car journey. That was it. She was still on a high from the past few days. The deal had finally completed after a two-day completion meeting which had involved hanging out at the lawyers' offices whilst documents were amended, tweaked and eventually signed. She had assumed that after the big issues had been resolved at the all-party meeting, they could have signed on the dotted line then, but as Alex had warned her that wasn't how things worked. The final sale price had been agreed between Tom, Lawson and, to her surprise, her. She had more than held her own in the discussions and had held firm at one point sensing how keen Equinox were to get a foothold in the UK. She had persuaded Tom they shouldn't agree to reduce the price and ultimately Equinox had agreed. As she and Ian had discussed, the amount of work Equinox had already put into the Beau Street deal would have to be incurred again on their lawyers, accountants and numerous trips to the UK for Ryan and the team if they were to ditch Beau Street and look for another UK business and, after all, Beau Street had always been their first choice. It made sense to recognise that despite all the Lloyd, Albert and Karen issues they were in a strong position. As a result, all Stella's financial issues had been solved overnight. Tom's original estimate of her payout from the deal had actually been conservative and Stella was now feeling like a lottery winner.

'Come on, gorgeous. Are you ready to go yet?' Ian grabbed her from behind and kissed her.

Stella zipped up her wheelie bag and plonked it on the floor before turning to face him and return his kiss. She sighed as she lowered her shoulders, relaxed into their embrace and realised that for the first time in her life she was secure financially and emotionally. Seeing Ryan again over the past week had cemented her conviction that she and Ian were right. She had noticed Ryan's flirtations with the banker Meredith and yet there had been no let-up in his overfamiliar approach to her. That was something she would need to watch going forward now he was effectively a colleague.

As they headed up the motorway with Ian singing away at the wheel she continued guessing where they were heading.

'Lake District? Nice chalet and a bit of walking?'
'*Non.*'
'A five-star hotel in the Yorkshire Dales?'
'*Nein.*'

'We're not heading to John O'Groats are we? That's a trek and a half.'

'Stop guessing and don't get your hopes up too much. We are in a hotel but it isn't an obvious holiday destination.'

★★★

Stella finally woke up from the inevitable slumber which had overwhelmed her as the last few days of work caught up with her. She rubbed her eyes in disbelief and tried to suppress the slight disappointment as she stared at the skyline of Newcastle approaching her. She had always loved Newcastle. It was the fun party town of her youth but wasn't exactly a new place for her to explore.

'Flipping heck. Newcastle! Is this where we're staying?'

'*Si!* Is that okay? We're in a lovely hotel right in the centre and there is another surprise this evening.'

Actually, she thought, *this isn't bad at all*. She could walk the streets and do a bit of shopping. She knew all the places to go and the burning hole in her pocket was palpable.

'Ian, it's perfect.'

'And if you don't mind, I need a couple of hours to myself this afternoon so are you happy to entertain yourself? The hotel has a spa and a gym.'

'And the streets have numerous lovely shops! Ian, don't you worry about me. I'll be fine.'

'Don't suppose I can restrain your shopping today really. Go for it. Get an outfit for tonight. Treat yourself. You deserve it.'

After checking into the hip hotel overlooking the River Tyne, Ian made his excuses and left Stella to relive her teens on the shopping streets but with a slightly larger budget. He told her he was going to visit an A&E consultant who wanted some tips about London hospitals and a potential transfer down south.

Stella made the most of her afternoon and browsed all the boutiques and department stores. For once she didn't purchase a single item. She mused over her latte in a high street coffee shop at how, now that she had the freedom to buy pretty much anything, she had ended up with nothing. Was it that the forbidden fruit had always been attractive? Or had she finally grown up and realised she had a full wardrobe, dozens of handbags and shoes for every occasion. She had spoken with her sister earlier in the week and without giving her the specifics she had made it clear that her financial situation had changed radically. She had also updated her on the situation with Ian and had been touched when Michelle's response had been even more ecstatic when she had heard they were back together. The relief at not having to tell her parents that they had split up hit her too.

She wasn't enjoying her latte so left it and decided to make her way back to the hotel. She was conscious that she was feeling a bit nauseous again. She smiled as she fell into the usual pattern of thinking about pregnancy tests. She really should buy the tests in bulk online, she thought, as she queued in the pharmacy.

As she entered the hotel reception the concierge came over to her.

'Mrs Maynard?' he asked.

'Er, yes.' Ian must have booked them in as husband and wife.

'We have moved your baggage to a different room. An upgrade.'

'Oh. Okay.' Thank God she hadn't unpacked anything.

'Let me take you to your new room. I think your husband is already there.'

The concierge in his three-piece suit ushered her into the lift and pressed the button for the top floor. He then escorted her to a large double door at the end of a polished wooden corridor and knocked on the door before tapping the room card on the panel. He held the door for her.

'Ian?' she called as she walked through a large hall area with a fancy glass table with a huge bowl of orchids on it. Beyond the hall was a lounge area with glass doors leading onto an outside terrace with views across the river and the city.

'Wow, this is amazing.'

'Mrs Maynard, it is the best suite in the hotel and the one that all the celebrities stay at,' said the concierge.

'Ooh, who's the most famous person who's stayed here?' She couldn't help herself.

'I'm afraid I can't breach customer confidentiality. But seriously, a proper A-lister.'

'Yeah. It's me,' said Ian as he poked his head round the sliding door which presumably led to the bedroom.

The concierge momentarily checked out Ian's face before realising he was joking.

'I hope you have a lovely stay. Here's your key.' He handed the room card to Stella and left them. Ian came out of the bedroom in his boxers beaming.

'So. What do you think?'

'Am loving your outfit,' Stella smiled.

'No! The room. Do you like living the high life?'

'Ian, it's amazing. Thanks so much for booking it.' She kissed him.

'No shopping bags?'

'Nope. I'm a new woman. No idea what's happened. Now I have money I don't seem to want to spend it.'

'Brilliant!'

Stella plonked herself on the beautiful corner sofa and took in the view.

'Let me get you a drink.' Ian disappeared into the bedroom and emerged with a silver champagne bucket and two glasses.

The day was getting better and better.

'Just give me a minute to make myself respectable.' Ian disappeared again. Stella grabbed the bottle of fizz and worked away at the cork until it bolted from the bottle and hit the ceiling.

'Oi. Wait for me,' Ian called out.

Stella was already sipping her champagne when Ian reappeared looking very smart in a linen suit and shiny shoes. Stella held out his glass as he seemed to fall to the floor in front of her, fumbling in his pocket.

'Are you okay?' She leant down to see him pull out a small box from his pocket.

She gasped and held her free hand to her chest as her heartbeat suddenly escalated. He opened the box and looked up at her.

'Stella. Please will you marry me? Please.'

There was no hesitation in her instinctive response. She almost threw the champagne onto him as she leapt up from the sofa, jogged on the spot and said yes over and over again.

Ian leapt up too and they both hugged and jumped up and down.

'I went to see your mum and dad earlier and asked for your hand in marriage.'

'Really? Seriously?' She couldn't believe he had been so traditional in his approach but she knew that her dad would have loved that.

'Yes darling and they both said yes!'

'Of course they did! They absolutely love you. And so do I.'

The bottle of champagne was gone within an hour and Stella was finishing her make-up before heading down to dinner. She kept admiring the diamond solitaire set in a sparkling platinum diamond band. It was perfect and, true to form, Ian had apparently done his research by tying a cotton thread round her finger whilst she was asleep, so the size was perfect.

'Come on darling,' Ian called as he waited in the lounge area for her as she finally emerged from the bathroom all ready for dinner.

'Ah, here's my fiancée. I have to say you look ecstatic!' He put his arm round her and led her out of the room and into the lift. As they reached the ground floor Ian directed her to the very fancy restaurant where he had booked a table for dinner.

'Now darling, I have one last surprise left for you.' Ian pointed towards a table in the corner. Fenella and Max were waving across the room at them and raising their glasses.

Stella was thrilled to see them but was already anticipating that this could be a difficult night to manage without one more bombshell.

'I have just got another surprise too. I am going to have to tell you now before Fenella gets me back on the fizz. Ian, we need to get that wedding booked pronto. I have just found out that I'm pregnant.'

As Stella took in Ian's look of utter delight, she knew this would be the easiest night ever to celebrate without another drop of alcohol.